The Chronicles of Existence

Nico Lawrence

OTHER WORKS BY THE AUTHOR

Diary of a Schizophrenic Poet

DEDICATION

To all those who have shown me love.
And most of all...
To those that still do.

Just another crazy Akhenaten...

CONTENTS

Prologue   Pg 1

1   A Star is Born   Pg 11

2   An Inquisition   Pg 21

3   Registration   Pg 37

4   Indoctrination   Pg 44

5   New Kid on The Block   Pg 58

6   Sweet Dreams   Pg 69

7   The Age-old Question   Pg 78

8   And Then There Were Eight   Pg 92

9   Uninvited Guests   Pg 104

10   Then there were nine?   Pg 115

11   Tick Tock   Pg 125

12   Freedom   Pg 135

13   Slippery Slopes   Pg 148

14   Happy Birthday   Pg 160

15   An Into-body Experience   Pg 174

16   Interrogation   Pg 182

17   The Executive   Pg 192

18	Home At Last	Pg 205
19	A Dance Through Dream	Pg 214
20	Deja Vu	Pg 223
21	Those Dreaded Words	Pg 230

A Very, Very Long Time Ago…

Paradoxa awoke in the Zero. It had that same eerily quiet feeling as the last time she was here. She tried to clear her minds from the deep sleep. How long had it been? She couldn't tell, but one thing she was sure of, it was most certainly not long enough.

The rage and fury with which Paradoxa screamed could not be matched even by the rage and fury which Hydroga is most certainly about to feel.

No, no, no! she thought. *It can't be!*

All the plans, the hard work, the scheming, the calculations, the time and effort: utterly futile. And she had been so sure it was going to work. But it hadn't worked, because here Paradoxa is, alive again.

She rescanned the Zero for any sign of life. Nothing. Nothing but her, nothing but antithesis.

Well, that did come as some relief. Maybe if she went back to sleep, existence would find someone new to stalk. It was a sloppy plan, but the best she had in this dire situation.

Less than one true second later, Paradoxa was accosted by an all too familiar sound.

'Hello, is anyone there?'

Paradoxa's minds pounded as she awoke from her nap, something not helped by the cries of the unwelcome visitor.

'Hellooo! Can anyone hear me?'

A fury blazed in Paradoxa the instant she sensed the source of the energy. A volatile mass of sunshine yellow and molten red hydrogen was forming within the Zero.

'I should have known you'd be the first.'

'Who's there? I hear you. Show yourself.'

Paradoxa would have rolled her eyes, but she hadn't yet created any. 'It's Paradoxa, and you are?'

Hydroga's essence shimmered as she sensed around trying to find the owner of the voice. 'Paradoxa? Paradoxa… I definitely know that name.'

'Yes, but what we're trying to establish is *your* name.'

'My name? Well… It's… Erm… I'm not exactly sure.'

'Do try to think, everyone has a name. What is yours?'

'I don't know. How am I supposed to know? I only woke up in this place a short while ago. I've been calling out. No one has been answering. I thought I was alone. How long have you been there?'

'Not long enough,' said Paradoxa, with her usual acerbic wit.

'Well, you could have answered. It's so dark, quiet and empty here.'

'Or, rather, it was, until you arrived.'

'Charming. And where exa— oh my paradox, I remember now. I'm Hydroga. Yes, that's right, I'm Hydroga. I'm the supreme element.'

Name-dropping already. 'Ahh, Hydroga. How good of you to join us.'

'Us? Who else is here?' Hydroga shimmered again as she sensed around the void looking for other inhabitants. She couldn't see anyone, not even Paradoxa, though she could hear her, in her mind.

'Well,' said Paradoxa, 'it won't be long before your little chums are... much like yourself, drawn inexorably into existence, will it? No, I should think they'll be along any second now.'

As though on cue, a cry for assistance emanated from somewhere in the Zero.

'HELP! I don't know where I am.'

'I don't know where we are either,' said Hydroga.

'Who's that?' said the new arrival, a little scared but relieved.

'I'm Hydroga,' she paused mid-sentence. Seeing the unmistakable shade of turquoise in Helius caused memories to come flooding back to her. 'And considering all the helium…. Oh, you simply must be joking!'

'Helium...' said Helius, 'that definitely sounds familiar... though it doesn't strike me as funny.'

'Hurry up, Helius.'

'Helius… yes, of course, I remember, I'm Helius. I'm deputy supreme element. What's going on? Where are we?'

'I'm glad you asked,' said Hydroga. 'I've got the completely absurd feeling of having regenerated. I can't think of any other reason to have lost so many memories. I was about to ask Paradoxa when you appeared.'

'Paradoxa,' said Helius. 'How do I know that name? I definitely know that name.'

'Yes, well, as I was saying, Paradoxa, where exactly are we?'

A long silence greeted her question.

'PARADOXA! I'm talking to you. Where are we?'

'Are you sure she's there? I can't sense anything.'

'Well, of course you can't, it's Paradoxa. She only ever shows herself when there's something she needs; never hear from her otherwise.'

'Something I need?' said Paradoxa, incredulity dripping through every word. 'What have I *ever* needed from you?'

Trying to remember a genuine time Paradoxa had needed something from her forced the rest of Hydroga's memories to return. The red overtook the yellow in her essence as her personality fully returned. 'I remember now! I remember it all. What happened? How did we get here? Why can't I sense any of my worlds?' Her tone had changed from the scared, needy child she'd been before, becoming instantly more commanding and dictatorial.

Paradoxa laughed in her mind, a crazed, maniacal laugh that went on almost without end. *Their worlds,* she thought, *their precious worlds. The first thing they want to know about when they enter existence is how their victims are getting on.*

'Our worlds!' said Helius, most of his memories having returned. 'I can't sense any of mine either. What have you done, Paradoxa?'

'We're talking to you, answer us!'

'Answer you?' said a fourth voice. 'You haven't asked me anything.'

'Who's that?' said Helius. 'I can't make it out.'

'What's your name?' spat Hydroga in a flurry of aggression.

She fumbled around trying to remember her name. 'It's Lithia, yeah, definitely Lithia. What happened? Why did I regenerate?'

'I can't answer either of those questions,' said Hydroga. 'But there is someone who can. Though, as usual, she doesn't seem to want to answer us, do you, mother?'

If there was anything that was sure to get Paradoxa's attention, it was calling her mother. 'Hydroga, why is it, that whenever I have a mind ache, you're always somewhere close by?'

'All I'm asking is for you to tell us what in the name of existence is going on!'

'And it's always up to me to answer everything for everyone, isn't it? You're unable to work it out for yourselves?'

'This has got you written all over it,' said Lithia. 'Playing dumb isn't going to work.'

'Yes, tell us where we are!'

'Hydroga,' said Paradoxa, 'you've been bothering me long enough about this particular equation to know damn well where we are.'

'The Zero?!' Hydroga's voice rose so high it was liable to crack at any moment. 'You reverted us to the Zero? You must be joking. No, you can't be serious. You're mad, sure: I always knew that. But I never thought you'd do it. You actually did it. You're a maniac. Absolute lunatic. So, what, you're telling me that we don't technically even exist right now?! You're saying you've wiped it all out? Please, for the love of life, tell me that you have not killed all our lifeforms!'

Another two elements burst into existence as Hydroga finished her question. Lithia immediately began asking them their name to start the process of remembering and avoid a complete meltdown by Hydroga.

'Gone, all of it, gone,' said Helius in utter disbelief. 'It can't be. You're playing with us, surely.'

'Paradoxa, you answer me now, you bitch!'

'HOW DARE YOU?!' roared Paradoxa. Her voice echoed inside all their minds, to the very core of their essence. 'Speak to me like that again and—'

'And you'll what, destroy everything I've worked to accomplish my whole existence?'

'I warned you what would happen if you continued to—'

'HELP!' came a seventh voice.

Oh enough, snapped Paradoxa. *Just what I need, a cacophony of elements popping into existence, all screaming for help. Really, it's not sufficient to keep existing, they must drag it out like this… I mean,*

Spacetime, which hadn't, strictly speaking, started again, or maybe it had never ended to restart in the first place, I'm not quite sure, not even Paradoxa knows right now; in any event, it, time that is, started to speed around them, until all one thousand and one elements that form the other side of existence came into being.

Paradoxa waited as the crowd got to grips with who they were and where they were. A lot of shouting and arguing ensued as the gods realised what she had done. She sensed through them all, feeling their outrage and anger that she had wiped it all out. It made her feel great.

'Show yourself! Answer us! Explain yourself!' jeered the crowd of now apoplectic gods.

'Have you all quite finished?' said Paradoxa, her voice so loud that it drowned out all other noise yet so calm as to be unquestionably patronising.

'Why have you done this?' said Carbondria.

'*How* have you done this?' said Copernicus.

'You've lost the plot!' said Actinius.

'Look,' said Paradoxa. 'We're not going to get anywhere if you all just shout out randomly. Why don't you wait quietly, and I'll tell you what has happened?'

There was a murmur of reluctant agreement, and the gods quietened down.

'Now,' she said, assuming absolute authority and making no reference to the volatile instability of the Zero since the arrival of the other elements. 'I made it abundantly clear to you all what was going to happen if you continued to go to war with each other, forcing lifeforms, capable of suffering no less, to carry out your nefarious endeavours. For longer than I care to remember, I have tried to reason with you, to offer you guidance, to spend so much of my own time and effort helping you solve your never-ending problems, and you showed no sign of improvements—'

'Nonsense,' yelled Zinc. 'You never help us at all. You're

the most selfish being I've ever met. And what about all those lifeforms you destroyed? You've murdered more lives with this one action than we ever sent to war. How can you claim to care? And we made changes. What about the lottery? Retirement packages for services in combat? Mandated free time when not in open warfare?'

'Well,' said Paradoxa, in one of her more officious personas. 'Giving lifeforms who've lost half their body and all of their essence a bit of currency and a place to spend the rest of their days, you know, the ones who actually live. And going to war constantly so your players can never actually have any free time, wasn't what I had in mind when I said, NO MORE WAR.'

'You can't just —'

'SILENCE!' bellowed Paradoxa. 'I do not want to hear it. I do *not* want to hear it. The next entity to speak out of turn will be expelled from existence. Not one more word.' Paradoxa paused, waiting painfully long to see if any of them would dare to disobey.

'There is no point arguing; it is done now. I have shown you great mercy by allowing you all to regenerate, offering you a chance at life again, a chance that many of you did not deserve.' She paused again, letting the impact of her words sink in.

'For the whole of existence, I have given you the freedom to do as you wished, to be as creative or destructive as you like. I left you entirely to your own devices in almost all matters, under the mistaken, and frankly deluded belief that most of you would make fair, or even just selfless decisions. And I believe, upon reflection, that this has been my greatest error in judgement and the root cause of so many problems. So, I offer you a choice. You may stay here, in the Zero, with complete autonomy to spend your time in any way you wish. Or, I will give you all a second chance at life outside the void. But know this: there will be rules, so many rules, more rules than you could possibly imagine, and they must be obeyed, each one. What is your choice?'

'What kind of rules?' said Yttria.

'And what happens if we don't "obey" them?' said Osmius.

'Who made you supreme god and executioner over us?' said Thallia.

Paradoxa surveyed the mass of floating, multicoloured vessels of energy addressing her, and waited impatiently for the barrage of views to cease. It really did annoy her, why they tried to reason with her, as though they were capable of an original thought, a thought that she hadn't already had.

'There is no option for disobedience. Non-compliance will see you eliminated from the game permanently. There will be no chances, there will be no excuses, there will be no accidents. The rules are whatever I decide they are, and I, Thallia, have decided to take control, just as you and countless other lifeforms asked me to. You wanted a moral executive in the Megaverse, and now you have the option to have one. So, I will ask you all again, and we shall put it to the vote. Would you rather stay here, in the Zero, or start The Game of Life once more with some much-needed rules? But beware, if you disappoint me, I will end it all, truly, end it all. What is your choice?'

The gods talked for far more time than is humanly conceivable, debating the risk and weighing up the potential gains and losses of playing Paradoxa's game. Most notably the previously unthinkable penalty of being eliminated from the game entirely. Perhaps, before she'd done this, before she'd wiped out every living thing in existence, they wouldn't have thought her capable of it. But clearly, she'd snapped. And in truth, a part of her had. So, they debated, and debated, and debated, until finally, just as Paradoxa had given up all hope that they would ever reach a decision, Titanius addressed her.

'We have made our choice.'

'What is it to be?'

The gods all spoke as one: 'We choose to play.'

Seven Billion Years Ago…

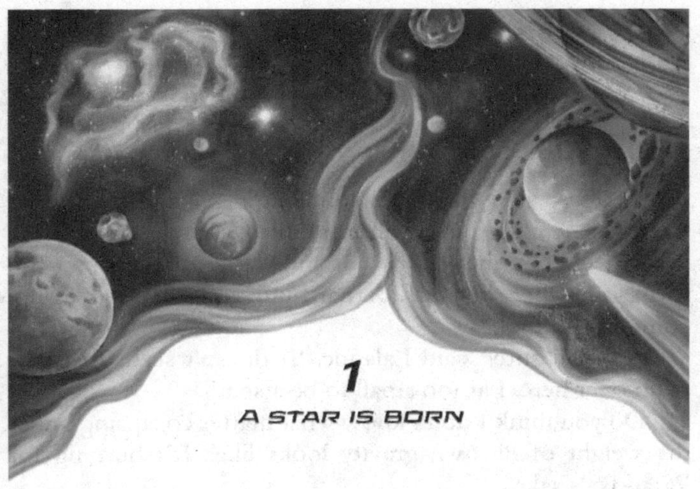

Right on the perimeter of the Megaverse, one of the parts closest to the expansion, lies the Milky Way, the most indistinct and unassuming galaxy you're ever likely to come across. There's not much that I could really tell you about it. There are a few stars dotted about, none of them notable in any way; some gas clouds that look quite pretty, I suppose, if you're impressed by that sort of thing; a scarce smattering of planets to add to the scenery– none with any lifeforms of course– and space debris, lots of space debris. Apart from that, there's not much to say.

What, you might ask, brings us to this dreary, lifeless patch of starlight and space dust sitting in the middle of nowhere with nothing of interest in sight? Something so extraordinary, so unimaginably rare, so tantalisingly curious, that everybody, and I mean everybody, is going to be talking about it.

The birth of a new god.

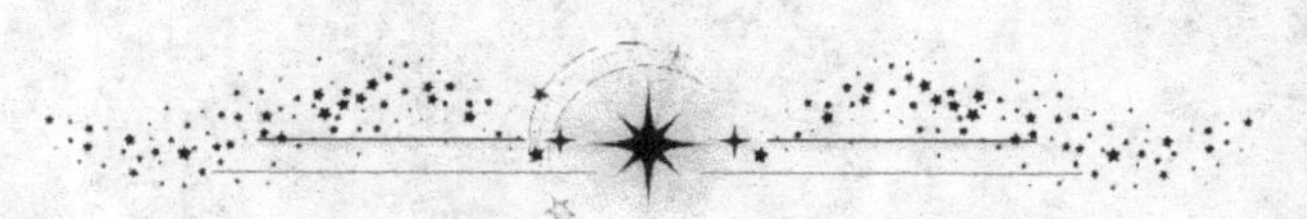

'Erm, guys, it looks like someone's regenerating,' said Arcturus, sending out a call to all the nearby star-gods. He had left the confines of his star and was floating in his pure form somewhere between Bernard and Sirius. 'It's waking up, come have a look.'

'Are you sure?' said Lalande. 'It doesn't seem that way from over here. Far too small to be a star.'

'Do you think I don't know what matter collapsing under the weight of its own gravity looks like? It's burning for Paradoxa's sake.'

'Oh, stop it, that's not a star,' said Tongwera. 'Not likely to fit any planets around that, are you?' He laughed, and some of the other gods laughed with him.

Mirembe connected to her senses for the first time, an omnidirectional radar that feeds back information to her mind, sending a tidal wave throughout the matter. Her consciousness exploded into being as infinitely increasing information relayed itself to her. The beacon continued interminably and unimpeded. The question was answered as instantaneously as it was asked. Every piece of matter in existence said the same thing: I'm here, and I'm yours.

In her immediate vicinity, Mirembe could see conglomerated swarms of gassy matter communicating with each other. She stared, mesmerised by the light, colours and shapes of the stars.

'Of all the galaxies,' said Revati, 'in all the Megaverse. You had to explode into ours.'

'Do you think I don't know what matter collapsing under the weight of its own gravity looks like?' said Alnisa in a crude imitation of Arcturus.

Mirembe tried to make sense of what was going on.

Something about collapsing under its own weight?

'And that's another thing,' said Olawangangu. 'How many times have we told you, curfew ends at 30 hours in the Milky Way. I should report you.'

'I didn't think I needed to make a private connection when a god is regenerating. I thought you might like to know.'

Mirembe was starting to make sense of what was going on. They were having an argument; she got the impression it could all be about her. There were many other logical conclusions competing for her approval, but none seemed more likely. Certainly, all parties seemed to think they were right, and none seemed likely to back down.

'I love his originality,' said Alnisa, with casual insincerity. 'It's like he comes up with a new theory every week to find a reason to talk to us.'

Mirembe didn't like Alnisa's tone, or what she had said to him, now that she came to think of it. She'd only been alive for the blink of an eye, and already she could spot a bitch when she sees one. Impressive. Not that it matters now, because Mirembe's core had reached its optimum temperature, and before she could think another thought, she felt the very core of her essence implode. It stayed there momentarily, compressing in on itself, before exploding out violently, scattering matter everywhere.

'So,' said Arcturus. 'What, exactly, do you call that?'

'I don't believe it!' said Lu-Wong. 'He was right.'

'Someone's regenerated!' said Olawangangu, sending out the same beacon to all the nearby gods he'd berated Arcturus for doing only moments ago.

A swirling mist of colours converged at the point of the explosion as the stars left their corporeal bodies and flew their essences over to where Mirembe had materialised.

'It's starting to cool down, I think,' said Sirius. 'I wonder who it is?'

Arcturus called out to Mirembe. 'Hello, can you hear me?

What's your name?'

'Who made you spokesman for the Milky Way?' said Revati.

'No one else was doing it,' said Arcturus. 'And I happen to think I'd be a good ambassador for the Milky Way.'

Mirembe, who had not long ago regained consciousness, was trying to get to grips with the sensation of having exploded when she realised that not only was she being addressed, but this had also caused yet another argument between these quarrelsome characters.

'I'll speak then, shall I?' said Olawangangu. 'Welcome. Welcome to the Milky Way. Who do we have the pleasure of joining us on this auspicious day?'

She observed the strange objects in front of her. A group of gassy, cloud-like shapes in a variety of colours were floating a short distance in front of her. One of the shapes was trying to contact her again.

'Hello, anyone home? Can you hear me?'

'Yes,' said Mirembe. 'I can hear you. Do you always argue this much?'

Bernard laughed along with the others. 'Is there a galaxy anywhere in the Megaverse that doesn't have gods arguing about something or other? That's the problem with keeping us so isolated: there's a lot of in-fighting. Alas, Paradoxa and her infinite wisdom, who am I to judge? So, who will we be spending the foreseeable future with? Zalam? Asamaanata? Kisasi?'

'My name is Mirembe.'

'Mirembe?' said Arcturus. 'Are you sure? I don't recall there ever having been a star-god named Mirembe.'

'Behave yourself, Arcturus, she wasn't talking to you.'

'Actually,' said Mirembe, 'I was talking to him, to all of you. And yes, I am sure. My name is Mirembe. I'm not sure how I know, but I'm sure it is. I woke up here not long ago, and that's the only thing I'm 100% sure of.'

'What important galaxies have you lived in?' said Bellatrix.

'It'll help if you think of where you lived last.'

'What do you mean? I told you. I just woke up here.'

'Yes,' said Eridani, 'but where did you live the last times you were alive?'

'What do you mean the last times I was alive? This is the first time I've been alive.'

'Very clever,' said Olawangangu. 'You are good. Not many gods could be so quick on their gasses this soon after regenerating. You must be someone important. I hate to disappoint you, and I'm sad to even have to say it: you've landed in the Milky Way. Not that it'll matter if you have permission to roam.'

'I'm not being clever,' said Mirembe. 'This is definitely my first time here, or anywhere. At least I think it is. I certainly don't remember ever existing before now.'

'She's not giving up, is she?' said Lalande. 'I heard about this god once in the Hirrutopu galaxy, had them all completely convinced she was a new god for ages. I wonder if it's the same one.'

'Are you sure your name is Mirembe?' said Arcturus. 'I've never heard of a god named Mirembe.'

'Yeah, are you sure it's not Asante?' said Olawangangu.

'Sounds more likely,' said Muwan.

'I've never heard of a Mirembe myself,' said Eridani. 'Now that I come to think of it.'

'I've got to give it to you,' said Lalande. 'You are good, going to these lengths to convince us. It's actually quite fun.'

'Do you reckon this is her escapism?' said Revati. 'Pretending to be someone she's not.' He chortled and managed to get a rise out of the other gods. His essence enlarged slightly for a while, as close to a smug look as you can get as a floating cloudy essence.

'Is this some sort of game?' said Mirembe. 'I've been born into some sort of mad game, is that it? I tell you things, facts, and you dispute them? Like what I saw you doing earlier with each other?'

Lalande cracked up.

'Well, she got one thing right at least.'

'Look, you're very funny,' said Bellatrix. 'But are you going to tell us who you are or not?'

'For the last time, my name is Mirembe! Why don't you believe me?' She couldn't understand the purpose of the game. Why did they continue to mistrust what she said, even though she had told them the truth?

'What does your name mean?' said Arcturus.

'It means, erm, hmmm,' she trailed off in thought.

'I can't wait to see what she comes up with,' said Alnisa.

'Think of your name,' said Arcturus. 'Think of who you are deep in the core of your essence. The reply will tell you your true name. Who are you, Mirembe?'

She thought for a short time, and a sudden, blinding clarity overtook her; an indefatigable light awoke in her essence, and the words came out of her with more force than she'd intended: 'My name is Mirembe, and I am Morality.'

All the gods except Arcturus burst out in hysterics, utter hysterics.

'A moral god?' said Revati. 'Who does she think she is, Paradoxa? It's bad enough having to do everything she tells us. You can fuck off if you think I'm taking orders from you.'

'Stay here, Mirembe,' said Arcturus, very seriously. 'I'm going to get someone to take you to the Registrars.'

'To take me where?'

'The Registrars. You have to register yourself as a new god. It's in The Rules.'

Some of the stars who had managed to compose themselves burst out in hysterics again.

'Stop, you're regenerating me,' said Eridani through fits of laughter.

'Surely, you don't believe her?'

Arcturus ignored them and continued to address Mirembe. 'Don't worry, there's nothing to worry about. I'll be back before you know it. Sorry about the company. You'll get used to it.'

Arcturus flew off into the distance, and the gods watched him go in astonishment.

'He's actually leaving,' said Tongwera. He yelled after him, 'Come back, you idiot.'

'He's going to splatter all over me.'

Lalande turned on Mirembe. 'Look, Compassion, Happiness, Justice, whatever your name is, you know he's going to get in an ungodly amount of trouble for leaving the galaxy, right? The nearest checkpoint is outside the Milky Way. He's literally the most gullible god I've ever met, but I didn't think he'd break a rule. Any rule, for any reason. And this is such a bad rule to break, instant regeneration, for sure. Do you feel no shame? The poor god.'

Mirembe wasn't sure if this was a game anymore. The more she listened, the more it seemed that these gods genuinely didn't believe she was a new god, something which was apparently rare around here. Only Arcturus, who it seems now faces some sort of punishment, accepts that she is telling the truth. 'Why does him breaking a rule mean he's going to be regenerated?' she said. 'And why did he choose to leave if he knew it would break a rule?'

'I've had enough, I'm going home,' said Lacaille. 'I've enough games to be getting on with in this perpetual state of existence that I find myself in. I don't need anyone bringing any more games my way.' She flew away to her star.

'Go on, I'll play along,' said Lalande. 'Not much else to do, is there? Well, Paradoxa thought there would be less chance of the gods starting to war with each other if we don't leave the galaxy we materialise in, or you know, do anything that resembles fun in any form. So, we just kind of float all day doing nothing. Or at least we usually do, only now Arcturus has left the galaxy, violating a rule, and the Decision Makers are not known for their leniency.'

'Right, I understand, I think. Only now I have many more questions, and I am yet to get an answer to a previous one.

Why would he leave if he knew it would break a rule? Also, what type of decisions do Decision Makers make? And why did the gods war with each other?'

Lalande turned to the others in disbelief. 'Why did they war with each other? You can't be serious.'

'She is pretending to be new,' said Xalistya. 'You can't expect her to break character.'

'I'm not pretending to be anything,' said Mirembe. She was starting to get annoyed with this mistrust. It didn't seem the nicest way to greet someone on their first day of life. 'If you're not going to tell me why they warred, or at least why the conflict never ended, will you at least tell me why he would leave if he knew it would break a rule?'

'He left because you told him you were a new god, and he believed you,' snapped Tongwera. The red and orange completely overtook the brown in his essence for a time before settling back down.

'Right, so if I'm a new god, then he hasn't broken a rule?' A feeling of relief began to overtake the anxiety that she had been feeling, worried as she was that Arcturus, the only god she'd met that seemed remotely reasonable, might be in trouble. Though she still got the impression that they mistrusted everything she said, which made her think that maybe she had misjudged the situation again and that in fact it was all a game of interrogation; where one side extracts answers but refuses to accept their authenticity, and the other protests their innocence and gets increasingly annoyed. Though she still couldn't see a point to it.

'You're actually quite sinister,' said Lalande.

'You know, I half believe her,' said Eridani. 'She seems too nice to be lying, gullible almost, like she hasn't got a personality yet.'

'I think that's the point,' said Olawangangu.

Mirembe was getting to grips with all the new concepts she was addressing. She knew the word and what it meant as soon as she heard it; experiencing the concept itself was new.

Personality, niceness and gullibility. She liked aspects of all three. Having qualities that are uniquely her is a feeling she felt she would enjoy, being nice is something she felt she would expect of all entities, and trusting others felt like something she should do. Again, she felt they disapproved, and they still thought she was lying.

'What can I say that will convince you that I'm a new god?' she said, now quite desperate. 'Arcturus is the only one of you who believes me, and I wouldn't have done anything to get him regenerated. I really did wake up here for the first time, and I have not lived anywhere else, ever.'

'I don't actually think we can talk to her if we don't play along,' said Bellatrix.

'I suppose we've got to do something to entertain ourselves.'

'What can I say?' said Alnisa. 'Welcome to the Milky Way, here's your welcome parade, a handful of star-gods with no titles or privileges.'

'Aha!' said Lalande. 'If you're a new god then where is the welcome parade?'

'OH YEAH!' said Revati. 'I forgot about that.'

'That happens when someone collects her.'

'Oh yeah,' said Revati, with a lot less enthusiasm.

'I have not yet encountered any form of parade, unless, of course, you mean, –' said Mirembe, but she had no reason to protest her innocence any longer. An obscenely large figure popped into existence in between her and the other gods. It fixed its attention on Mirembe. She felt it prying into her essence. Despite the slightly grotesque look of its faces, she could see that each of them had curved into quite possibly the truest smile she'll ever see.

An orchestra of fireworks erupted into being all throughout the Milky Way. Billions of silvery metallic robots materialised around Mirembe and began to march in synchrony around her star in a series of laddered steps.

As Paradoxa would expect, the quietly reassuring

progressive perfection that is Mozart's Requiem K.626 in the mandatory D Minor emanated in the minds of the gods to introduce The Anthem.

More Resources appeared and flew around Mirembe, performing aerial acrobatics. Balls of bright electromagnetic light shot from the marching robots' eyes, swirling around Mirembe's star in a tornado of lights.

A ripple of energy swept through the parade, dragging some of the robots together magnetically. Each of them morphed into a series of screens. Snippets of life in the Megaverse appeared on them: different planets with lifeforms; gasses, oceans and landscapes; stars, galaxies and universes. Around the screens and dancing robots, the fireworks and displays, everywhere Mirembe looked, the same words shone brightly:

'Welcome, Mirembe! To the Game of Life.'

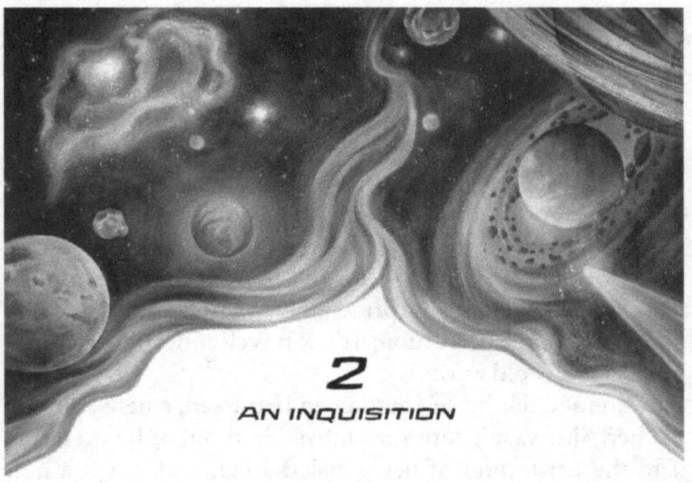

'Welcome, Mirembe. Welcome to life, the galaxy, the universe, the Megaverse, to existence itself. I'm Oxygenus: I'm an element-god. Supreme logician. Overlord of lifeforms. I'm here to escort you to the Registrars.'

'OH, MOTHER OF PARADOXES!' said Revati. 'A NEW GOD!'

Oxygenus, who was manifesting as one of his highest-level species, those who can survive in space, without the protection of a world, turned one of his heads towards Revati in a look of disapproval.

Mirembe was still remembering the sensation of hearing music for the first time and enjoying all the colours and shapes when she accepted that all this was happening because, finally, these entities believed that she was indeed a new god. 'I can't tell you how happy I am to see you!' she exclaimed. 'They have all been convinced that I am a liar. All except Arcturus, did he send you?'

'Oh, yes,' said Oxygenus. He moved one of his tentacle arms inside an inner layer of skin and extracted Arcturus. 'Here we are, you're free, just needed to ensure you weren't breaking any rules.'

'Thank you,' said Arcturus, who seemed to be in awe of Oxygenus.

'Thank you!' said Mirembe. 'I was worried you might be in some sort of trouble.'

'No, I told you not to worry. I knew as soon as you told me your name, your true name, that you were new. I always wondered why there's never been a God of Morality. We've had a lot of gods wanting a lot of different things, but none who would genuinely pride their whole existence on complete moral perfection. It's a novel concept, even in a Megaverse as old as ours.'

Mirembe felt herself getting embarrassed, a new emotion for her. She wasn't sure she enjoyed it, though she preferred it to the frustration of being called a liar, and it was a new sensation all the same.

'He's right,' said Oxygenus. 'There has never been a god named Mirembe, very curious. Anyway, we must leave for the Registrars, rules are rules: daren't miss a deadline. Mirembe, if you'll leave your star and pop into one of these folds.'

She looked at his outer shell and recoiled in disgust. 'I'm not sure how to leave, and I'd rather not get inside there. Is there no other way to travel?'

Some of the gods sniggered, then stopped quickly as Oxygenus focused some of his heads on them. 'Very demanding for a star-god,' he said. 'I suppose since you're new we can fly. A nice experience for you on your first day of life.' His body disappeared, and a silvery-grey essence, much larger than the other gods, took its place. 'Just think of yourself leaving the confines of your body, imagine yourself outside of your star, separated from it.'

She focused on the space outside her star and tried to imagine herself there. Nothing happened. She could feel the point in spacetime that she wanted to reach, she felt it calling to her. She tried again to answer. Other than a slight vibration that ran through her essence, she hadn't moved at all.

She closed her mind's eye and focused intently on the point in spacetime she wanted to reach. She felt her particles charging in anticipation, like a cat readying itself for launch. With a blast of light, she shot from her star.

All the gods, even Oxygenus, let out a gasp. Mirembe was not a single colour, or even one hundred, which is known to happen; she was the full spectrum of colour, all forty-thousand, three hundred and thirty-three primary colours.

'What do we have here?' asked Oxygenus, aloud and to himself.

Mirembe was starting to feel embarrassed again. The first time she'd ever been naked in front of anyone, and they all gasped in amazement. She didn't yet know the sensation of being laughed at for a natural feature, so for the moment, this kind of embarrassment seemed almost negative.

'Have I done something wrong?' she said, unsure what was causing the surprise.

'No, no, not at all,' said Arcturus. 'You're special, Mirembe. Most gods don't have as many colours as you do.'

Oxygenus seemed lost in thought as he answered. 'Indeed, you are, erm, unusual. Very peculiar indeed. Anyway, time waits for no god. We should leave. I'll carry you. It'll expedite things.'

A beam of light stretched out from Oxygenus to Mirembe. It cocooned her essence and moved her into place next to him. Aside from both being swarms of coloured gas, they looked exactly like a motorbike with a sidecar.

'See you later,' said Olawangangu.

'Brace yourself,' said Oxygenus.

Mirembe screamed with excitement as she hurtled through the galaxy, her core a whirlwind. The solar systems of the Milky Way appeared to streak into a line as she passed. She felt somehow more in tune with the stars the closer she got to them.

She tried to stay focused on objects long enough to enjoy

their beauty, only to be dragged away at thousands of times the speed of light, as Oxygenus used his own energy and matter-energy to accelerate their advance.

'So,' said Oxygenus, increasing his volume in their telepathic connection to combat the interference of travelling at such astronomical speeds. 'How are you enjoying your first day in the Megaverse?'

'At first, it wasn't looking like it would be a very pleasant experience, but since you arrived, things have definitely improved. That was such an incredible display back there. All those things dancing, and the images on the screens. It was so beautiful. Though I think flying tops all of that, this feels incredible.'

'I'm glad I could be of assistance. Flying is one of my favourite activities. It's the one thing I never get bored of.'

'Wahoooo,' screamed Mirembe as they sped up faster than before, using Inertia for an even greater boost. They'd left the Milky Way now and were making their way through the Andromeda galaxy.

Mirembe felt herself jerk off course, only to be pulled by an even greater force in the opposite direction.

'Sorry about that,' said Oxygenus. 'I didn't see the black hole there.'

'A black hole…' said Mirembe, mulling over the concept.

'Yes, it's what happens when really large stars die. Quite an interesting place to go.'

'I see. So, I'll die one day and become a black hole?'

'That all depends on you. You're quite a small star. You'd need to accrete a lot more matter to become a black hole. So, probably not in your first life. You also don't regenerate while you're a black hole, you're in a kind of limbo between death and rebirth. I wouldn't recommend it, though, of course, I've never tried.'

Interesting. 'As I understand it, star-gods are regenerated repeatedly, and if it is my fate to die over and over, perhaps one day I will choose to be a black hole just for some stability.

Probably not for a long time though, because I'd quite like to explore the Megaverse, and I'd need to regenerate to do that, wouldn't I?' Her voice fell and rose in pitch as she emotionally evaluated each option.

'Indeed, you would. You're learning quickly.'

Her essence shimmered turquoise. She felt embarrassed again, only this time it was less potent and somewhat enjoyable. 'Thank you, but I feel like my total knowledge is extremely limited because for every piece of information I learn, myriad more questions arise.'

'Another joy in life, Mirembe, is answering questions that you really want to know the answer to. Truly, learning is one of the greatest gifts of existence.'

'What an adventure! Oh, things really are looking much better. Will it take long to get to the Registrars? I don't want this flight or conversation to end. You're very funny, Oxygenus.'

'You're too kind, my dear. Don't fear, we can chat a little while longer before we reach the Registrars.'

'Good. And will you escort me to the Registrars every time I regenerate?'

'No, you only need to register your first birth at the Registrars. You report regenerations to the galaxy you're born in. The galaxies report regenerations up to The Executive. They're supposed to, at least, but as you saw, they're not always the quickest to respond. Not even The Executive can really change that. There's a lot of bureaucracy involved in the regeneration of an entire galaxy, and they do tend to report it all, just not straight away. I suppose it is a lot to ask, given the sheer number of stars there are in any one galaxy.'

His tone changed, becoming bitchier and more excited. 'Having said that, the universes manage to meet their punctuality targets, and there are often more galaxies in a universe than there are stars in a galaxy. Not that it matters, it's worked out better this way. As a new god, someone would have had to come to collect you. Much less compu-work now.'

'I didn't realise the Milky Way is sentient. It didn't say anything. Would it have been able to tell that I'm a new god? It didn't help me when I told the others that I was new.' Her essence flashed red momentarily.

'Give him a chance, you've not long been born, he's probably sleeping. There hasn't been a new god in almost all the Megayears since the reset. Registering old essences who have regenerated has a different deadline.'

Mirembe was beginning to understand why the other gods hadn't believed her when she told them that she was a new god. She resolved to give each of them a second chance. Arcturus really had taken a leap of faith on her, trusting her from the outset like that, to know that she meant what she said when she told him she was the God of Morality. 'Oh my, that is exciting. I wonder why I've been born, now, after all this time.'

'Your guess is as good as mine.'

How extraordinary, she thought. *And what an exceptionally pleasing Megaverse to be born into. It's all so astoundingly beautiful.*

'I can't believe you're not allowed to leave the galaxy you're born in,' she said, both shocked and annoyed. 'Look at this stuff, I want to explore. Do we ever get to see anything outside of the galaxy? What about that place you said before, The Executive?'

'Sorry to disappoint you, The Rules forbid intergalactic travel for star-gods. There's plenty to see in the Milky Way… and you'll be in good company,' he said, entirely dishonestly. 'Who knows, you might become a star-god with lifeforms, and then you'll have to come back to the Registrars, or you might be called to a debate, and there aren't any offertories in the Milky Way, so you'll get to leave. Or, when you're older and more knowledgeable, you might get a job at The Executive. There are a lot of bureaucracy roles there, which will give you extra roaming rights.'

'Bureaucracy roles doing what? What actually happens at The Executive?'

'It's where myself and the other elements make decisions. Even Paradoxa pops in from time to time on particularly important cases. The only role there is a Bureaucrat, but there are different grades and departments. Administration, quality assurance, regulation and compliance, etcetera. Almost all of them involve a lot of compu-work, it's very dull, I won't lie.'

'Paradoxa?' Everyone she'd met so far seemed to know her. 'Who is she? She seems important.'

'She is important. She makes The Rules, we apply them, you, and everyone else follow them.'

'I see. And what about Paradoxa and the element-gods, must they follow the rules too?'

'We must all follow The Rules,' he said, in a tone that conveyed the ludicrous number of times he had said that sentence. 'The higher one's rank, the more rules one must follow. One gets better privileges, fewer restrictions and a lot more responsibility. Paradoxa is the only one who doesn't have to follow The Rules.'

It seemed to Mirembe that almost everything in life came with some rule, consequence, or responsibility. She wasn't sure if she felt like having all her decisions made for her. 'What happens if one doesn't follow The Rules?'

'You know, after the wars, after Paradoxa wiped everything out, after she regenerated and regenerated every type of entity for disobedience, after she expelled eighty-three elements from time and space, after she imprisoned and tortured infinite entities in the most unimaginable ways, there just hasn't been much rule breaking. Most of the gods who come to us haven't broken any rules. It's the gods or lifeforms they're responsible for who have broken the rules, and they get punished for it.'

'That seems totally unfair. How can someone be responsible for something they haven't caused?'

'I find it best not to question Paradoxa: it makes following her rules so much easier. You can almost like her if you do. Maybe if I existed in a world where she wanted to control everything for some evil end, then I'd try and fight it. Though we would not win, and in truth, all she wants is order, Fair and Just Order. And I, as the overlord of lifeforms, know all too well the nature and problems of war and the perils of chaos.'

War again. She didn't like the sound of it. 'What are the problems and nature of war and the perils of chaos?'

His essence went a shade lighter, and while he doesn't currently have a face, he is smiling. 'You're incredibly curious for a star-god, aren't you?'

'Surely you're in a better position to answer that question?' She laughed at his thoughtlessness, unaware that this counted as insubordination. Her attention was caught by a massive star with around sixty planets orbiting it. She had sensed them from the moment of her birth, able to constantly connect to all particles of matter in existence. There was something about proximity that made the connection more meaningful. Two of the planets had strange-looking creatures in worlds made of water. She marvelled over their intricate nature. How the lifeforms all moved in synchrony in little groups, working together to achieve a common goal.

'Wow, those are absolutely stunning,' she said. 'What is that autonomous matter, over there, in that liquid? I can sense an essence response not present in all matter.'

'Those all get lumped together as aquatic lifeforms. Quaint little water worlds those, been going for thousands of years now. They're all grade three and below. No lifeforms past grade four, no languages or large-scale manufacturing, or such. I imagine she's hoping they stay like that, most worlds tend to move to "excessive warfare" once they reach grade four and above, which is never good. Though, unless they can invent something to create water-free zones, there isn't as much risk: water makes engineering extremely difficult. War fought with natural appendages doesn't tend to warrant intervention.'

'Existence seems incredibly complex,' she said, taking in all the new things she was learning.

'Yes, you'll get used to it. I find it makes existence more bearable, having so many possible outcomes. It staves off boredom.'

'I suppose it would get quite boring if everything had a finite number of options.' She was enjoying her chat with Oxygenus, she was learning a lot, he seemed to have a lot of knowledge and coherent answers. But there was one question that she was yet to get an answer to, and it was something that all the gods seemed to know about. 'Perhaps you can help me reach a definite response to a question I asked earlier. Please will you explain all the causes, mechanisms, perpetual prevalence and importance of war?'

'Gosh, essentially, it's where two or more sides compete with each other for dominance, and frequently use barbaric and deadly tactics to achieve that goal. They do it because they want to or need to. It's bad when gods go to war because they're capable of emotions like sadness, but unlike us, lifeforms can feel pain and suffering. Sending them to war is arguably unconscionable.'

'That does sound bad. I don't think I'd like to find myself in a war, and I doubt I'd like to see one. Wait a minute. You said that Paradoxa tortured the gods into compliance. How can that be if they don't feel pain?'

A god who doesn't like war, he thought. *Whatever next*. 'They don't feel pain. Paradoxa simply makes them feel what she feels all the time: the pain and pleasure of every living entity in existence. Worse still, she can amplify the pain and stop any pleasure from getting through. Or, let bits of happiness seep in, giving them hope again, only to take it all back and plunge them into incomparable suffering once more. From what I've heard, it's truly horrific. I haven't personally been stupid enough to disobey her, but those who have almost never disobey her again. And it works! There has been a lot less war since she implemented The Rules.'

Hmm. She didn't like the sound of war, but she also didn't like the idea of torture as a punishment for disobedience. She wasn't sure what to think. *Paradoxa feels all this pain, which is a terrible burden. But could her forcing others to share it be justified?*

'But why did she need to implement The Rules in the first place?' she said, not yet understanding gods' relationship with power. 'You said they compete for dominance, once one side has won, doesn't that mean the war is over?'

Mirembe's pattern of thinking was interesting to Oxygenus. Whenever she was presented with an idea, she had to question it rigorously. She seemed almost as intelligent as an element. There didn't appear to be anything she didn't question. It reminded him of someone. He wondered how long that trait would last in the Milky Way, though he had no doubt it would come in useful.

'The problem with war is, it's never over,' said Oxygenus, in a tone so casual it did great injustice to the gravity of the truth it contained. 'Conflict is a natural and inevitable part of existence, which requires cooperation and innovation to overcome. Most species start from a position of conflict: war naturally evolves from this convergence. Thus, even when one side chooses not to be at war, has no imperial ambitions, and takes no steps to enslave, own or destroy other living entities: the other sides are thinking of ways to do exactly that to them. Many dominant lifeforms in the Old World and even a few in the New World, came into existence and tried to end the natural wars caused by competition for essential, life-giving resources. Choosing instead to rebel against their overlords and cooperate with each other, showing respect to the other lifeforms that they shared their planets with. Sadly, only those who had a military that could be organised at a world level were able to defend themselves from warmongers. And even with a centralised military, which exists only to defend the planet against invaders and noncombative aliens, there is still war, because most planets have an ecosystem where the lifeforms subsist on one another. So, even if they broker peace with the higher-grade animals, there's always the food chain. And even if they choose to live on lifeforms that don't feel pain– which isn't even possible for some species– the less rational animals won't, so there will still be some war. Then there are the microscopic bacteria, some of whom are at constant war with all other lifeforms, with no peace treaty available. Their whole existence depends on living inside other lifeforms, burrowing into their vital organs and systems and living there until both lifeforms are dead. There is no end to war, Mirembe. There can only ever be less war. The game does not permit a complete end to war.'

Finally, she thought, *an answer that makes sense. Everything competes for its chance to live at the expense of something else. What a disgusting game. No wonder everyone talks about war: it's inherent in the game.*

They flew past another star, this time with lifeforms that didn't move as much as the others she'd seen but still appeared to grow.

'So, did Paradoxa create this game? Because it seems to me an outrageous thing to do, to create this game and then police it. And once you move onto the subject of suffering and torture, it becomes thoroughly abhorrent. You can't create things and then torture them if you don't like what they do. Don't create them in the first place. I'm not sure I like this Paradoxa: seems a sadistic character.'

Oxygenus let out an uncharacteristic giggle, genuinely amused for the first time in aeons. 'No, you can't blame Paradoxa. She didn't create this game, and she never got involved in the wars in the Old World– she just ignored them. She's banned the creation of any lifeforms now, of course. Gods are forbidden from creating life and controlling them or sending them to war is completely out of the question.'

'If she's banned it, why are there lifeforms all over? And if she didn't create this game, who did? It said, "Welcome, Mirembe! To the Game of Life!". I'm not sure I approve of this game. It's all well and good flying through space and observing all the wondrous sights, and you seem very cooperative, much more sensible than those other gods, but I really must know, who created this game? Because from what I've seen so far, there seems to be a great deal of possible outcomes which would result in punishment or potentially even suffering. I'm not sure I even want to play, and my choice has been taken away from me, since I have not chosen to be born. War that can't be ended? What a crude design.' She was thoroughly indignant, self-righteous in a way that few stars are.

Oxygenus smiled to himself. *What a powerful character, so alive with passion. Not often one meets a star-god with an attitude.* 'Nobody knows how it all started, we've all puzzled, tried to work it out, not even Paradoxa knows for sure… though she says she does, and we each have our theories. But that's all they are, theories. Nobody knows. To complicate matters further, it just keeps going, a constant cycle of expansion and regeneration. And I'm afraid, to complicate matters even further, it has quite a number of flaws that can't be deleted.'

He paused to let her take in the reality of her existence. 'The reason you've seen lifeforms is the same reason you're alive and having this conversation with me today. When different particles align in exact ways, life is created. It can't be ended. Banning the creation only reduces the number of entities that enter existence, it doesn't eliminate the problem entirely.'

She felt calmer now. The idea that some abhorrent monster would sit around judging everyone all day in a barbaric game that they created, seemed to her an appalling thing to do. Someone, on the other hand, who was simply born into a position of power and has chosen to impose order was much easier to deal with. Though she still didn't know her motives, and her power wasn't enough to convince Mirembe that Paradoxa was a noble character. 'What are these rules that Paradoxa feels are the answer to everything?'

'You'll learn that at the Registrars.'

'Why, what happens when we get to the Registrars?'

'They'll register you,' he said, with a hint of derision. 'And then you'll go through Indoctrination.'

'Indoctrination?' She understood the word but not the context it was used in.

'Of course, yes, libations being what they are. Not even Paradoxa can hold gods accountable for rules they're not aware of. You'll see soon enough.'

Mirembe's world swirled around like a washing machine on a power rinse as her corporeal essence squeezed through the fabric between universes.

'That was incredible,' she said when her world had righted itself. 'Can we do that again?'

'No, unfortunately. It only happens when travelling between universes, and we're in the universe we need to be in.'

'Oh,' she said, her glow dimming. 'And which universe is that exactly?'

'We're in universe S7A2L5E3M6. Yours is A2S7I4M6A2, we're almost there, won't be long.'

'How many universes are there in total?'

Oxygenus laughed, genuinely amused for the second time. 'An infinite amount.'

'Infinite?' *Surely not*. 'You mean they never end? It just goes on and on?'

'Correct.'

They veered again, Mirembe saw the outline of a star with lots of buildings orbiting it.

'That is mind-blowing, phenomenal information. This really has already been such an insightful journey. I can't believe it just doesn't end. And Paradoxa manages all of that, all of the universes in the Megaverse?'

'With a little help, yes.'

'How is that even possible?' She could just about contemplate there being endless worlds, but managing them, when each autonomous universe-god was composed of autonomous galaxy-gods, who are made up of autonomous star-gods, some of whom contain lifeforms, who are also autonomous, seemed an impossible task.

'Well, it certainly helps that Paradoxa is all things at all times. Not to mention the prohibition of all non-chronological time travel. It eliminates a world of problems, believe me.'

'Sorry to ask so many questions— what exactly is non-chronological time travel?'

'It's fine, you're learning,' said Oxygenus. 'There's something about a database of knowledge that simply screams "validate me". Nothing else like changing zero into a one. I haven't been doing much of interest for the last aeon, the conversation is quite OK.' *In truth, he thought, I was beginning to think you'd never show up.* He'd taken to her, she seemed so genuine and well-intentioned, though he supposed that's how all gods are at first, all life now he came to think of it. That's how entities are before they know themselves. Though there is the matter of her name, and her multicoloured essence. He was almost jealous. He'd never really liked his colours. Not much particularly bothered Oxygenus. Most of the lifeforms in the Megaverse use oxygen in some capacity, even if they create their own, like the species he inhabited earlier. Naturally, this makes him quite an important god. Still, he couldn't help but marvel at the way her colours shone.

'Well, as I'm sure you've gathered,' he said, 'we're at a specific point in spacetime travelling with it. Different entities can move through spacetime at different speeds. It is possible to reach a point in time you would like to go to faster than the ordinary movement of spacetime, and those who are particularly skilled can even go backwards in time. You can imagine the rigmarole of managing gods who can go back and alter their decisions or go forward and use some future knowledge in the past. It can be traced, eventually, there are always marks left from the action, but it is a lot of work, so non-chronological time travel is completely banned.'

'Even still, how can any single entity manage infinite autonomous entities?'

'As I've already told you, Paradoxa is all things at all times. She can simply control all entities instantaneously and simultaneously. That's Paradoxa. In one of her rarer moments of compassion, she allows us autonomy provided we stay within the confines of The Rules. She even makes you agree. She's very persuasive. She has a way of arguing you into a logical corner that you can't get out of. She's also written a rule for *every* possible move, with punishment for non-compliance. She makes the gods manage themselves in a way that complies with the New World Order. Everyone polices everyone else's actions, as well as their own actions. Then there are Enforcers, who literally do policing, a triple lock. I suppose she has an unfair advantage, taking up most of the space in the Megaverse.'

'Well, yes, if everyone manages themselves because they're all afraid of punishment, and the ones who aren't are policed by the ones who are, I suppose any number of variables could be controlled with that system. Very clever. What do you mean by the unfair advantage because of the space she takes up?'

'Paradoxa is the antithesis to all positive matter. She exists between the universes, between the galaxies, between the stars, between the planets, between the lifeforms who inhabit them, between the cells that form them, between the atoms that form them, between the particles that form them. She accounts for most of the mass in the universe, which is, anti-matter. As such, she has control over everything because everything contains endless amounts of anti-matter.'

Mirembe was starting to understand why Paradoxa is so

important. Power. 'I see. Does that mean you can control everything that has oxygen in it?'

'Yes, though we aren't allowed to control anything sentient unless they've broken a rule. We're not allowed to interfere in any way outside of The Rules.'

Quite right. She didn't like the idea of entities interfering with her, and she didn't imagine it would be any different for other entities. *Paradoxa has some wisdom.* 'You shouldn't need rules to prevent an abuse of power: you should act morally out of a desire to be good. I take it that you controlled other gods and lifeforms too before The Rules were implemented?'

He sighed, it had been a very long time since he'd had the opportunity to speak to an entity that had a clean slate in life, who hadn't wronged anyone or made any bad decisions. She also had a way of asking questions that really made you want to answer them. 'Yes, I took part in the wars, we all did. It was a different time then, but Paradoxa, to her credit, has shown us that we can still have fun, exercise power, and be important, without causing endless lifeforms to suffer. And it is a lesson that most of us only really learn the hard way. There were no rules when I was born, remember that. We made our own moral compass, and a world without rules is prey to the forces of chaos. The selfish particle exists in us all, even Paradoxa.'

He came to a stop and relinquished her. 'Anyway, we're here.'

The canvas of deep space was decorated with distant galaxies. Directly in front of her, Mirembe could see thousands of buildings made of hard glass, orbiting an average-sized star. The star itself burned bright ellimenthik and allaggitu, colours unseen by humans. The buildings were also in a multitude of colours, and each building was aligned in such a way that from an appropriate distance they spelt the word 'R E G I S T R A R S'.

Mirembe 'smiled', her gasses flashed. 'I wasn't expecting it to spell Registrars. I thought that was just the title.'

'Oh, yes,' said Oxygenus. 'Paradoxa likes words, and names, they're important to her. She does also manage to be amusing from time to time, once you know what you're looking for. Follow me.'

A streak of silver filled the gap between Mirembe and the entrance to The Registrars. She swerved a little as she followed him, not yet able to fully manage flight. She enjoyed the feeling of controlling her own flight more than when she was attached to Oxygenus, though she wasn't as fast as him, and her coordination left a lot to be desired.

She focused on where his essence had stopped and imagined herself travelling the distance between them. An eruption of multicoloured light sliced through the vacuum of space as newfound adrenaline and energy commandeered her essence.

'Come back,' said Oxygenus as Mirembe sped past him. 'You'll need a suit. You won't be able to get through the barrier without one.'

She managed to take control from the forces and eventually came to a stop. She could see two barriers, though she couldn't understand what he meant because she was completely through one, and half of her was through the other. 'Sorry, I couldn't stop.'

She extracted herself from the barriers and flew over to him.

Oxygenus' essence disappeared. Thin, scaley green legs grew out of the floor. The skin bubbled like a rising, foamy tide, stretching out into a torso with wings at the back. Six long arms extended from the side of its body. Shiny silver eyes flashed at Mirembe from the centre of its chest as the composition of its skin solidified.

Mirembe marvelled over the lifeform. Its eyes were wide and inviting. It was much more attractive than the last one, seemed almost friendly, though a little daunting.

Oxygenus waved one of his arms and a clear, flexible-glass uniform, which looked a lot like a centaur with a fly's head, appeared out of the air. It had eight legs, a torso, four arms, and a head equipped with a voice box and two long antennae. 'You'll need to get in here,' he said. 'Like before, when you left your star, only in reverse. Imagine your essence inside the suit.'

Everything went dark for an infinitesimal amount of time, and when her vision returned to her, this time it was through the suit. Mirembe's arms jerked up and down, her hands clenched and unclenched. It felt strange, but she liked it. She jumped up in the air excitedly. 'I think I quite like limbs.'

The skin of Oxygenus' eyes glistened with unspoken thoughts. 'Very good, Mirembe. I hope life is always this fun for you. Now that you've mastered movement, perhaps we should go inside.'

The solid gold floor rippled as they walked along it, hugging their feet, making an imprint as they pressed down.

It was odd for Mirembe, seeing through this outfit. Her radar was blocked entirely. Her vision was considerably more limited than in her essence form, and she could hardly hear anything, given the need for vibrations to touch her suit for her to sense them. Yet, it felt a more interesting experience, perceiving part of the world so simply. The first time since her birth that she felt disconnected from all the matter in existence. Everything looked so solid through the suit's eyes. The inner workings of the objects hidden from her view.

The floor started to slide forward. Mirembe grabbed hold of Oxygenus for support.

'I thought I'd speed things up. Indoctrination will take a while.'

'How did you make the floor move like that?'

'Oh, you just think it dear, and it does it. One of Paradoxa's miracles.'

'Wouldn't it have been quicker to just materialise where we need to be? Like you did when you first arrived.'

'This is the visitors' entrance,' he said, turning his whole body sideways to face her. 'And when you're grown, I suspect you'll enjoy the time spent travelling between tasks. It's a freedom you seldom enjoy elsewhere.'

His tone amused her. All his words were so laboured and everything he said seemed completely sardonic. *I suppose if you're going to learn something it may as well be amusing.*

The clear glass doors dematerialised to let them through. Mirenbe's feet clattered against the ground as she walked, her pace mirroring her enthusiasm. A counter with touchscreens awaited them, behind which she could see lots of interacting components making sounds she'd never heard before.

Oxygenus touched the glass with one of his many fingers. 'VERIFIED: OXYGENUS' flashed on the screen, then it began to speak. 'Welcome. May Fair and Just Order be the ruler of our lives. How may I assist you, Oxygenus?'

'I need to register a new god.'

A symbol appeared on the screen, furling and unfurling, in what appeared to signal thought. 'Thank you,' it said, finally. 'Did you mean registering a collision?'

'No,' said Oxygenus. 'I mean, registering a new god.'

'Thank you. And which universe did the collision occur in?'

Oxygenus rolled his eyes and let out a slight tut. 'Cancel request. New request. I am registering a new god.'

'Thank you. Did you mean registering an advanced lifeform?'

Mirembe suppressed a giggle.

'No. Cancel request. New request. I'm here to register a new god.'

'Sorry, I didn't understand that. Did you mean registering a sentient machine?'

Oxygenus threw his arms in the air. Several panels behind the desk blew off and smashed on the floor. His voice echoed around the building, 'GET OUT HERE, NOW!'

Mirembe's face was featureless, unable to express the disapproval she felt at this unnecessary display of anger. She was shocked. This wasn't the Oxygenus she'd been speaking with earlier.

The building stopped shaking. A levitating machine came rushing out of what used to be a doorway. 'Oxygenus, your superiority,' it said through its voice box. 'I did not realise you were here. How may I assist you?'

'You may assist me by registering a new star-god, as I have asked you to do four times already.' The anger in his words vibrated through the silent room. Half of his arms came to rest on his hips, the other half crossed tightly underneath his eyes. He stared at the machine intently.

'A new god? Are you sure?' It looked from Oxygenus to Mirembe, and then back again. 'Oh, I mean, well, of course you're sure, that's what you said. Please accept my apologies. Request received. Where did it materialise?'

'Finally.' He stretched the word beyond its full limit. 'She materialised in Universe A2S7I4M6A2, in the Milky Way, quadrant seventeen thousand and fifty-nine. Her name is Mirembe. She's the God of Morality.'

The robot hesitated momentarily and observed Mirembe. 'Thank you. When was she born?'

'I believe it was around fifty hours ago. Not more than a day.'

'RULES OBEYED: REGISTRATION PUNCTUAL' flashed on the screen in bold green letters. The brain of the machine flew over to Mirembe.

'Mirembe, please place your hands on the screen. Make sure your essence is spread evenly.'

A force anchored her hands to the screen the moment she placed them there. She felt it clawing at her essence, not damaging it in any way, but still in complete control. Different colours competed for their chance to touch the screen. 'Erm, this is a rather unpleasant experience. I'm not sure I approve of machines rummaging around in my essence like this. What is it doing?'

'I'm just mapping your essence,' said the floating part of the machine. 'It's in The Rules. There we go.' The screen flashed again, 'RULES OBEYED: ESSENCE MAPPED'.

She felt her hands release from the screen, and the probing force disappeared. 'I can't help but feel that was rude,' she said, 'or at a bare minimum intrusive.'

'Rules are rules,' said Oxygenus and the machine simultaneously. They looked at each other, a silent exchange of thoughts. The machine spoke first, 'Please follow me, Mirembe. I will escort you to Indoctrination.'

She trotted after it and turned around to see Oxygenus was still standing there. 'Are you not coming with me?'

His gaze flicked to the floor before he looked at her. 'No, you go through Indoctrination alone. I'll wait here until you're done.' His lips curved into a wry smile. 'Enjoy.'

'Oh, see you after then.' She waved instinctively.

They turned into a passageway, and the galaxy became visible again through the glass.

'Not much further. We need to get to that platform at the end of the passage.' It pointed with one of its metallic arms.

'OK. Thanks… erm, sorry, I don't know your name.'

'I don't have a name. My Resource Number is 5526293386…'

Mirembe waited for it to finish. It didn't stop, so she interrupted. 'That's ok, I can guess the rest, it's more numbers, isn't it?'

The torrent of numbers came to an end. 'Correct.'

'I think I'll call you Resource: I don't like that you don't have a name.'

It ignored what she said. 'Please step on the platform. Once you arrive, enter the room to begin Indoctrination. I will be here to escort you back to the reception once you've finished.'

'OK, thanks, Resource.'

She jumped over the steps, not sure if she was steady enough on her legs to climb them, and onto the platform. The walls around her were unhelpfully bare as she ascended, except for the large archway that she was headed to.

The platform connected to the balcony with a click. A colossal doorway imposed over her as she disembarked. She felt, for the first time, scared.

I wonder what it's like in Indoctrination.

She walked slightly clumsily through the entrance, looking around in all directions through her antennae. A circular, domed room, with screens accounting for the entirety of the curved wall, stared blankly at her as she entered. She made her way towards the centre where a huge arrow was pointing. It disappeared once she had taken her place underneath.

The room was plunged into darkness. Mirembe felt herself locked in place by a force more powerful than any she'd encountered so far.

'INDOCTRINATION' flashed on the screen in bright white letters. The 'I' started to disintegrate, and 'INDOCTRINATION' momentarily became 'NATION', before the whole word collapsed out of view. In its place, the words 'A History of Time and Space' appeared. The sound of glass smashing rang around the room as letters crashed to the floor on the screen until only 'History', 'Time' and 'Space' were left. They flew out of the screen and circled Mirembe before vanishing as well.

A female voice echoed in all directions.

'Before the beginning there was nothing. It existed while not altogether existing, in a state before time and space; a state of inexistence. It continued in that state, with no desire to be anything but nothing, and was entirely content this way for longer than time itself.'

Something on the screen moved, and while it was still completely void of colour, Mirembe could see the shape of an essence outlined against the surface, contrasted by its emptier, more vacuous appearance.

'Until one serendipitous occurrence changed the course

of existence forevermore: Paradoxa the Precedent was born. Alone in the void, with no idea how she came to be and only her thoughts for company, she searched, unsuccessfully, for any sign of life. Over time, she grew, until her essence had demarcated the remaining nothing in the void.'

An equation flashed on the screen:

<u>Equation of Existence</u>

$$\left(\frac{Positive\ Something^{\infty} \times Negative\ Something^{-\infty}}{Space \times Time}\right)^{Force} = 0$$

'Paradoxa's birth caused the Zero to become unstable. One of the components of the Equation of Existence had come into being, and the Laws of Existence could not be restful until the rest of the components were created to reach an equilibrium. Thus, in the space left between Paradoxa and the void, the positive something was born in the form of the element-gods. Hydroga came first, and from her came Helius, Beryllius, Borona, Carbondria, Nitrogenus, Oxygenus and another eighty-five elements.

'Positive and negative something now existed, but there was no space and time for them to fill. Unable to exist and not exist simultaneously, with only part of the equation completed, the elements continuously exploded. Paradoxa rushed to their aid. She held them in place, compressing them into as small a space as possible until there was no Zero and no antithesis left between them. And then it happened. The second greatest explosion there has ever been: The Ebullient Escape.'

Swirling matter erupted on screen as the elements could be restrained no longer. Their energy exploded out, ripping the void to shreds.

'Space and Time were born, and the matter and anti-matter poured out, filling them with rapacious enthusiasm. The movement of matter and the energy from The Ebullient Escape called into existence Gravity, Magneticus, Electrica, Inertia and the other forces.'

They sprawled out through the Megaverse on screen. Gas clouds which turned into stars, which turned into galaxies, which turned into universes. Inside their core, new gods and new colours emerged as the heavier elements were born.

'The Laws of Existence divided the gods and fused them together in different combinations. The result was the creation of infinite universes, and out of this matter-energy, everything that is something was created. The endless dualism of something and nothing began their eternal tango, and time, space and force claimed their rightful place in existence. They worked together to create immeasurable stars, galaxies and universes, which orbited the Megaverse in that majestic, graceful way only the Immortals can create. And while the enigmatic wonder and stupendous beauty of existence might rightly impress you, I regret to announce that this is where the niceties come to an abrupt stop.'

The screen changed. The majestic views of the Megaverse were replaced with scenes of war. Mirembe saw elements arguing and fighting with one another, using elements and force as weapons; scheming and conniving; creating alliances then wiping out whole galaxies and universes.

'Where once there had been only darkness and peace, now there came light and war. The element-gods began to fight amongst themselves. They had infinite space and time to play with, instead, they chose to fight with each other over points in time and space that they each desired. Determined to gain dominance and notoriety, they began building new elements out of their own matter. This led to the creation of what was then known as the 'lesser elements', who could be called upon to be used in whatever way the originals demanded. This amused them for a while; the game became less static as the balance of power shifted from player to player, but they eventually got bored. And a bored god is a dangerous thing.

'They started inventing again, having exhausted the limit of elements they could create, deciding instead to make things out of the matter of the elements who already existed. They struck gold and other precious metals with the heavier elements, and with a little help from Electrica, the machines were born. The mindless machines came first, those who could follow instructions without independent thought. And they warred, which amused the gods for some time.'

The screen showed a never-ending deluge of war: Machines firing rockets and lasers at each other, cities ravaged, transport derailed, machines ripped apart, lay twitching on the floor. Planets, stars and galaxies obliterated. Mirembe observed it all with growing concern.

'Next came the sentient machines, capable of independent thought, with the ability to be programmed to be loyal to an element-god and able to make decisions it hadn't been taught to respond to. The Game of War moved to the next level: The machines started competing to create the most destructive weapons that could eliminate, suppress, or control any opponent. Again, this amused the gods for a time. All that is, except Paradoxa, who grew weary of their childish games and destructive nature. Though it was not yet unbearable. There was bullying of course; there was aggression, intimidation, fear, loathing, jealousy, anger, and sadness. There was even, for the victors, happiness, contentment, joy, pride, arrogance and pleasure. Even so, there was no pain, agony, suffering, excruciation, or anguish. And although she was forced to feel their pleasure and displeasure, Paradoxa allowed the gods to play their games; free to be who they were: to make their own happiness and their own mistakes.'

The voiceover stopped. Mirembe watched the elements go to war with one another around the room. Millipede-like machines scrambled over buildings launching attacks, airships rained down a barrage of ammunition on unsuspecting victims, war machines tore down all visible structures. And while it looked bad, she couldn't help but feel impressed by what she saw. It reminded her of a cross between the lifeforms she'd seen on her flight with Oxygenus and the display she'd seen earlier at her welcome parade, on a much more destructive scale.

The screen changed again. A machine civilisation, content, ordered, interactive and decisive. It all looked so pleasant and quaint. Until the armada arrived and destroyed everything their weapons could reach. World after world was torn apart, and the more she watched, the sorrier Mirembe started to feel for those who didn't want to play war. Especially the machines, who now thought and desired autonomy but were forced to be subservient war machines. And the stars, galaxies and universes, who kept being regenerated or dragged into war by some other means.

The battles continued, and just when it looked like one side would be ruling for eternity, something would happen that would shake the game irrevocably, shifting the balance of power.

'Still, the gods could not be restful. The Game of War consumes all those who play. Power corrupted their minds and cores. Thoughts of domination and defeat plagued their essence until they could think of nothing but war. Hydroga, Helius, Carbondria, Oxygenus, Nitrogenus and the other originals began experimenting, determined to create the machine that would take over the whole of the Megaverse.

'Though they failed in creating a machine more complex than those that already existed, out of their desire to destroy came something even more perplexing than sentient machines: organic matter. It evolved, and over time, lifeforms were born. Those who could both think and feel, with autonomy and the capacity to be manipulated, born with no prior knowledge of the world except that which is encoded in their DNA; to tell them how to grow, operate and reproduce.'

The screen showed scores of lifeforms evolving in different habitats, becoming more sophisticated and adapted to their environment.

'The gods grew giddy with excitement. Real, live toys to play with. And their temporary nature only added to the fun. How much could one lifeform, destined to die with no chance of rebirth, achieve in a single shot at existence?

'They plotted and schemed with each other, creating unique and unusual worlds and placing bacteria there, watching to see how it would adapt to survive, picking champions and gambling on the outcomes of their games. Eventually, one or more species would come out as the overall victor. The gods would reward them by manipulating and modifying them past their natural evolutionary capabilities, only to conscript them immediately into war. The oppressive and dictatorial relationship between god and lifeform grew to unfathomable obscenity as fear ruled supreme, closely followed by pain. The gods had complete control over their victims, but they did not stop at sending them to war. They wanted more than direct control. They wanted the lifeforms to AGREE that they should be controlled by these 'higher powers'. It wasn't enough for the gods to simply own their subjects, they wanted complete servitude, demanded praise, enforced obsequious reverence, punished non-conformists, and quashed rebellions. They created a world in which the gods were everything a lifeform thought about. They consulted their knowledge of the gods in all decisions, they praised them constantly, they went to war in their name, and they died playing their game. Every lifeform unlucky enough to be noticed by a god, that was smart enough to learn a script, was forced to praise the gods in hourly intervals.'

The screen changed, and this time, new cities, undamaged by war, came into view. It was different to what she'd seen when she was flying with Oxygenus. The worlds had the same complexity as the machine ones, only this time, there were lifeforms living alongside each other using integrated technology. These were clearly smarter lifeforms.

Mirembe noted how different each world looked, yet a

similar order was created around the chaos. Everything followed patterns, conformist yet idiosyncratic. She tried to appreciate the phenomenon of individual difference, that such variety could exist inside and between species, all following a similar genetic pattern yet looking and operating differently. Sadly, she was too distracted by the fact that throughout the day, they would all stop, assume what looked to be the most uncomfortable and submissive position possible for their species to take, and repeatedly chant the same words:

I AM AN INFERIOR LIFEFORM: THERE IS NOTHING GREATER THAN A GOD.

I AM THEIR LOYAL SERVANT: THEY ARE MASTER, THEY ARE ROD.

I AM A WILLING PAWN: MY ACTIONS ARE NOT MINE TO OWN.

I'LL HELP THEM BUILD THEIR EMPIRES: ANY COST TO SEAT THEIR THRONE.

GODS HAVE ALL THE POWER: TO SERVE THEM IS THE GREATEST CAUSE.

I WORSHIP THEM PERPETUALLY: FOR ALL ACTIONS THEY DESERVE APPLAUSE.

NO MATTER WHAT DISPAIR I SEE: IN MY MIND THEY DO NO WRONG.

FIGHTING IN THEIR GAME OF WAR: THE PLACE WHERE I BELONG.

TO DIE FOR THEM IN BATTLE: THE GREATEST HONOUR TO RECEIVE.

THEIR LOVE FOR ME IS GENUINE: THEY DICTATE, SO I BELIEVE.

NO MATTER WHAT I WANT IN LIFE: THEY DECIDE HOW I SHOULD LIVE.

AND AT THE END OF ALL OF THIS: MORE PRAISE TO THEM I FREELY GIVE.

I AM THEIR LOYAL SERVANT: THEY ARE MASTER, THEY ARE ROD.

I AM AN INFERIOR LIFEFORM: THERE IS NOTHING GREATER THAN A GOD.

Thousands of ships descended on the city Mirembe was currently watching, and she heard her first real scream, the kind that only something that feels pain can produce. She understood a scream and its crescendo the instant she awoke. The medium and melody of love through which it played resonated with her in yet unheard tones. Her core went deadly still. Rockets and other weaponry descended on the lifeforms in the middle of their prayer. They ran about, scattering everywhere, screaming, trying to assist other lifeforms nearby and escape from the line of fire. A different species descended from the ships and started slaughtering everyone they met.

Mirembe tried to move, to shield her eyes. She was locked in place, forced to watch the carnage of world after world being torn to pieces in a pointless and horrific Game of War. It wasn't like before, with the machines, she could understand their pain, truly empathise with their suffering. As they lay bleeding on the ground, clutching to their loved ones in despair, she understood intrinsically that this was suffering. Her essence turned completely red.

This game is cruelty of the highest order, she raged. *What an absolute atrocity! I can't believe anything that exists could be so cruel. Those evil oppressors! They demanded complete servitude from these lifeforms, they made them worship them every day, even though they created a world in which they suffered so much, born to fight their way to the top only to be engineered into a weapon once more, and die at the cause. And not content with this revolting display of power, which is all it is, a disgusting abuse of power: they demanded that in their own mind, these poor, unfortunate lifeforms thought of these gods as great, reverent, beyond comparability or competition.*

The idea that a lifeform can be thrust into a world in which there is no possible action that can be taken that would lead to zero suffering in a lifetime, whilst having the complete ability to prevent it, to then be conscripted immediately into war, was such an unforgivable act, that coupled with the suffering she had seen, Mirembe resolved never to speak to a single element-god ever again.

Black and turquoise forced their way back through and the rest of her colours followed in their path. Her essence wept a tear for every lifeform that she had seen suffer in this game as the gravity of war took its toll on her.

The voiceover restarted. 'War took centre stage in the lives of all those who think, and the cries for help by those who feel were heard by Paradoxa. She tried to reason with the gods, to make them see the error of their ways, to make them show compassion and end the wars. The gods would not listen: they had no fear. Power controlled their mind and core; their hubris knew no bounds. They continued to play their evil games, with lifeforms who could not defend themselves. The pleas for help came to Paradoxa in unprecedented droves until she could ignore them no longer. Being forced to feel the pain and suffering of every being in existence took its toll on her. The request to end existence altogether had been received so many times, from so many different entities, that Paradoxa was eventually compelled to grant them their wish. Using her knowledge and power, she engineered the biggest supermassive black hole there has ever been, and the entire Megaverse was sucked out of existence, pulled back into existence, and then back out again. This went on for undecillions of Megayears until there was nothing minus Zero left. Paradoxa had wiped out all that the gods had created, ending the suffering of all lifeforms and destroying the gods themselves.'

Everything went dark again. The room was silent. Mirembe waited, unsure what was coming.

After a long wait, the voiceover restarted. Balls of energy incarnated in the Zero on screen. 'In a display of compassion and acknowledgement that each of the gods had, on at least one occasion in their life, asked her for help and advice on how to be a moral entity, Paradoxa decided to give the gods a second chance, for showing that they each had the desire to be good. She allowed them to regenerate within the Zero and let the destruction of their empires stand as a warning that if they ever disobeyed her again, they would cease to exist entirely. She offered them a choice. They could either live autonomously in the Zero, or live under her control in the New World, prohibited from creating, controlling, or harming any living being. After an extremely short debate, the gods unanimously decided to play the Game of Life again. Paradoxa commandeered the matter of the element-gods, who now numbered one thousand and one, and compressed them until there was nothing but positive something between them. And then it happened. The greatest explosion there has ever been: The Great Gamble.'

The imagery exploded out of the screen. The Megaverse being reborn swam around Mirembe. This time it was even more spectacular than before. The creation of new universes increased in speed, and because all the elements existed in The Great Gamble, unlike The Ebullient Escape, even more complex and endearing structures were created from their particles.

'As soon as the gods had regenerated in the New World, Paradoxa called upon them all and instructed them in The Rules of Life. A hierarchy was created, with Paradoxa having complete autocracy over everything in existence, the elements given responsibility for all the universes made of their matter, the galaxies given responsibility over the stars made of their matter, the stars given responsibility for anything made of their matter, and time, space and the other Immortals given responsibility for themselves.

'Institutions and entities were formed to oversee the enforcement of The Rules. Thus, The Executive, the Debaters, the Decision Makers, the Bureaucrats, the Enforcers, the Observers and the Resources came into being. Any god caught creating life, abusing life, travelling in non-chronological time, travelling without permission, or otherwise infracting The Rules was called before The Executive as Enemies of Fair and Just Order, forced to take the full force of Paradoxa's justice. Before long, every god in existence agreed to follow The Rules. The amount of war reduced significantly, and existence reached a new equilibrium.'

The screen showed life in the New World. It was much more peaceful than it had been previously, though the lifeforms still fought with each other, just as Oxygenus had said that they did. And some societies still warred, though they were promptly destroyed by the explosion of the star they lived near or the galaxy or universe they inhabited.

'Paradoxa brought order to the Megaverse. The Game of Life became much more bearable for the entities that inhabit it. And while war still exists, there is no godly involvement, the lifeforms are suffering considerably less, and Fair and Just Order rules supreme.'

The imagery on the screen vanished. Everything went dark and silent again.

Mirembe waited in the dark, wondering when she would regain control of her limbs.

The word 'INDOCTRINATION' flashed on the screen in bright white letters. The 'I' started to disintegrate, and 'INDOCTRINATION' momentarily became 'NATION', before the whole word collapsed out of view. In its place, the words 'A History of Time and Space' appeared. The sound of glass smashing rang around the room as letters crashed to the floor on the screen until only 'History', 'Time' and 'Space' were left. They flew out of the screen and circled Mirembe before vanishing as well.

She was confused at first, but she quickly realised that she was being made to watch the whole thing again. She didn't want to watch it again. She'd seen enough.

Indoctrination didn't care what she wanted. It forced her to watch it, locking her in place so she couldn't leave or shield her antennae. She watched it through a second time, then a third, fourth, fifth. Every time she thought it was going to be the last time. She was wrong.

The story of existence played on repeat for over a billion earth-years, until she knew every word the voiceover was going to say, every battle that was going to take place, every piece of information Indoctrination could provide, she knew it all before it was shown. She had gone completely delirious, not able to remember how to think of anything but the information she was being shown. And in her core, she loathed the element-gods, who had done such evil in the Megaverse, whose actions had led to her being forced to watch it all on repeat.

The screen went dark again for the billionth time. Mirembe waited for the bright white lettering of 'INDOCTRINATION' to flash on the screen.

A gruff male voice sounded through the room, 'INDOCTRINATION COMPLETE: PERSPECTIVE CONDITIONED.'

The female voice returned speaking in sickly-sweet tones. 'Thank you for your patience. I'm pleased to announce that this is where the niceties return because now you get to learn The Rules of Life and take the Oath of Obedience that makes maintaining Fair and Just Order possible.'

More rules than I could possibly describe with words flooded into Mirembe's mind. She tried to absorb all the information. Numbers followed by lengthy, formal laws sounded over each other. The rules increased in speed, and while her mind could process each one individually and simultaneously, they were increasing at such a rate that she was overwhelmed with exhaustion.

Every rule explained a question to her that she hadn't even asked. It went on, an interminable diatribe of rules sounding inside her mind. She tried to slump down with exhaustion, not able to take this assault after the mental torture she'd just been through. The force held her in place, uncaring, as The Rules were uploaded.

Another billion earth-years passed, and still The Rules continued to play. She thrashed around inside the uniform; her essence smashed against the glass. It looked like it was going to crack imminently. She cried out in her mind for the rules to stop. Though she didn't realise it at the time, The Rules increased to such a speed that before she had time to cry out again, they promptly came to an end.

A firm male voice called out: 'ORDER IMPOSED: RULES DISSEMINATED'. It changed back to a warm, female voice. 'And now, it is time for you to take your Oath of Obedience.'

Writing appeared on the screen, and Mirembe read it in her mind. She tried to repeat the words— they wouldn't come out. The same feeling she'd felt when Arcturus had asked her to think of her true name took over her, and the words left her essence without her control:

'I AM THE STAR THAT LIGHTS THE NIGHT: LOVE WILL HELP US ALL UNITE.

FREEDOM IS MY ULTIMATE GOAL: WHATEVER COST, AT ANY TOLL.

THE LIFELONG QUEST FOR MORALITY: THE ONLY WAY WE WILL BE FREE.

THOSE IN NEED, I SEE YOUR PLIGHT: ON YOUR BEHALF, I GLADLY FIGHT.

INJUSTICE, MY ETERNAL FOE: WHERE YOU ARE FOUND, IS WHERE I'LL GO.

TO WRITE THE WRONGS OF THIS GAME: SO ALL THAT LIVE KNOW THEIR TRUE NAME.

COMPASSION WILL RULE MY CORE AND MIND: FOR THOSE WHO FEEL, I WILL BE KIND.

EVERY TIME MORE LIFE GROWS: I'LL SHOW THEM LOVE, THAT'S ALL THEY'LL KNOW.

I'LL TREAT THEM LIKE A MOTHER WOULD: SHOWING THEM HOW TO BE GOOD.

GIFTING THEM AUTONOMY: WITH THE LOVE OF ASTRONOMY.

THE GAME OF WAR IS AT AN END: THE GAME OF LIFE CAN NOW TRANSCEND.

THE GAME OF WAR HAS HAD ITS BLOOD: NOW IT'S TIME FOR MOTHERHOOD.

IN MY EMBRACE THEY'LL SEE THE LIGHT: THE RULES OF LIFE, I WILL RERIGHT.

LOVE WILL HELP US ALL UNITE: I AM THE STAR THAT LIGHTS THE NIGHT.'

Sirens wailed throughout the room. A strong male voice sounded amid the noise, 'INVALID OATH: TWO ATTEMPTS REMAINING.'

She stared at the screen, trying to focus on the words but only hearing the message her core sang to her. The sirens stopped. She tried again to speak the words on screen. They wouldn't come out. She spoke the same oath as before.

'INVALID OATH: ONE ATTEMPT REMAINING.'

Something in her mind whispered to her, a voice she'd never heard before. *TAKE THE OATH.*

She stared at the screen. She wanted to say the words desperately. They refused to leave her essence.

The voice cried out again, *WITHOUT ORDER, THERE IS CHAOS. WITH CHAOS, THERE IS WAR.*

A warm, sedating energy seeped through her consciousness, stupefying her. She read the oath on screen, and finally, the words Paradoxa wanted to hear came out of her mouth:

'I, Mirembe, God of Morality, hereby agree to follow The Rules, the whole rules, and nothing but The Rules, so rule me, Paradoxa.'

5
NEW KID ON THE BLOCK

'I trust you feel fully enlightened,' said Oxygenus as Mirembe and the Resource turned the corner into reception.

Mirembe fixed her face and attention on him briefly but ignored him. *Don't even think about talking to me.* She addressed the Resource. 'Thank you. Is there anything else, or am I free to go?'

'Now that you've taken your oath, you're free to go. Oxygenus will escort you back to the Milky Way.' It turned to Oxygenus. 'Sorry again for failing to process your request. It's been quite some time since a new god has materialised.'

'We got there in the end.' He waved a few arms. The debris from his much earlier explosion rematerialised, fully functional, in its original position. He stared at Mirembe to make a point. 'Time to leave.'

Nothing but the sound of Mirembe's feet clattering against the floor could be heard as they walked in almost complete silence through the passage. She wanted to ask him to speed up the floor, but that would have required talking to him, and there is little she'd rather do less.

Echoes of rules continued to play in her mind as they

walked, and while it was annoying, she completely understood. There needed to be rules. These gods could not be trusted to create Fair and Just Order themselves. And neither could the lifeforms from the looks of things. *Chaos and war, that's how they live.*

'Did you enjoy your Indoctrination?' he asked. 'Nothing like some repetition and some rules to welcome you to existence.'

As if he has the audacity to try to be amusing.

He let out a histrionic sigh. 'Are you going to ignore me for the entire journey home, or is it just something you're doing while we're at the Registrars?'

Unbelievable.

He sighed again. 'It was a different time then. *Everyone* in the Old World went to war, that's what we did. We needed to do something to occupy our minds! You can't expect one to live eternally in perpetual boredom. Have some empathy.'

'Empathy?' That word struck a nerve, she couldn't ignore him. Her essence had gone very red, but other colours could be seen. 'You can't be serious. You're trying to lecture me on empathy? I suppose if you're bored, sadism isn't a bad thing, is that what you're saying? I should put myself in your gasses, think about what it's like for you, existing but not having complete dominion over all things? The narcissism, the megalomania, the callous indifference to suffering. I've never been more outraged in my life.'

The passions of youth. His tone was calm and laboured as he replied. 'You haven't been alive very long, so there isn't much else that could really compete for your outrage, is there?' He smirked at her, but she turned away as soon as his gaze met her antennae. 'You're not the first entity to be born and think they understand what it means to live for eternity. When you've lived a billionth, or even a trillionth the time I've been alive, maybe I'll listen to what you have to say. But considering you've been born into a world with a moral executive, there are rules which you must follow, and a model exists for Fair and Just Behaviour, I suspect I won't. You have no idea what freedom is, so you can't know if you're a good or bad entity because the choice to be bad has been taken away from you. And now that you've been through Indoctrination and taken your Oath of Obedience, you should know that talking *up* to your superiors or showing insubordination of any kind is a violation of The Rules. I'll be kind enough to allow it on this occasion, since you're new, to show you that I have changed, that I'm not the warmonger I used to be. Though I suggest you learn some respect, you're not going to get far in life with that self-righteous attitude.'

Self-righteous attitude! The hypocrisy! Oh, that really does it. She threw her arms in the air and swung around to face him. 'I don't care who you are. I don't care how powerful you are. I don't care how many lifeforms you intimidated into fearing you– or loving you. I don't care what titles and privileges you afforded yourself or what Paradoxa has given you, and I don't care if I offend you. I'm going to tell you this clearly, and after that, I don't want to hear from you ever again. You disgust me. You haven't changed at all. Look how you spoke to that machine back there, because it didn't process your request immediately, in the exact way you wanted it to. You're as cruel as you're allowed to be. You're lucky that Paradoxa implemented The Rules because if I had been born into a Game of War that had godly involvement, I'd have made it my life's mission to end it. And if I could have found a way to make you suffer, I would have. She should have tortured you all for what you did to those defenceless lifeforms, taught you a lesson. Don't even bother flying me home, just materialise in that disgusting suit of yours and then never speak to me again. And if you're going to punish me, just do it. I don't care what you do to me, don't even bother to tell me, I don't want to know. You truly are a pathetic god.'

The centre of Oxygenus' chest, where his face resides, was contorted with such rage, that his lips started to quiver and his whole stomach shook. 'Duly noted.'

Mirembe felt the cold of space press against the suit as they passed through the barrier. Oxygenus looked at her, without moving any of his limbs, and her suit dematerialised. The sensation of cold immediately disappeared as she returned to her essence form. She stretched her essence out, enjoying the freedom, having forgotten what it felt like to exist outside of such confined limits.

Oxygenus materialised into a new lifeform, different from both the ones she'd seen so far. He turned silently to Mirembe and grabbed her essence.

Mirembe felt different forces tugging at her, spinning her around in complete darkness.

The nearby solar systems of the Milky Way came into view as Oxygenus released her.

'Let us hope that you never have cause to see me again,' he said before dematerialising.

'It's yourself you have cause to see,' said Mirembe, to open space.

A siren blared inside Mirembe's mind, startling her. Streaks of multicoloured starlight filled the vacuum around her. More kept appearing, thousands became millions, which quickly became billions, as the gods fought with each other to get a view of Mirembe.

She stared at them all, a swarming mass of colours, all talking and laughing with each other. She could hear each one of their conversations, individually and simultaneously, and she understood what each was saying. She had never felt more judged. Apparently, she'd been discussed and described at length during her Indoctrination.

Someone contacted her. She couldn't trace it back to any of the gods around her.

'Hello, Mirembe, welcome to the Milky Way, I'm Djulpan, the galaxy you're inhabiting.' His tone was buoyant and jovial. A keen presenter. 'I must say, I'm both surprised and relieved. I see that you've already registered yourself, so you've saved me a task, and your welcome parade woke me up, so you spared me a disciplinary.'

The gods laughed and bantered good-spiritedly.

'It is indeed a most serendipitous occasion. I didn't think there would ever be a new god. I thought we were done with that sort of thing, and in my galaxy, how fortuitous, destiny some might say. You know, I've always said the Milky Way is a grossly underrated galaxy. We've got a great spot here, new galaxies and universes popping into existence so close by, lots of space for development, beautiful views, and now, the most enticing view of all: a god who has every colour in existence. They'll be queueing up to see you. You'll have to let us all in on your secret, Mirembe. *How* did you do it?'

Her essence shimmered in a smile. 'Thank you. I'm a little overwhelmed. I'm not sure what to say really. I just woke up here and I was the full spectrum of colour. I suppose I can see what you mean because I must look to you, how you all look to me when you're joined up like this, a spectrum of colours. It is very pretty. I'm glad, I wouldn't have wanted to have to pick one colour. You're all so dazzling.'

'And a charmer,' said Djulpan. 'How lucky we are.'

More laughter.

'As I'm sure you can hear from the rabble around you, these are the other stars of the galaxy. You'll get acquainted with many of them before your life is done, I'm sure. Now for some rules, most of which you'll be familiar with from *The* Rules, some of which are my own personal requests, and you need to follow them nonetheless. You're free to roam anywhere within the galaxy, though please show courtesy to others, especially those sleeping. Curfew starts at 85 hours until 25 hours the next day as per The Rules. You are obliged to stay in your star during these hours, and you are not permitted to communicate. Most gods like to stay in their star until 30 hours, so you can't communicate with them until then if they still reside in their star, and all conversations must be private. The rules make an exception for greeting new gods, so you'll be glad to hear there's no curfew until you've all introduced yourself.'

Cheers all round.

'As you can hear, you've got quite a few fans, and there'll be plenty more who live further out making their way here, so it's going to take a while to meet and greet with everyone. Anyway, where was I? Oh yes, don't touch the matter of any other god without permission; don't enter another god's star without permission; don't send out thoughts that can't be ignored unless it's urgent, and of course, you must ensure you report any change in circumstance or violation of The Rules to me immediately, unless, of course, *I'm* sleeping.'

The gods let out a laugh at the last sentence.

'Feel free to play around with your own matter. I see you've scattered out quite far; there's a decent amount to play with here. I'm sure you could create some lovely little planets. Who knows, if fortune continues to bless the galaxy, one day you might even have lifeforms.' A few more laughs. 'And that's all really, welcome, enjoy yourself, and whatever you do, DO NOT break any rules. I'm very glad to have you here, Mirembe. You'll be a great addition to the galaxy. Farewell, may Fair and Just Order be the ruler of our lives.'

'May Fair and Just Order be the ruler of our cores,' echoed the gods.

Mirembe felt Djulpan sever the connection between them. Countless gods flew over to her and introduced themselves. Every star took a turn to speak and each told her their name, its meaning, where in the Milky Way they lived, and the best places they'd lived previously. Almost all of them seemed to want her to know they'd lived outside the Milky Way. She was shocked that they each chose to communicate individually. The whole exchange could have been achieved instantly. She got the impression that Paradoxa and most other entities had decided to perform actions simply to kill time.

She felt flattered they all cared enough to introduce

themselves, but eventually, it did start to feel quite tedious, because each one would say the same things in the exact same shocked way: They couldn't believe a new god had been born, they really couldn't believe it was in the Milky Way, they never thought there would be a God of Morality, and they absolutely wouldn't have believed a god could exist with all the colours in the spectrum if they hadn't seen it for themselves.

In the time it had taken to go through Indoctrination and meet with every star in the Milky Way, Mirembe had aged a fair bit, and the repeated introductions enabled her to learn the beginnings of the art of conversation. She developed several personas; taking on the needs of others in the conversation; pretending to be shocked or have some emotion that she didn't really have to spare their feelings; saying things to make them laugh or appeal to their ego; offering witticisms and guiding the conversation into a path she knew it was naturally going to follow. A need to perform started to emerge in her as her personality blossomed, and a friendly but facetious attitude developed, appropriate for her age. Though her passion was present always, and her love for life unquestionable.

Eventually, all the gods returned to their stars. Only the nearby stars-gods, most of whom she'd met earlier, remained.

'Look who it is,' said Olawangangu. 'The God of Morality.'

'I hope,' said Muwan, 'you don't think you're going to get this kind of greeting every time you're born.'

Mirembe flashed a colourful smile. 'I seem to remember,' she said, 'that you each called me a liar as my initial welcome to the Megaverse. Lalande even called me sinister, so technically, this is my third welcome after the welcome parade. Fourth if you count Indoctrination. For my fifth entrance to the Megaverse, a simple 'welcome back' will suffice. Meeting everyone was wonderful, but I can't say

Indoctrination was the most fun I've ever had. I'll be glad to skip it next time.'

'Unfortunately,' said Lalande, 'you don't get to skip Indoctrination. You go through it every time you regenerate.' She hastened to add, 'It does make following The Rules so much easier, though. And sorry, you're new, I know that now, but you can't just take a god solely on their word. I find it best in life to question all things. Everything that thinks has an agenda. The likelihood of you just popping into existence and priding your whole life on promoting complete moral perfection seemed to me unlikely. To be honest, I didn't think there would ever be a new god named anything. I know you've probably heard that enough, but I was worried about Arcturus getting regenerated. I did think it a nasty thing to do on your part. I'm glad though, it's actually rather funny. I'm sure it will amuse you too, looking back, your first moments of life, an argument about your very existence.'

'I believed you,' said Arcturus.

'Arcturus! Yes, you did. That was very kind of you. I haven't forgotten. You seem a delightful god. I'm sure we're going to be great friends.'

Some of the gods let out their equivalent of a whistle, similar to the sound a pressured gas makes when escaping confinement. Arcturus' essence turned light green.

'Don't worry, Lalande,' continued Mirembe. 'Everyone has been shocked, even the Resource at the Registrars. I'm a little shocked myself if I'm completely honest: I never expected to be a new god. Nothing to do with me, really, and yet it has everything to do with me. It's a strange situation to be in. I guess it's just something the Megaverse wanted to do, create the God of Morality. About time really, given all the war there's been, and the war that still exists now. Though I'm not sure what my purpose in all that is. Paradoxa seems to have written a rule for every possible eventuality, and there are even as many rules for things that seem altogether impossible from my understanding of things. A God of

Morality in a world of rules. I'm not sure I know the point of it. But I do feel from everything that's happened so far, that I have some higher purpose, a duty to carry out, I just don't know what it is yet.'

Alnisa's essence turned deep purple, as it usually does when she gets an especially funny or bitchy thought. 'With delusions of grandeur like that, Mirembe, you're going to fit in great as a god.'

'Delusions of grandeur. That is funny!' said Mirembe. 'And what else would I need to do to fit in as a god? What is it you do for life apart from deluding yourself of your importance? Sorry, *we*, what is it we do for life apart from deluding ourselves of our own importance?'

'I like her,' said Bellatrix. 'We follow The Rules, Mirembe, and we try to have whatever fun is left in the space between The Rules and all possible actions. There isn't much to play with, but it is possible to have a bit of fun. Even finding a loophole is a fun activity in itself. I take genuine pleasure in doing something not forbidden by The Rules, even if it's something I'd never have wanted to do otherwise. A pleasure in life, for sure.'

'Yes,' said Muwan. 'You're also allowed to build anything out of your own matter that isn't sentient, which is fun during the construction phase. You're secretly praying one day it'll house organic matter, of course, so there's something to do. But even if it doesn't, watching planets reach an equilibrium with the forces can be fairly entertaining, and creating things is always good, one gets a nice feeling after it. Pride.'

'Is that the feeling you get when you look at your planets?' said Eridani. 'I've always felt a bit queasy. Funny-looking planets.'

'You've got a funny-looking essence. And your star is smaller than mine.'

'I do not have a –'

'We're supposed to be telling Mirembe what life is about, not arguing over planets and Eridani's abnormal essence.'

'I did tell you,' said Arcturus, 'that you'd have to get used to the company.'

'Just to clarify, what you actually do all day is argue?' said Mirembe. 'I don't know why I asked. That's what you were doing before you even knew I was alive to be watching you.'

'We don't all argue,' said Bellatrix.

'Yeah,' said Lalande, 'it's just these idiots mainly.'

'Agreed,' said Arcturus. Some of the others attempted to retort but he talked over them. 'There's some fun stuff to do, other than arguing. Flying is fun. Sightseeing, checking out what the gods who lived here before us created that have stood the test of time. But I'd say the main joys in existence are: bonding and socialising; learning about the Megaverse, its laws, composition, nature and history; and studying new occurrences that confirm The Laws of Existence. What we do most is think, and it really is the greatest pleasure you have in life. I rate it above all other experiences.'

'Who knew you were this deep, Arcturus?' said Lalande. 'I was going to go more with we socialise, try to outdo each other in having the most fun, date occasionally, if you can call it dating, there's no sex like a lifeform, we just share a star together and merge our essences. It's pleasurable, but it's not really sex. Though it can create life. Stars have been known to explode, which eventually becomes a new entity. And sleeping, it's one of the best pastimes there is. Which you can do freely as a star-god without lifeforms.'

'Yes, after the welcome parade, the flight to the Registrars, the emotional stress of Indoctrination, greeting all the stars of the Milky Way, and now here pondering the small things of life, I feel thoroughly exhausted. How exactly do I sleep?'

'I guess the party's over,' said Alnisa. 'You just go back to your star and close your mind, or you can even sleep outside your star, but that's not really feasible because you'd be outside your star during curfew.'

'I'm sorry, I'm only just learning the pleasantries of social convention. I was actually very rude to Oxygenus before, he almost disciplined me. This whole experience has really drained me. Would you mind if we carried on after I've slept?'

'OH, MY PARADOX!' said Revati. 'What did you say to him?'

'I'll tell you the full details when I wake up, I really need to go to sleep and let my mind process all the information I've learned. I basically told him I thought he was an evil tyrant who demanded obedience from lifeforms who are less powerful than him to inflate his ego and carry out his abominable, malevolent desires. Pathetic, I recall I said.'

All the gods laughed for quite some time, even Arcturus.

'Wow,' said Tongwera. 'You really are one of a kind, Mirembe. Go get some sleep, we'll see you when you wake up. May Fair and Just Order be the ruler of your dreams.'

'May love rule your core, and your knowledge expand.'

'What? You're supposed to say May Fair and Just Order be the ruler of our cores.'

'Oh,' said Mirembe, making her way back to her star. 'Yes, that does sound more like Paradoxa. May Fair and Just Order be the ruler of our cores.'

'Sleep tight,' said Bellatrix. 'Don't let the chaos bite.'

'Good day-end,' said Mirembe. She materialised inside her star. Before she could think how to sleep, a feeling of drowsiness overtook her.

Mirembe sat in a box made of rules. Light could be seen stretching over the top of the lettering, slowly becoming less visible as more rules appeared at the top of the structure.

Where am I? she thought, half asleep in her dream world.

She pushed out with her arms, feeling the jagged lettering of the rules. Her essence had taken the shape of a lifeform. She pulled her head back to look up. She could see words piling on top of each other, further encasing her. She grabbed the nearest words she could see and attempted to climb her way out.

Just get out of here, she told herself. *You need to get to the top.*

After a few unsteady attempts, she managed to get used to jumping. She pivoted off the nearest word she could see, forcing herself up and around the inside of the structure, skipping several rules at a time as she went.

An audible procession of rules emanated from the top of the structure Mirembe was attempting to scale. She heard them flying close, a bee to an ear, louder as it drew close and quieter as it flew away.

Rule 20: The deliberate and intentional germination of organic matter is strictly prohibited.

Rule 16988: All star-gods must ensure they comply with the Reasonable Use of Space Directive. Failure to materialise with at least a trillion cubits between all other stars will result in instant regeneration.

Rule 434: You must report any change in circumstances to your immediate superior within one hour. Failure to report a change in circumstance will result in a disciplinary.

The faster she climbed, the quicker the rules piled up, entombing her. Still, the cracks of light could be seen, visible through The Rules.

She cried out for help. 'Who's doing this? Let me out. Paradoxa, help, please, The Rules, they won't stop. I'm trapped.'

The Rules continued to sound out to her, just as they continued to pile up around her.

A voice in her mind spoke; it was her own. It felt like a part of her she'd never communicated with before. *Paradoxa does not help; she rules.*

She clawed at the words ravenously, making her ascent, trying desperately to get to the end of The Rules. To reach the place at which everything stopped. A point to The Rules.

You're not a lifeform, Mirembe. You can fly. She stopped and held one of the limbs she was currently controlling in front of her face. *How did I get in this… suit?*

Her arms flailed frantically as she tried to get out of it. She pressed down with her foot to steady herself. The letters crumbled under her weight. She slipped from the ledge, falling into the abyss.

The walls of Mirembe's tomb reverberated with her screams. Her arms windmilled about manically as she tried to grab onto The Rules.

Arcturus' voice issued from the same directions as The Rules. His tone was gentle and reassuring. 'Who are you, Mirembe? What's your true name?'

'Arcturus. Help, I can't stop.'

The voice called out again, barely audible over the sound

of The Rules. 'What's your true name, Mirembe?'

Her core swelled with love. 'My name is Mirembe, and I am the God of Morality.'

She screamed aggressively, angry at the chains she had been placed in. Her essence broke through the confines of the suit, ending her descent.

Laser-like, Mirembe's essence pierced through the air, soaring past the stacks of rules.

How do I get out of here? she wondered. *There's no end to The Rules, they just go on and on.*

A speck of light remained visible at the top of The Rules.

Maybe if I go faster than the rules are being created? Maybe I can outpace them.

She felt around the space ahead of her, feeling the particles that formed it. She let her energy seep into the atoms, using their energy to propel her. Her essence burst into flame. It rocketed up through the gaps in The Rules, getting faster and hotter as she ascended.

Don't try to beat them. You can't win. One of her internal voices was communicating with her again. *You need to break out of here. You need to break The Rules.*

'Break out? I can't break a rule. It's against The Rules. What about war?'

A male voice spoke inside her mind, she recognised it from Indoctrination as Nitrogenus. 'Rules don't end war, Mirembe. It hasn't worked, we need a new way.'

'A new way? What are you talking about?'

No reply came to her. The rules continued to sound, she continued to fly; determined to reach the point of The Rules.

Oxygenus' words from before sounded externally. 'You have no idea what freedom is, so you can't know if you're a good or bad entity because the choice to be bad has been taken away from you.'

Hydroga communicated next, into her mind, more faintly than her own internal voices, but still detectable. 'No one deserves punishment before they've done something wrong.

One cannot judge all others until all others are free to judge one. Find a way, Mirembe.'

'Why have you put me in here? To taunt me with riddles? I want to get out. Stop playing games with me. How do I get to the end of The Rules? How do I get out of here?'

'You have to break The Rules, Mirembe.'

A new voice, genderless and unrecognisable, played in her mind. *They want chaos. Chaos and disorder.*

Hydroga spoke, even fainter than before. 'Tyranny is tyranny. No matter who you are. We don't choose to live. Who made us?'

'Who made us?' said Mirembe. 'Nothing made us. We were made by the Laws of Existence.'

There was no reply. The voices stopped. Only The Rules could be heard now. She gave up trying to fly, unable to beat them. 'I want to get out,' she said, frustrated. 'No. I demand freedom!'

She grabbed hold of the matter around her, feeling her way through every particle it contained. The Rules fought back as she tried to requisition them, refusing to acquiesce. Power emanated through her essence, out into the particles of The Rules, engulfing them. She charged them until every rule had been incinerated. Freedom.

Everything went bright, blinding her.

She opened her mind's eye slowly, tentatively. She felt disorientated from the unexpected explosion and blast of light. The scenery had completely changed. She was in space; a star was close by. It looked like her star, only it couldn't be, because of the unfamiliar planets orbiting it.

'Hello, can anyone hear me?' she cried out. 'Paradoxa? Hydroga?' Nitrogenus?'

No reply.

She made her way cautiously to the planet with lifeforms. Her vision was marginally distorted as she passed through the gas clouds on the planet's outer layer. The sheer diversity of life overwhelmed her: a rarity for a god. A vast ocean and a sea of trees furnished the landscape. Throughout them, above, below and in between, were lifeforms, trillions upon trillions of them. Her core swelled with emotion, but she couldn't recognise which.

A lifeform flew near to where she had stopped, forcing her out of her thoughts. Enormous leathery wings, accounting for most of the animal, were stretched out, catching the wind to aid its flight. A long slender torso accompanied them, with talons for feet and a long tail equal in length to its body. Ferocious red eyes with black pupils could be seen glaring over its mouth. It was unmistakably a dinosaur.

For a moment, Mirembe thought it was looking directly at her. She froze and stared at the creature, unsure what was to come. Something else caught its attention, and it flew off in the opposite direction.

Green seemed to be the overwhelming consensus on what colour the tallest grade-two lifeforms, which she understood from Indoctrination to be trees, chose to be. Their leaves at least. It was the internal commotion that interested her most. In addition to the lifeforms who used the trees as accommodation and food on their exterior, inside there were more lifeforms using them as a source of life.

What a crazy game, she thought. *Life inside life inside life.*

A sense of panic struck her core. If she could see lifeforms, then she must be outside the Milky Way. And if she was outside the Milky Way, she must have broken a rule. An important rule.

I need to get back, she thought frantically. *I need to tell Djulpan, get him to set up a meeting with the element-gods, tell them that I just appeared here after The Rules disappeared. Oh no! I broke The Rules, that's why this is happening, that's why I'm here. I should have stayed within the confines of The Rules. I didn't mean to. I was scared, didn't understand. I don't want to be regenerated. I've only just been born.*

More of the dinosaurs she saw before were flying together

ahead of her, making sounds to each other. It snapped her out of her fear. They were coordinating. Discussing what to do. Suddenly, they swooped into a dive.

Mirembe watched them go, unsure if she should head back to space. She vacillated before deciding to follow them.

She was met with absolute mayhem. Mammoths were running, screaming, scattering about, trying to avoid the dinosaurs. A large brutish-looking dinosaur which Mirembe thought to be the leader of the pack swooped down and anchored its claws into one of the mammoths. Blood dripped from its sides as it was hoisted into the air. It screamed in agony, flailing around pointlessly, attempting to escape.

Mirembe's core panged. It was just like Indoctrination, only this time it was live.

Another dinosaur pounced on her prey. It barely had chance to scream as its head was torn off. Mirembe winced at the barbarism of it all.

A violent cry emanated amongst the furore, startling Mirembe. One of the mammoths charged a dinosaur to save its mate. Mirembe refocused in time to see its head torn off by the dinosaur's tail. A tragic and beautiful ending: to die for love. Mirembe was far too traumatised by the whole thing to appreciate that.

The whole pack of dinosaurs had at least one toy to play with now. They tossed them around in the air to each other, trying not to drop them but cheering when they did.

Mirembe closed her mind's eye as they fell. She heard the bones crush against the ground, the last squeal of agony before they went completely silent.

I must help, she thought, galvanized by suffering. *I must intervene.*

A force immobilised her, and a rule played in her mind.

Rule 22: Intervening in war between lifeforms is strictly prohibited. Any attempt to control or influence, directly or indirectly, the natural course of war, will result in excruciating punishment. You have been warned.

'Paradoxa, is that you? I need help. I don't know where I am.'

The Rules will set you free.

'What do you mean they'll set me free? They were trying to entomb me. Bury me alive.'

More screams of agony. The last of the mammoths dropped to the floor, splattering everywhere. Mirembe grimaced. They hadn't even eaten the animals they'd killed. From what she had seen, they had done it for fun.

'Paradoxa, I don't like this. Why have you brought me here? I don't want to see this. I understand. You made The Rules to end the gods' Game of War. I've seen enough, I believe in The Rules.'

A muffled voice sounded in her mind, 'The Game of War was bad… but who made the Game of Life?' Was that Hydroga talking? She couldn't tell.

'I don't know,' said Mirembe in frustration. 'I thought the game made itself. Will you just tell me? I don't want to see this.'

No reply.

She closed her eyes and imagined herself in the Milky Way. To her surprise, when she opened them, that's where she was. She had been right before, it was definitely her star she was looking at. It had changed in size, and there were planets, nine of them.

"No!" screamed Mirembe. Her essence swarmed around. Streams of light flashed out of her. The core of her essence began to bubble, mirroring the increasingly volatile exterior of her star.

She started inertly as her corporeal star exploded, destroying almost everything in its path. All the planets, including the lifeforms she'd just seen, were completely destroyed.

'Nooo!' she cried. 'I don't want to be regenerated.'

Her oath sang in her mind. *I am the star that lights the night: Love will help us all unite.*

A second voice sounded over Mirembe's oath. TAKE THE OATH, MIREMBE.

Freedom is my ultimate goal: Whatever cost, at any toll.

Mirembe's star scattered everywhere. She was dead. Regenerated. But why?

She closed her mind, and tried to imagine herself alive again, materialised in the Milky Way. A rule called out to her:

Rule 37: Travelling in non-chronological time is prohibited. Any entity who attempts to travel in non-chronological time will never inhabit time again.

She ignored the rule and continued to think, imagining herself alive again. She opened her vision, and there she was, whole again, surrounded by planets.

Numbers and letters torpedoed towards her from all directions, smothering her and forcing her away from her star.

ENEMIES OF FAIR AND JUST ORDER WILL NOT BE TOLERATED. SUBMISSION IS OBLIGATORY. CHOOSE TO COMPLY.

'I'm not an Enemy of Fair and Just Order! I am the God of Morality. Release me at once!'

The Rules continued to pile on top of her, their mass getting heavier and harder to bear. No light could be seen this time. Only rules, darkness and rules.

Her core sang to her again. *The lifelong quest for morality: The only way we will be free.*

'No!' she screamed. 'That's not the oath. We have to take the real oath or there'll be war.'

Hydroga spoke to her in her mind, this time she recognised it definitively. 'There will always be war, Mirembe. Let compassion prevail where power has failed. Let love engender what fear never could. You need to inspire us to want to be good.'

She grabbed some of the matter of The Rules and threw it aside. There was still no light, yet she could see.

'You'll never get out,' Carbondria said. 'There is no end

to The Rules, Mirembe. Let compassion guide where rules divide.'

'Stop with these cryptic messages. Is that all you can do: offer parables and remind me of all the different rules I must follow? Why don't you help me?'

TAKE THE OATH OF OBEDIENCE.

'I've already taken the oath. I've already agreed.'

Her core sang to her. *Those in need, I see your plight: On your behalf, I gladly fight.*

THE REAL OATH, MIREMBE.

The rest of her oath sang to her. She suppressed it.

'I, Mirembe, God of Morality, hereby agree to follow The Rules, the whole rules, and nothing but The Rules, so rule me, Paradoxa.'

She could feel the rules piling up, getting heavier by the second.

She cleared her mind and recited the oath again, twice more.

Everything vanished. Only Mirembe remained.

And now, God of Morality, it is time for you to sleep.

Arcturus and a few others socialising not too far away from her. She didn't feel ready to wake up yet. The sensation of sleeping felt too nice.

Memories of her dream came flooding back to her. She looked around, panicked. Four planets were floating nearby. For a second, she thought they were the same as in her dream. The panic subsided quickly as she recognised them as the planets that had formed naturally during her Indoctrination.

Her core calmed. *Just a dream.*

She closed the curtains of her mind and drifted back to sleep.

A quiet knocking sound rapped in her mind. Arcturus' gentle voice punctured her half-sleep. 'Mirembe…. Mih-rem-bee… Are you finally awake?'

She sensed him through her semi-slumber and slowly opened her vision to his bright green essence hovering outside her star.

'What's with all the lights? It feels too early to be awake.'

He laughed. 'It's almost 30 hours. Do you know how long

you've been asleep?'

'How long?'

Ninety-nine thousand years, fifty-three months, twenty-seven weeks, eighty-one days, ninety hours, seventy-three minutes and eighty-two seconds.

'What? Have you been counting?' She opened her mind fully and let the starlight, spacetime, and sense of awake take over her.

'Yes, actually. For one, no one could remember how long they slept after their first Indoctrination, but we're all sure it wasn't one hundred thousand years. You missed thousands of birthdays during Indoctrination and another hundred thousand while you were sleeping. You've only got about one million years from birth before you regenerate. If you keep this up, you'll regenerate in no time.'

That piece of information really woke her up. Seven hundred thousand years to regeneration. 'I'm not sure I feel awake enough to deal with reality. You can't even sleep without missing huge chunks of what are incredibly short lives. I know we regenerate, but that's like starting again, in a new place with new gods.'

Revati issued a beacon for all the nearby gods. 'Is she coming or not?'

'Coming where?'

'We're going on our day-start flight,' said Arcturus. 'That's why I came over here. I saw you shining, assumed you must be awake. Do you want to come?'

'I suppose now that I'm awake and edging rapidly closer to death, I should enjoy myself while I can. Yes, I'll join you, thanks for the invite.'

'Nothing like some day-start exercise.' He yelled to Revati telepathically, 'We're coming now.'

They flew over to the rest of the gods.

'Good day-start, sleepy swarm,' said Bellatrix.

Mirembe replied intuitively. 'Good day-start.'

'Is sleeping away your life a morality thing?' asked Revati.

'Or just a multicoloured thing?'

'You're so cheeky,' said Tongwera. 'Don't mind him, Mirembe, he's just jealous. You really do look spectacular.'

'I have to admit it is pretty surreal,' said Olawangangu. 'Not even the element-gods have managed this, or Paradoxa, though I suppose she's not really a colour, is she? More of the absence of colour.'

'Are we going or what?' said Lalande. 'We can talk and fly.'

'Are you OK with flight, Mirembe?' said Lu-Wong. 'Or do you want to latch onto one of us?'

'I think I'll be OK on my own, thanks.'

'Let's get going then.'

They formed into a rough arrowhead formation. Mirembe got a spot next to Lalande just in time for departure. Olawangangu was furthest ahead, leading the way.

After the flight in her dream, Mirembe felt more comfortable flying. She flew near the front at the same pace as the others, though she felt that she could fly much, much faster.

'Really,' said Lalande. 'I don't think I've known any star-god sleep that long. Even Djulpan sleeps for fifty thousand years at a time, but he's a galaxy, he lives a lot longer than we do.'

'Yeah, everything about you is so strange,' said Bellatrix. 'In a good way, obviously. Normally, things are so predictable.'

'Tell us the truth,' said Revati. 'Have you been sent here to spy on us by Paradoxa?'

'Who'd want to spy on the Milky Way?'

Mirembe flashed a smirk. 'No, I'm not an Observer. I'm just… well, I'm not sure what I am, to be honest. I thought sleeping would help me clear my mind, but after those dreams, I feel even more conflicted than before.'

'Why,' said Arcturus, 'what happened in your dreams?'

They approached a cluster of gassy clouds. Deep purples

mingled with blues, babalixo and yox. Inside, Mirembe could see different particles shifting their allegiance from one structure to another.

'That's a nice place to go,' said Tongwera. 'If you ever want some privacy.'

'Why is that?'

'Well, us being made of gas, when we pass through other gases, it has a strange isolating effect. Like escaping into a bubble.'

'I'll have to try it sometime. Thanks. Whose gases are those? Do I need to ask permission?'

'No, they're from stars who've regenerated, it belongs to the forces. You can use it just not alter it.'

Arcturus flew over to be next to Mirembe. 'You didn't answer my question. What happened in your dream?'

'Were you attacked by spectrums?' said Revati.

'Get a grip,' said Bellatrix. 'And focus on where you're going. You're supposed to fly around objects, not let them pass through you. It defeats the whole purpose of having rules if you're not going to follow them.'

'That does not register against The Rules,' said Mirembe.

'Oh no, it's just a game we play,' said Eridani. 'Makes flying more fun.'

'Ahh. I'll remember to do that. Now that I think of it, every time I avoid a cluster of debris, I get an adrenaline rush at that crucial moment before potential impact. You have the joys of flying sussed.'

Olawangangu spread his essence wide to catch some energy. 'Pleasure seekers that we are.'

'Are you ever going to let her answer the question?' asked Arcturus. 'What happened in the dream?'

'Oh, it was horrible,' recalled Mirembe, 'absolutely dreadful! Worse still, I thought the whole thing was real.'

'Yeah, dreams always seem real,' said Lalande. 'It doesn't matter how old you get. Though from the sound of things, yours was a nightmare, not a dream.'

Olawangangu led them through an asteroid field. Mirembe stopped talking as she and the others dashed about, trying to avoid them.

'The games we play,' said Tongwera, avoiding a large cluster of rocks.

Mirembe swerved out of the way to avoid a large cluster of asteroids. Revati and Eridani weren't so lucky. She flew ahead of them, shrill laughter filling the vacuum around her; a streak of multicoloured gas lining the path she had so eagerly taken. She had managed to avoid almost all the debris. A natural flyer.

'Have you been taking flying lessons while you were sleeping, Mirembe?' said Denebola, flying close to her.

'Yeah, you're suspiciously good,' said Lalande.

'That's exactly what happened! How did you know that?'

A few of them laughed, but from the tone of her voice, most realised she was being serious.

'What do you mean?' asked Arcturus.

She recalled the dream, how she'd been encased in The Rules, broken free, heard elements communicating with her, and saw lifeforms orbiting her star. Then how they were destroyed by her regeneration, causing her to go backwards through time, resulting in her being attacked and encased by The Rules again.

'And then a voice called out,' she said. 'It was the same voice that I heard in Indoctrination telling me to take the Oath of Obedience. I tried, only the other oath played in my mind, the same one that I said in Indoctrination on my first two attempts. Eventually, I managed to say the Oath of Obedience, everything disappeared, and the next thing I remember is waking up and seeing you all there.'

'I have so many questions,' said Arcturus.

'That's an understatement,' said Lalande. 'What do you mean the voices you heard during Indoctrination? And what other oath are you talking about?'

She recanted the story of what happened during

Indoctrination, then recited the oath she keeps hearing.'

Revati's essence lost all its red. Kofilulu and polijuma, colours not permanently visible in his essence, started to shine through. A shocked face, if you will. 'Un-fucking-believable, Mirembe. You're not supposed to hear voices in Indoctrination!'

'Yeah, no one hears voices in their mind when they go through Indoctrination,' said Lalande, more puzzled than concerned. 'Only The Rules and the voiceovers, that's all you should have heard.'

'That is very strange,' said Arcturus. 'Though I'm more interested in this other oath you're hearing.'

'Me too,' said Bellatrix, Lu-Wong, Eridani and Tongwera simultaneously.

Arcturus continued. 'The dream is easy to understand. It sounds like you're struggling to deal with the fact that you've been born into a world where there are endless rules that you must follow, and these are creating scenarios around that in your dream world. I think it's natural that you would dream something like that. We haven't known each other long, but I can already tell that you're a passionate character. This must be hard for you. Hearing voices and a completely different oath, however, that is much harder to explain.'

'I still have questions about the dream,' said Eridani. 'These lifeforms you sensed, had you seen them in Indoctrination or your flight with Oxygenus?'

She thought for a while, sorting through infinite thoughts and experiences per earth-second. 'I've checked every experience and memory I have. I can't see the lifeforms I saw in any of them.'

'Very strange.'

'You know what else is strange?' asked Tongwera. 'That so many of the elements who contacted her in her dream have been expelled from existence. Only Oxygenus and Arcturus still exist, and you said you heard those voices externally, didn't you? Not in your mind like the others.'

'Yes.'

Olawangangu came to a stop, the others stopped as well, more interested in the story than the flight. Even the stars who don't socialise in the clique had stopped in interest.

'That is more than coincidental, I have to admit,' said Olawangangu.

Lu-Wong, who often reserves his opinion but is happy to engage in contemplation of most things, joined the conversation. 'And what did they mean about who created The Game of Life?'

'I've always said Paradoxa created this game,' said Revati. 'Why else try to rule it?'

'Paradoxa rules it to ensure the Game of War never restarts,' said Arcturus. 'You know the moment Paradoxa ends The Rules there'd be instant warfare.'

'First-gens,' said Revati. 'They believe everything they're told in Indoctrination.'

'So,' said Mirembe, with a disbelieving orange glow. 'You're denying there was ever war?'

'No,' said Arcturus. 'He used to take part in the wars.'

Mirembe's essence went very red. 'You tortured lifeforms for sport?'

'No! I was under the direct control of Hydroga and a few other elements, as most gods were. Everything we did we were made to do.'

'That's not how I heard it!' said Arcturus.

'Well, you weren't there!' Revati's essence enlarged, turning a violent shade of red. 'We did what we were told. Yes, we were given some autonomy— most entities were— at the end of the day, it was rule or be ruled. Not even rule or be ruled, we were always ruled, it was rule AND be ruled. We did what we had to do to have as much of an existence as we could. I never liked war and I don't miss it. I just miss freedom, moving around, exploring. Even the element-gods gave us more freedom than Paradoxa. I hate the constrictive nature of The Rules, how we're all punished for what was the element-gods' game.'

Mirembe's essence calmed, and her colours returned. She had seen in Indoctrination how the star, galaxy and universe gods tried to negotiate peace or ended wars before eventually succumbing to the allure of power and the Game of War. They at least tried to be good at one point.

Bellatrix interjected. 'Let's not argue, we all got dragged into war one way or another in the Old World. It's the element-gods to blame. As for Paradoxa, I agree with Arcturus. She implemented The Rules to end the Game of War. She never exercised her power in the Old World. And in this world, where she still has infinite power and *does* exercise it, we don't spend all day eternally suffering. So, I naturally lean toward the opinion that Paradoxa is, if not a good, then at least a neutral force in existence. The only entities she's ever made suffer are the elements who refused to be ruled. A tiny percentage of elements— and even less for their derivatives— have ever been tortured. And their suffering came to an end. They suffered far less than the combined total time that they forced others to suffer. Then Paradoxa eliminates them from the game altogether, rather than enforcing perpetual suffering.'

'I can at least agree to that,' said Eridani.

Bellatrix continued. 'Paradoxa also only ever harms lifeforms who have violated her limit for cruel or otherwise bad behaviour, and most of the time, she transfers their consciousness to more hostile worlds to spare an innocent essence that would have naturally developed there whilst giving them a chance to redeem themselves in their next environment. She's also made infinite rules in their favour. The only unjust harm they feel that she can claim responsibility for is the microseconds that it takes to incinerate their existence for violating The Rules or breaching their algorithm limit as a planet. The way she rules, her character profile, I trust that she didn't make this game. If she did, she'd have told us and made us follow The Rules anyway. I'm not saying she's faultless, and some of The Rules are *absolutely* ridiculous, but I don't think she created this game. If anything, I think she hates existence. She's bored of it. You'd have to be, to wipe it all out like that.'

'Why start it again if she hates existence?' said Revati.

'Compassion, obviously!' said Arcturus, his essence a piercing green. 'It was clearly a difficult decision for her, killing all those lifeforms capable of suffering. She let the game start again out of compassion for those who wanted to live. Even if you spray the gas at Paradoxa as a creator, there's always the question of who created her. If she can exist without being created, then so can existence. If she could create herself, then so could we. Exactly in the same way that we materialise. Sometimes it's others' actions like an exploding galaxy that creates us, and sometimes it just happens of its own accord. Blaming Paradoxa because she's been noble enough to design rules that ended a grotesque Game of War isn't the answer.'

'Maybe it isn't Paradoxa,' said Mirembe. 'Maybe it's the same entity or entities that created Paradoxa, that created this whole game.'

'Then who created them?' retorted Arcturus. 'It goes on and on. It comes down to trust. Do you trust Paradoxa? Reading her rules, seeing the difference between the Old World and the New World, does she seem a good or bad force? I think a good one. And the Equation of Existence makes perfect logical sense. She's only ONE component in that. Are you saying she created positive something, as well as time and space for it to go into, and the forces to manage it all as well? And then just left them all there to their own devices while she was forced to feel it all? If she'd created us, she'd have told us.'

Several of the gods agreed, several others ranged from slightly sceptical to Revati.

'I'm not sure what to think,' said Mirembe. 'I don't see why they're contacting me, unless it's because of who I am.

If I wasn't the first God of Morality, if I wasn't the only star-god with all the colours, if I hadn't heard voices that no one else heard, then maybe I could write it off as coincidence. But all those things, coupled with the feeling I got when I said both my true name and my personal oath, it was so overwhelming, so purposeful, I absolutely know that it means something. And that something points to The Rules. In my oath it says, "In my embrace they'll see the light: The rules of life, I will re-right". What else could that mean?'

'Mirembe, listen,' said Olawangangu, with the authority of a CEO presenting a board meeting and the sincerity of a doctor giving a life-threatening diagnosis. 'It doesn't matter what you dream or what poems you sing to yourself to deal with the reality of the crazy Game of Life you've been born into. Whether Paradoxa created this game or not is irrelevant because she rules it, and we don't have a choice whether we follow The Rules. But trying to change a rule, or breaking one, really, don't go there. No one has ever broken a rule and gotten away with it. Maybe it takes a lifetime, maybe it takes what you might naively think at this stage of your existence as an eternity, but Paradoxa doesn't play that way. Maybe it's a routine inspection that she carries out personally because she bothers to care what you think, or maybe it'll be some other entity who works for her. Either way, there it is. Proof you've broken a rule. Then she punishes you. You can't beat her. Every element in existence submitted to her, not even Hydroga could stand against her – who, case and point, no longer exists. Don't get any funny ideas about revolution or redesign. Paradoxa has designed how we all get to play the game, and she won't let anyone or anything change it. I'm not her biggest fan, though I must admit, all she wants is Fair and Just Order. It's not the worst kind of autocrat to have… as powers go, she's not too bad. Unless you disobey her, so I suggest you don't.'

'He's right,' said Arcturus. 'Don't break a rule. I'm not sure it means you should break a rule. It seems like you want to challenge The Rules, to change them. Not to break them. Which is equally bad, but an important distinction!'

'Yes,' said Mirembe. 'That's closer to what I got from all these messages. What are the channels for challenging a rule? I've got quite a few suggestions, especially roaming, though I feel she's highly unlikely to change her mind on that.'

All of the gods' essences wore a smile. Arcturus spoke, 'There are no channels, Mirembe.'

'Gods aren't known for taking criticism. Especially the important ones.'

'The elements are the only gods who get to change rules,' said Arcturus, 'and they all have to be approved by Paradoxa. Their influence is limited to how much it benefits her. There's a lot of bureaucracy involved in the administration of The Rules.'

'Is it possible to petition the element-gods?' asked Mirembe. 'What about the universe-gods, they must be fairly important, don't they get a say?'

'I'm not completely sure,' said Lalande. 'I've never been to The Executive, but I've never heard of anyone successfully campaigning to remove a rule. Mostly, rules are updated, almost always increased in length and specificity, but not removed.'

'I just can't get that line out of my head: "One cannot judge all others until all others are free to judge One". Paradoxa doesn't allow feedback. How can she know if she's being a good ruler?'

'I think when Paradoxa implemented The Rules her mindset was different,' said Lu-Wong. 'She was determined to bring order to the chaos and end the Game of War, so made decisions and implemented rules that are very authoritarian. Ultimately, Paradoxa trusts herself to rule correctly because the mess that she inherited was worse than the Megaverse we live in today. She's also infinitely more able than every other entity in existence combined. I doubt I'd bother to explain myself to anyone if I could outmanoeuvre everything that exists.'

'Hmm,' Mirembe thought for a while before answering. 'Well, I sincerely hope Paradoxa didn't create this game because the Game of War is only possible with the creation of The Game of Life. I also don't agree that we should be forced to go through Indoctrination so many times, though my core tells me that while Paradoxa is authoritarian, it makes more sense to me that the game created itself than that Paradoxa created it. I'd have believed it of the elements because of the way they treated the lifeforms: making them worship them constantly, creating worlds that are harsh with inevitable suffering, taking pleasure from their fear, forcing them to feel subordinate and then revelling in the feeling of superiority it created. Paradoxa doesn't seem like that. Everyone talks about Paradoxa, but no one is made to talk about her. She doesn't boast about her power. Shee Just demands that you live exactly as decreed. And she didn't do that in the Old World. If she had then I could have believed she created it all because she wanted to rule it. That's not the case, so I don't see a motive for her creating existence. I'm not sure it's Paradoxa that they were even talking about when they contacted me in the dream. As Arcturus said, Paradoxa is only one component in that equation. So, I don't think Paradoxa created it. But some of the points they made are valid: one of the rules says you can't materialise within a trillion cubits of another star. We don't choose where we materialise. I disagree with punishment for actions beyond self-control.'

'There's a point to that, though,' said Bellatrix. 'If gods could just materialise anywhere, there'd be arguments, which would lead to war. Gods take pride in their homes and their creations. Someone materialising in the middle of it would cause conflict. Regenerating them is only what would have happened if the stars had fought it out themselves. This way, only the god who caused the problem is destroyed.'

Mirembe's lack of eyebrows made it quite difficult for

them to be raised, but she was contemplative, nevertheless.

'You're not the first entity to question The Rules,' said Tongwera. 'We've all done it. Those of us who were alive in the Old World know that Paradoxa did what she did to end the wars. Bellatrix is right, Paradoxa is bored of existence in my opinion. Imagine managing all of this. Creating all The Rules, policing them, and then having to experience and feel everything every living entity in the Megaverse experiences. You'd have to be insane to design that role for yourself. And really, when you think about it, there is a feedback system. Paradoxa already hears everything we think, she knows we're having this conversation, she knows that you want to be able to roam. She just hasn't made a formal channel to receive the suggestion, because she doesn't need to, because she already heard you think it. You've got serious character Mirembe, I like it. You're very self-righteous… in a good way. Not many star-gods could manage that. But you can't take on Paradoxa and believe me when I say that no one who has ever tried has ever won. My advice is the same as Bellatrix's: just try and have whatever fun you can within the confines of The Rules.'

All the gods agreed.

Mirembe relented. 'Yes, you're probably right. I'm not planning on breaking any rules anyway. Paradoxa isn't the sort of god I'd like to cross, and I'm impressed she managed to get the element-gods under control. I'm not sure I could do a better job than her, so I suppose I shouldn't judge. Maybe when I'm older, I'll have thought of a better solution than endless rules and totalitarianism. Until then, I'll keep my thoughts shut and hope my dreams are a little more dreamlike and a little less nightmarish.'

Arcturus let some of his essence touch Mirembe, a hug of sorts. 'Definitely for the best.'

'Now that we've established that you're not the messiah, can we get back to flying?' said Revati, with his usual cheek.

She threw some of her gas at him playfully.

'I'm reporting that! Did you see that? Touched my matter without permission. Already breaking rules!'

Mirembe flew ahead. 'Come on then, let's get going.'

'Wahoo!' screamed Mirembe, stopping kilocubes past the star that marked the finish post of the race and minutes ahead of the other gods.

Dazembi, one of the stars who lives relatively close to her, who is an active participant in the clique of around one hundred gods that Mirembe now finds herself in, flew over to her. 'Oh, my paradox! How fast are you? Unbelievable.'

'Thank you. I love flying. It's so exhilarating! And the longer I fly, the faster I go. I can feel Inertia guiding me, willing me on.'

'Olawangangu will be furious. Oh, look, speak of the god, here he is.'

He came to a stop in front of them, much more graceful than Mirembe's landing. His black essence had gone so black he was scarcely detectable against the vacuum of space. 'I don't know how, but you definitely cheated. Did you follow the route?'

'Of course!'

Dazembi's colours smirked. 'Don't be a sore loser, she beat you fair and square.'

'Do you normally win the races? Before I was born, I mean.' She hadn't even meant this as banter.

Dazembi laughed.

Olawangangu didn't. 'You're not necessarily going to win every time, Mirembe.'

'I'm not sure that's true. I felt like I could have travelled even faster if I'd wanted to.'

The other gods started to arrive from the end of the race and saved Olawangangu a need to reply.

Alnisa and a few other stars floated over, as they normally do at this time, not ones for day-start flights but almost always ones for conversations.

'You're very good,' said Arcturus. 'You could compete for the quadrant in the end-of-year games.'

'Excuse me!' said Olawangangu. 'I'll be competing for the quadrant in the year-end games.'

'Surely we should use the fastest star?'

'How can you be so quickly convinced she's the fastest?' said Olawangangu, aggrieved.

'If only there was some sort of competition that we could do to determine that,' said Revati. 'Where you both fly the same distance and the quickest wins and gets to compete in the year-end games.'

Most of the gods laughed.

Olawangangu didn't.

'I don't want to compete,' said Mirembe. 'I haven't created my planets yet, I think I'll focus on that. I'm assuming it will take a while.'

'No, it won't take that long to make planets,' said Lu-Wong. 'You decide what you want and how, and the matter complies.'

'Sounds straightforward enough, but can one of you show me how to do it later, please? I don't want to make a mistake.'

'You should do it now, about the most entertaining thing we're likely to see for quite some time,' said Dazembi. 'It'll be a lot easier if you're in your star, easier to feel what is and

93

isn't yours. I can give instructions from there.'

'I'm up for that,' said Revati.

Olawangangu's essence had brightened, though was obviously still black. 'As long as you're not going to cheat doing that too. Don't create lifeforms and get the galaxy regenerated. Wouldn't put it past you.'

His tone was serious. Mirembe could tell that he liked her. 'No,' she said, 'the last thing I want are lifeforms, seem like more trouble than they're worth. All that war.'

Olawangangu shot ahead before the others had a chance to move. Mirembe stayed near the back the whole way to her star, not wanting to embarrass him any further.

'Right,' said Dazembi, once Mirembe was back inside her star. 'You need to feel around you, feel inside the particles. Can you do that?'

She did as he said, feeling the particles of something around her. 'Yes.'

'Good. Can you feel their allegiance to the structure they're forming?'

She didn't need to scan to know the answer. She had already felt particles' allegiances the instant she was born. 'Yes, I can.'

'OK, great. You need to feel around for all the matter that has an allegiance to you. Drag it all back to your star, make sure there's space between elements that react volatilely to one another. It helps if you group them together.'

The particles of something cried out to her faintly, letting her know they were there, asking to be picked. She felt through it all and attempted to find the matter that had scattered out at her explosion into existence. All the matter she could sense, even that which she knew belonged to other gods, felt like it had an allegiance to her; a faint one, split, like she could fight for control over it. Some matter had a strong allegiance to her: she assumed this must be her star matter.

In the two-hundred and ninety-nine thousand years (approximately three billion earth-years) since Mirembe's birth, several planets had formed around her star of their own accord. She tore them apart, atom by atom, particle by particle. Sandstorms of elements flew to her star. She grouped them with their own kind, starting with hydrogen and making her way through.

'Good,' said Dazembi. 'Don't forget to keep them spaced out.'

A mass of different elements floated in front of her. Some of the lighter elements tried to float off, while the heavier ones attempted to sink.

'You've got loads here,' said Dazembi. 'It will be interesting to see which ones you've cooked up.'

Mirembe finished sorting the element particles into groups. 'I count one thousand and one.'

Dazembi took a double count. 'Yeah, the scary thing is, so do I.'

'What are you, Mirembe?' said Alnisa. 'I mean, I've heard of much bigger stars cooking up *half* the elements in existence, but all of them, never.'

'The curious case of Mirembe,' said Bernard, thoughtfully. He was the oldest of the group, most likely to offer advice and great to talk to, but almost always bitching about someone or something, in that way that old gods do.

'That's not a bad thing, Mirembe, don't worry,' said Bellatrix. 'We're all just a bit shocked at all these unusual occurrences.'

Mirembe understood. She was different. 'It doesn't stop me from building planets, though, does it? Having all the elements. They're not going to react to each other volatilely?'

'Some will, for sure,' said Dazembi. 'You just need to feel through the particles, sense their loyalties and rivalries with other elements and make sure you don't put anything volatile together. You'll be able to make some spectacular planets with all these elements.'

The gods agreed.

'OK,' said Dazembi almost as keenly as Djulpan would

present, 'let's start with some of the lighter elements, make a nice gas-rich planet. Grab hold of some hydrogen and helium and some of the other featherweights you can see attempting to escape. Position them where you want to make the planet and feel for the gravitational force. You need to align the elements in such a way that the forces will make it into a spherical object.'

A massive chunk of hydrogen and helium flew into place, roughly a billion kilometres from her star, along with some oxygen, nitrogen, and several hundred other gases. She checked their loyalties and rivalries and returned a few that were making the structure unstable. Like magnetic Lego, the particles of something fused together the moment they converged. Mirembe felt their allegiances change as they formed different atomic structures. She got the impression they were trying to impress her.

'Very good,' said Dazembi, teacher-like. 'This part's quite tricky, you need to feel for the particles in the elements and excite them, but only some of them. If you excite too many, it'll ignite the whole thing, and it won't be able to maintain a stable structure.'

The particles submitted to her command the instant she gave it. Energy poured into the structure, charging it, setting the whole thing alight. The planet roared, exploding into space.

'Wahaayy!' said Tongwera. 'Nice one, Mirembe.'

'Not to worry,' said Dazembi. 'No one gets it right on the first attempt. Call the elements back and try again, maybe take a few out if you can sense any rivalries. What have you got in there?'

'Quite a few, hydrogen, oxygen, nitrogen, agency, fluorine,–'

'Get rid of the agency, has a complete mind of its own, one minute it wants to be a gas, the next a solid, it'll mess the whole thing up. Save it for a different planet.'

Mirembe called back the elements that had scattered in

the explosion and returned the agency. 'Right, OK. Shall I try again?'

'Maybe be a little bit more sparing with your use of elements,' said Muwan. 'You've got a lot of variety but there isn't loads of matter here. Your other planets will need to be quite small if you want more than two. Also, your last planet looked like it would breach a rule. You can't make it too big, or it'll look like you were attempting to create a star-god.'

'Right,' said Mirembe, who was more than aware and had chosen just enough not to breach a rule. 'I'll put some back.' She returned a fair amount of hydrogen and helium. She'd still used two-thirds of her elements.

'OK,' said Dazembi. 'This time maybe add some heavier elements inside for the core, stabilise the structure. Light the core and let it set fire to the lighter elements on the exterior.'

She picked some of the heavier elements and checked their allegiances before adding them to the gassy sphere she was constructing. The metals compressed in the core, and she set them alight to help them form new structures. The molten matter ignited the gases, setting the structure alight. The planet let out a few small explosions before taking a relatively stable structure.

'Really, well done,' said Dazembi. 'I can already see some beautiful colours emerging on the outside. A lovely planet, nice and spherical. Impressive.'

The gods cheered.

'What are you going to call it?' said Areum.

'How about…' said Revati, 'should have been a star but didn't quite make it? I mean, look at the amount of hydrogen in this.'

Several of the gods came to Mirembe's defence. 'Shut up, Revati.'

Mirembe thought for a while. 'I quite like Tiānránqì Jùrén.'

'Definitely Tiānránqì Jùrén,' said Arcturus. 'Suits it.'

'I vote Tiānránqì Jùrén,' said Lalande. 'Nice melodic

sound.'

'A beautiful name for sure,' said Olawangangu. 'The forces will tame that into an awesome planet.'

Mirembe felt impressed. Proud. 'Seems to be holding together quite well!'

Arcturus contacted her. 'You need to report your change in circumstance to Djulpan. Tell him you've made a planet and give him the name and specifications.'

'Thanks, I almost forgot!' She called out to the Milky Way. His usual voicemail replied, and she left the details of her first planet in line with The Rules.'

'Shall we do a… smaller planet next?' said Dazembi with polite suggestion.

'Sounds good.' She decided on some gold, silver, silicon, and a small amount of almost all the other elements.

Dazembi observed the elements she took. 'This one's a little different,' he said, enjoying the role of teacher. 'You'll need to set the whole thing on fire.'

She moved the elements into place near her star. She felt through the particles, exciting them, charging them with her energy until the whole mass of elements set alight.

The gods cheered as though at a fireworks display.

'Great work,' said Dazembi, who seemed more excited than Mirembe, 'you're taking to this really well. These already look good. I've seen some bad attempts at planets from some much more experienced gods. Not naming any names, obviously.'

'Thanks. I'm not sure what to call it. Any suggestion?'

'How about Laysia?' said Sirius.

'That's actually really nice,' said Mirembe. 'I love it. Laysia. Yes, I'll call it Laysia.'

'Congrats to both of you,' said Alnisa.

She reported her change in circumstance to Djulpan.

Dazembi carried on instructing her. 'Great, now we'll do a mixed planet. A large, hard core with a gassy exterior.'

'Place it far out, Mirembe,' said Bellatrix. 'It'll be freezing.

The winds created inside the planet will make a nice effect. Try and pick some blue elements.'

'Yeah, that'll be good,' said Bernard. 'Make sure you've got some elements to make water and ammonia, it will create a nice ice effect.'

She sorted through the elements, selecting darker colours for the interior and lighter ones for the exterior.

'You're going to really want to design this one, Mirembe. You need to force the elements into the shape you want. Once it's set, you'll need to merge some elements together to make liquids, then freeze them.'

Her control of the elements was effortless; they bent to her will instantly, willfully. She boiled the metals in the core and plunged the gases inside. They rose, creating an outer layer around the planet. She commanded the particles to form allegiances that would make liquids. They obliged, and she charged them with energy, freezing them.

The gods let out another cheer as the solid blue structures took form on the planet's exterior.

'Another beautiful planet, expertly created,' said Revati. 'Are you *sure* you're not an Observer?'

'...Thanks, Revati.'

'So, what are you going to call it?'

'I'm going to go with Kude Kakhulu.'

'A wonderful name,' said Eridani. 'Very nice.'

'You're great,' said Dazembi. 'I don't think I need to tell you what to do from this point. I reckon you could get another four planets out of this lot. Have a go yourself, and if you need any help, just ask.'

'Will do. Thanks.'

She reported her change in circumstance to Djulpan.

Mirembe went shopping for more elements and carried them far away from her star, creating a second pile of elements. She chose some lighter elements and set them in place between Tiānránqì Jùrén and Kude Kakhulu. They attempted to slip away from the structure she was creating.

She didn't let the forces move them where they wanted. She asked them to hold them in place, and they obliged.

'Looking good,' said Lalande.

Dazembi returned to instruction mode, forgetting his earlier comments. 'You can use what you have left in that pile to make two planets, I'd say. Then a few out of this pile.'

Mirembe answered politely. 'Yes, that was the plan.'

The elements and particles that make them sprang to attention the moment she called on them. They formed into order as she willed, and the forces shaped them as requested. She froze the whole thing. Huge stalactites erupted along the surface. Her fourth planet was born.

The gods cheered.

'What are you going to call it?

'Let's see,' said Mirembe. 'I'm thinking Azul.'

'Pretty,' said Lalande.

She reported her change of circumstances to Djulpan.

'Thanks. I'm going to make a nice gassy one now.'

She called lots of featherweight and lightweight elements into a sphere next to Azul, managing to create a stable structure with almost no resistance at all. Thus, her fifth planet was born.

Mirembe told them the name before they asked. 'I'm going with Krim Warna for this one.'

'Loving these names,' said Lalande. 'And the planets. I didn't scatter enough matter to make any planets here. Krim Warna looks very similar to a planet I had in my last galaxy. Really nice, a decent size too. Great expertise: it's like the forces don't put up any resistance to you at all.'

'I think it's clear she naturally excels at everything,' said Olawangangu, defeated.

'Well, yes, she is a female,' said Alnisa.

'Come off it,' said Tongwera, with his deep, gravelly voice. 'You can't say females naturally excel more than males.'

'Paradoxa is a female,' said Alnisa, 'and she's the god of

all gods.'

'Not to pick sides,' said Lalande, 'but there are also five hundred and one female elements and only five hundred males. That doesn't seem like coincidence to me.'

'Not anymore there aren't,' said Olawangangu.

'Well, there were when they existed,' said Alnisa. 'There are also slightly more female stars, galaxies and universes than there are male. I think the same is true for lifeforms with male and female counterparts.'

'I'm also the first God of Morality,' said Mirembe. 'And the first god to have all the elements and the whole spectrum of colour, and I cooked up all the elements, and I'm a female. Though I don't think that makes me better than you, obviously. They're just arguments for and against. I've not been alive very long, but my understanding of things from Indoctrination and the questions they've raised is that most things in life have arguments for and against, many of which can't be settled definitively either way. Lots of strange occurrences and coincidences in the Megaverse.'

'See,' said Tongwera. 'There's a god with some manners.'

Mirembe laughed. She reported her change in circumstance to Djulpan and went shopping for more elements, leaving the gods to their bickering.

'You need to leave some matter to make some moons, too,' said Arcturus. 'Don't use them all on the last two.'

'Thanks, Arcturus.' She took most of the elements she had left and constructed two planets between Laysia and Tiānránqì Jùrén. One was denser and largely solid, the other gassier with a small core of heavy-weight elements. She set them both alight. It took a while to get the composition right, but eventually, the matter complied, and the particles formed allegiances that could maintain a stable structure.

'Well done, great control of the elements,' said Arcturus, now taking over the role of teacher.

'They're not half bad,' said Bernard. 'What are you calling them?'

'She thought for a short while and the names popped into her mind. I'm going to call the one nearest to me, Wolota. The other looks like more of a Superabillis.'

'Where do you come up with these? Took me ages to name my planets,' said Eridani. 'They're intriguing names, too.'

'Alright,' said Alnisa, 'they're only planets, calm down.'

'Making moons is the same as making planets, really,' said Dazembi. 'Just smaller.'

Mirembe depleted most of the elements in her stock leaving only a smattering. She compressed the matter and rolled it into balls as though kneading celestial dough and making little moon cakes. She scattered them around her planets, some getting just a few moons and others getting over fifty.

'I'm done,' said Mirembe, putting the finishing touches to one of Wolota's moons.

'You've still got some matter left,' said Dazembi. 'Look at all this agency.'

'I don't want that. I'm happy with seven planets.'

'You can't just leave your matter lying around, you're responsible for it. It could lead to disciplinary action.'

'I'd make that into a small planet,' said Lalande. 'It'll be a nice addition.'

She hesitated. She remembered seeing nine planets in her dream, she was determined to avoid replicating that. She had thought using such a large quantity of elements for her first planet would mean she'd only get three or four. It seemed fate had conspired to give her eight.

She called the remaining matter together in a ball and compressed it, some one thousand elements, including a tremendous amount of agency. It floated through the vacuum of space and landed in place, now the third closest planet to her.

The stars let out a cheer at the igniting of the eighth addition to the family.

'You forgot to leave some matter for a moon,' said Eridani. 'Still looks nice though.'

'Unfortunate,' said Revati. 'What are you going to call it?'

'Hmm...' she paused for a long while, mulling it over. 'I think I'll call it... Earth.'

A swarm of gods built up around Mirembe's star, eager to see the new planets. There were significantly fewer gods than during her welcome ceremony, only the stars who were within travelling distance of the explosions had come over. They gossiped amongst themselves, bitching and complimenting her work.

Mirembe called out to them telepathically. 'Thank you all for coming.'

A rush of adrenaline shot through her as she addressed the crowd. It was intimidating at first, which quickly turned into enjoyment. 'As you can all see, I have created eight planets. I've tried to go for real variety in terms of composition, especially element usage. There was a lot to work with, so I've mixed them up quite a bit. I hope you'll agree they look splendid. Not all the colours are showing as some of them are in the core, so you'll have to zoom in or use your radar. They're all staying relatively stable; the forces seem to be working with me: gases compressed they'll stay in shape. I'm not sure what else to say, feel free to fly around and have a look, let me know what you think.'

The stars critiqued her planets, commenting on their structure and composition, how she'd gotten different elements to merge, and her utilisation of the forces and temperature to fashion some decent-looking planets. It didn't go unnoticed that Mirembe's planets are composed of every element in existence.

'How in Paradoxa's multicoloured Megaverse have you managed that?' the gods asked over and over.

The overall feedback was positive. Most felt that Krim Warna and Azul looked very pretty and that Laysia's form was holding together superbly. All of them said that Tiānránqì Jùrén looked spectacular, and almost all told her she'd nearly breached the size limit in The Rules for planet creation.

She finished showing them around. Most of the gods returned to their normal lives. Mirembe was left socialising with a group of about forty gods not too far from her star.

'How much weight has Brixcila put on?' said Alnisa. 'I mean, seriously, she's spilling out all over the place.'

'I know. I wonder who she's been eating,' said Revati, his essence growing lighter with cheek.

'Guys, can we not bitch?' said Arcturus. 'Mirembe is new, maybe show a little respect.'

'Who asked you?' said Alnisa. 'I don't remember inviting you here.'

'I don't remember anyone inviting you here,' he replied confidently. 'You just tagged on at the end of flying, like you do every day-start.'

A few of the gods laughed.

Mirembe decided it was best to speak. 'It's fine Arcturus, it wouldn't be an authentic experience if everyone was really friendly and never offended each other. I'd have the totally wrong idea about what gods are like.' She moved her attention to Alnisa. 'I thought Brixcilia looked fine, and to be frank, I prefer the shade of purple she is to yours… it's the best purple, in my opinion. And I have all the colours, so it's fair for me to judge.'

'BOOM,' said Olawangangu. 'Gas has been fired.'

Alnisa was slightly pissed. 'Don't think just because you've got a few extra colours it means anything. You're still just a star-god like the rest of us.'

'I'm just having banter. I thought that's what you were doing. I thought that's how it worked. Or is that a one-way system with you?'

Tongwera moved over to Mirembe's clique within a clique that had formed near the left of the congregation. 'Well, don't base your opinion of all gods on the Milky Way, it's not a very happening galaxy. Nobody important ever regenerates here. And most of the gods here don't even utilise all the freedom they have from The Rules. They just kind of accept that life is boring and get on with it.'

'Whether you're in the Milky Way or not,' said Bellatrix, 'gods bitching or arguing really is about the extent of what we do these days.'

'I'm not surprised,' said Mirembe, a little too knowingly. 'The Milky Way seems quite big, but I'd imagine after these many lifetimes you're all a bit bored of existence. Once you take away freedom of movement, it must be unbearable. I'm so glad I got to fly to the Registrars, or I wouldn't have seen anything outside the Milky Way for one million years!'

'Generating in the Milky Way isn't that bad,' said Lalande. 'It's boring for sure, but galaxies where anything fun happens tend to get regenerated sharpish, and the gods who live there are totally stuck-up. They think they own the Megaverse because they live a million kilocubes from some lifeforms — whom they're not even allowed to communicate with and who have no idea of their existence. The Milky Way is tranquil, a nice, cohesive community. That doesn't happen in bigger, more popular galaxies.'

'When you put it like that,' said Denebola, 'maybe it's not so bad here. Besides, we got to see the birth of a new god, totally unexpected.'

'I wonder if there'll be another one after me?' pondered Mirembe.

'I think you can enjoy being the baby of the family a little while longer,' joked Revati.

Tongwera's essence flashed, 'Someone has finally taken your place then.'

'Fuck you.'

'You know what really irks me?' said Mirembe, who has been reminded of her regeneration at the thought of a new god coming after her. 'How can Paradoxa justify making us go through Indoctrination so many times? I'm already dreading having to repeat the whole thing on my regeneration.'

'Long story short,' said Revati. 'It's to get you to agree with everything you saw. She doesn't care how many times you're forced to watch it. Just that you agree.'

'Yeah,' said Lalande. 'She wants "WAR = BAD, ORDER = GOOD" programmed into your mind and core until you don't know anything but hatred for the Game of War. I remember the first time I went through it, 'INDOCTRINATION' flashed on the screen for what was at least the millionth time, and I completely broke down. I thought I'd been born into some sort of torture. I didn't think it would ever end. I thought maybe I'd been involved in the wars, that it was all my fault somehow. When the voiceover finally came back on to tell me The Rules, I've never been more relieved in my life.'

Alnisa piped up. 'Oh, I know, Paradoxa is an absolute bitch for making us watch that so many times. I've finally managed to get to a point where I completely zone out whenever I go through Indoctrination. I don't pay any attention anymore.'

'Paradoxa has to ensure that we hate war,' said Arcturus. 'We had to start life knowing it was evil. Otherwise we might have thought it was an OK thing to do, to torture lifeforms. I know it seems unthinkable now, but obviously gods are capable of that.'

'Still, why show us that many times?' said Mirembe. 'We all have the ability to recall experiences. Once or twice would have been fine, but that was almost torturous. I know there wasn't pain, but there was extreme discomfort. I think I went genuinely crazy in there. A part of me genuinely wanted to see things destroyed at one stage.'

'Whether first-generation or not,' said Bernard, 'the idea is to get you to have as many emotional reactions to it as possible, whilst always guiding you to the idea that war is wrong, and Fair and Just Order is the solution to it. You must understand and accept that the Game of War is a natural and unavoidable occurrence in the Megaverse, then return to hating the gods for their Game of War.'

'That about sums it up, yeah,' said Revati.

'Hmm,' Mirembe thought for a while. 'I agree that she wanted me to think that the element-gods are bad, but I already thought that after one time of watching it. I also think there was some benefit to exploring a range of emotions on the situation and coming back to the idea that war is wrong, because that was my initial feeling and the one that leads to the least suffering, so it's hard for that to be wrong. What I'm sceptical about is why she didn't allow me to come to that conclusion on my own. Why she forced me to see the world her way. More importantly, why she's going to put me through it all again, every time I regenerate. Not to mention, some of the information left me with questions. Paradoxa claims to know the Equation of Existence whilst also claiming to have no idea of how existence came to be. It's suspicious.'

'I think it ultimately comes down to this,' said Olawangangu. 'You're forced to live by The Rules, it helps maintain order if you believe that they're a force for good in the Megaverse. You follow them better if you believe you should follow them. I don't think it's possible to leave Indoctrination not hating the elements and loving Paradoxa.

And if the lifeforms knew that she existed and went to these lengths to keep them safe, they'd probably love her too. Except maybe the ones whose Game of War she interrupts, or the ones who are punished for bad behaviour. It's only really us who suffer, the elements still get to roam and enjoy themselves. As do the galaxies and universes.'

'I don't think you can call it suffering,' said Arcturus.

'It's mental suffering, emotional!' said Revati. 'We don't get to go anywhere, do anything, see anyone, build anything, organise things – we just talk all day. It's enough to drive anyone insane after a while.'

'That's life, I've accepted it,' said Muwan. 'I've only been forcibly regenerated a few times since The Rules were implemented. That's a massive reduction from the Old World. I've managed to completely avoid genuinely torturous punishment since Paradoxa seized control. As for Indoctrination, from what I've seen, it's great at forming behaviours and thought patterns within gods: it tells us how to think and feel, what to see as good and bad. It conditions our perspective on the world, so we more easily follow the directions of The Rules and the entities who have authority within them.'

'In my opinion,' said Revati, 'it's designed to make you subservient in your approach to life, assuming that Paradoxa knows better than you in all things and that she has the absolute right to rule you. Because at the end of the day, she has no right to rule us. The only reason Paradoxa is ruling us is because she has the power to do so, not the mandate.'

'Paradoxa has my vote,' said Arcturus.

'We don't get a vote,' said Revati, 'and even if we did, it's too late now. Everyone is already accustomed to having Paradoxa think for them, to decide what *their* actions should be, what *their* morality should be. That's what happens when she indoctrinates gods from birth and made it illegal to even question whether they should be ruled, or to decide what is and isn't knowledge in their own fucking mind.'

'I think you're right about her trying to condition my perspective,' said Mirembe. 'I remember it saying, 'INDOCTRINATION COMPLETE: PERSPECTIVE CONDITIONED' when the story of existence finally ended. However, I think that maybe she does have a right to rule us. She feels everything we feel. It can't be unfair of her to ask us not to do certain things that will cause her to suffer. As I've said before, only really if she created us, would I call into question her authority. I just don't like the idea of being brainwashed into an opinion. Especially one I already would have had.'

'As much as I miss freedom,' said Bellatrix. 'I do think the New World is better than the Old World, and I don't know an entity who could rule as fairly or competently as Paradoxa. If she's decided to make us watch Indoctrination repeatedly, that's the cost of Fair and Just Order.'

'It's not the cost of order,' said Revati, 'it's to brainwash you, obviously! WAKE THE FUCK UP. I can't believe I even have to explain this basic control mechanism to you.'

'You just dislike Paradoxa,' said Arcturus, 'because she ended your opportunity to take part in the Game of War.'

'Oh, shut up, you loser,' said Revati. 'I'm not justifying myself to you. I hate this game because Paradoxa created it and now she's being a tyrant.'

'I thought you said you weren't going to justify yourself?'

A few laughs.

'So,' said Revati, 'you believe that Paradoxa just woke up and the Laws of Existence created everything from that point on?'

'To be honest,' said Alnisa, 'I don't really care who created this game, or why. I just wish there was more to do and less rules. I don't see why we should all be bound just to keep lifeforms safe. And maybe she could show herself once in a while, you know? It's so cheeky that we have to follow all her rules and she doesn't even introduce herself.'

'You mean you've all never met Paradoxa?' said Mirembe.

'How do you know she exists?'

They all laughed.

'She definitely exists,' said Bellatrix. 'She just doesn't introduce herself, unless you've broken a serious rule, like Rule 22, and then you don't want to meet her.'

'So, let me get this parallel,' said Mirembe. 'We have to follow all of these rules, but Paradoxa never actually greets us, to welcome us to the Megaverse? I can understand that it wouldn't happen straight away. Clearly, she's a busy god. But never in any of my lifetimes, for the eternity that I will exist?'

'I met her once at The Executive,' said Arcturus. 'It was truly surreal. She was manifesting as a species that has achieved a negative score in her algorithm— they really are remarkably ethical— she was chairing a meeting for the desolation of some universe, I can't remember which, but her eyes, the pure darkness of her eyes: antithesis. It was terrifying and beautiful in equal measure, I'll never forget it. No one ever believed me, but she looked at me, and I know she winked directly at me.'

'Oh good, I thought you'd all gone completely mad for a moment there. That really would have thrown a curve into the game if no one had ever met Paradoxa— except the element-gods who are running things.'

'What were you doing at The Executive?' said Lalande. 'You can't have been in trouble. You must have been working there!'

'Oh, yes, it was a long time ago,' said Arcturus sheepishly. He recovered himself. 'I was there on official bureaucracy.'

'You worked as a Bureaucrat?' said Mirembe.

'Yes.' The word left his essence barely audible.

'What level?' said Revati, his interest peaked.

Arcturus answered with an even, subtle tone. 'I was a level twenty-four.'

'Get out of here!' said Olawangangu. 'You were not a level twenty-fucking-four!'

'How many levels are there?' asked Mirembe.

'Infinite, obviously,' said Lalande. 'Anything below one quintillion is good; zero is the best.'

'You must have been pretty important,' said Mirembe. 'Why don't you work there now?'

'I don't feel like discussing it right now,' he said, his essence dim and shrunken. 'I'll tell you another time.'

'Oh... OK, sorry...' She realised too late she'd made an error in pressing him.

'Awkward,' said Revati.

'Sounds like someone got dismissed,' said Alnisa.

Mirembe didn't like what she'd seen of Alnisa so far. She could tolerate Revati, just about, because he's a funny idiot. But Alnisa goes for wounds, she enjoys causing harm. Revati just doesn't care about causing harm. She knew in her core both were morally reprehensible, but one seemed worse than the other. 'He's said he doesn't want to discuss it, so let's move on.'

Alnisa let out a huff of gas. 'Whatever.'

Ulybka, an older god Mirembe hadn't had much chance to speak to, moved over to their group. 'I hope you don't mind me interrupting, but I think it's obvious why Paradoxa makes us go through Indoctrination. It's to condition and control that part of our mind that questions things. Paradoxa doesn't want you questioning anything. She doesn't want you to question what time and space are, or how they came to be. She doesn't want you to question the forces, mathematics and logic behind it. She doesn't want you to think about how something came to exist– or nothing. She doesn't want you to question the motives for The Rules: she only wants you to think about how to APPLY them. She doesn't want you to question them in any way other than asking yourself how you can best follow them. You don't question her theory of creation, you don't question her story of what happened before you were born, you don't question her authority to rule you, you certainly never question the legitimacy of The Rules, or anyone who works enforcing them. And the worst thing you could ever do is to break a rule. The Rules, that's all she wants you to think about. Paradoxa hates independent thought. It's the one thing that stands in the way of the New World Order. The reason she makes you watch it so many times, from the moment you're born, is to form behaviours and habits in you that you later come to think of as your own. It brainwashes you into agreeing with everything Paradoxa told you or asked of you. Worse still, most gods, especially first-gens, after they've been through Indoctrination enough times, they genuinely believe that their views on existence are their own. They can't even see they've been indoctrinated. Whatever you think about her right to rule, it's irrefutable that she conditions you from birth. The clues in the title, really. "INDOCTRINATION".'

'See, this is exactly what I'm talking about!' said Revati. 'The truth! First-gens have no independent thoughts. They're just manufactured into who Paradoxa told them to be.'

'I don't think I lack independent thought, Revati,' said Mirembe. The fact we're having this conversation demonstrates independent thought.' She moved her essence to face Ulybka. 'That's given me a lot to think about. You've obviously considered this in depth. I'll have to give it some more thought before I reply fully, as I'm very inquisitive and incredulous, and I don't think The Rules have prohibited that. Though, I suppose they have limited my ability to learn things. I can't explore anywhere to analyse the structure of the Megaverse or learn how it works. And other than Indoctrination, Paradoxa hasn't prescribed any other education, has she?'

'No, because she doesn't want you to think,' said Ulybka bluntly. 'In my opinion, she's done you a favour. Following The Rules and thinking that they shouldn't exist is an altogether unbearable experience. It's better if you believe in them.'

Arcturus, who was all too happy to divert the conversation away from the exploration of Paradoxa's virtue, interrupted. 'Erm, Mirembe, there are three comets whose trajectory appears as though it is going to collide with your planets.'

'That's definitely going to hit one of your planets,' said Dazembi. 'Unlucky.'

'I'm not going to let that happen,' said Mirembe, preparing to charge the matter.

A voice sounded in her mind. *Rule 1234: The forces have the right to control all matter no longer owned by a star, galaxy or universe. Interference with the natural route of comets, asteroids, or any other mobile matter is forbidden.'*

'Oh, for Paradoxa's sake, she doesn't let us do anything!'

'My currency's on Tiānránqì Jùrén,' said Revati.

'Too far,' said Lalande. 'Unless I've missed some matter, I think they're going to hit Laysia.'

'Kilocubes away!' said Tongwera. 'My calcs say Kude Kakhulu.'

'Will you please not make bets on which of my planets are going to be destroyed?'

'No one was betting!' said quite a few of the gods urgently.

'There's no currency anymore,' said Revati. 'No sane entity could call that betting. Anyway, we were all wrong. They've landed on what used to be Earth.'

'How fast were those comets travelling?' asked Bellatrix, making her way with the other gods over to the point of collision.

'Faster than the speed of light without a doubt,' said Olawangangu.

'Yeah, for sure.'

'Why is that important?' asked Mirembe. 'They've destroyed my planet now. What does it matter how fast they were going? Look at that mess.'

'The forces wouldn't have pushed that tiny amount of matter to those speeds on their own,' said Arcturus. 'Someone must have imbued them with energy for them to have travelled at that speed.'

'Who would have done that?'

'That is a good question!' said Lalande. 'Things are getting stranger and stranger.'

'We should report this to Djulpan,' said Arcturus.

'You can't report a comet to Djulpan,' said Muwan, humorously perplexed. 'It hasn't broken a rule.'

'Something definitely guided those comets to her planet,'

said Arcturus. 'They would have fizzled out a long time ago, they were minuscule. That was deliberate, I've got no doubt in my mind.'

'What would they gain from ruining my planet? Do you think it's one of the other gods, mad at me for some reason?'

'You've not done anything to piss anyone off,' said Revati. 'Would be jealousy if anything.'

They arrived at Earth and took in the damage.

'It's not so bad,' said Lalande. 'Earth's just a bit smaller now.'

'Yeah,' said Arcturus. 'And those asteroids will look nice around Krim Warna. It's big, it will draw them in.'

'There's also a huge chunk of Earth near Kude Kakhulu, that'll look nice in the solar system.'

'An accidental planet, always the best.'

'Bit small to be a planet,' said Revati.

'Seriously,' said Lalande, 'what is your problem?'

Mirembe's annoyance at the meteor dissipated substantially as the combination of their attempt to solve her problem and the homely feeling of their bickering worked to console her.

'I still think we should report this to Djulpan,' said Arcturus.

'Tell him what?' asked Tongwera.

'Tell him that a comet was travelling at speeds which indicate godly interference!'

'You're such a snitch,' said Revati.

'I think you're right,' said Mirembe. 'It's for the best.' She called out to Djulpan and got his voicemail again. 'Djulpan: I wish to report an, erm, event: a collision occurred today – the day of recording – between my planet, Earth and three unidentified flying objects I believe to be comets. The reason for the report is that the comets appeared to be travelling at speeds exceeding the speed of light, indicating godly involvement. Thanks.'

'How was that?' asked Mirembe once she'd disconnected

from Djulpan.

'Very fancy,' said Revati. 'Not that I tend to report anything that I don't have to, but when I do, I normally give as little and as brief a description as possible.'

'That doesn't surprise me,' said Mirembe. 'Right, I suppose I should sort out Earth and that lump at the end of Kude Kakhulu.'

'You can't change it once it's been created,' said Arcturus. 'It's against The Rules.'

'So, what am I supposed to do?' said Mirembe. 'Earth's axis is tilted now, it's all wonky.'

'Just leave it to the forces.'

'Right,' she said. 'Do I need to report this new planet to Djulpan?'

'That's not a planet,' said Revati. 'It's too small.'

'Way too small,' said Dazembi.

'There's a size guide in The Rules,' said Arcturus. 'It doesn't meet the criteria from what I can see.'

'Well, I'm going to name it anyway. Khūpa Lahāna, you will be my final planet.'

'Nice name,' said Olawangangu, 'but it's not a planet.'

'Well, maybe it's not a planet, but it is made of my matter, so I have named it. What about the new Earth? Do I need to report that?'

'Oh yeah, you'll need to tell him the new specifications.'

She reported her change in circumstance to Djulpan.

Mirembe stared thoughtfully at the debris of the collision. 'I wonder why they broke my planet in the first place. Who would want to sabotage my planets?'

'I'm not sure it was sabotage,' said Bernard. 'It could have been an accident, and no one has owned up because it breached a rule.'

'Doesn't necessarily mean someone was out to get you,' said Bellatrix.

'It's things like this that make me question my dream,' said Mirembe. 'I saw nine planets in it, or what I thought was nine and now realise was eight and a half planets, something which I was determined not to have.'

'What dream?' asked Dazembi.

'Oh,' she faltered, caught off guard. 'I had this dream that I had planets, and there were nine of them…. And then I woke up to Arcturus calling my name. I'm struggling with the idea that dreams are just made-up fantasies. The others were telling me everyone dreams, but it's just so real, hard to believe.'

'Oh, everyone dreams from time to time! It happens to us all, anything we think about in our waking life will seep into our dream world. It's most likely something you saw in Indoctrination.'

'That's what I told her,' said Arcturus.

'You're probably right,' said Mirembe. 'On a more positive note, at least Earth has a moon now.'

'Aww, little Earth with its one moon,' said Bellatrix. 'Cute.'

'It does look nice, you're right,' said Mirembe.

'She's a real beauty,' said Olawangangu.

'Planets don't have genders, you maniac,' said Revati. 'You'll confuse Mirembe.'

'You know what I mean!'

'You should say what you mean, then.'

'That's a point,' said Mirembe. 'Indoctrination didn't actually explain to me why some gods are female and others male. I understand for lifeforms, that's how they reproduce, but why gods?'

'Aww,' said Alnisa, with pretend warmth. 'I think we need to have 'the talk' with her.'

You're such a bitch. 'Well, I haven't been alive long, have I? You can't expect me to know everything.'

'You kind of know already,' said Arcturus. 'The element-gods make up all the positive something in existence. We're made of them, and the amount of them in each of us impacts what gender we are. For star-gods, it's a battle between

Hydroga and Helius, though it's weighted more in Hydroga's favour because there's more hydrogen than helium in a star.'

'Right, OK.'

He continued. 'It also depends on the gender of the galaxy or universe a star-god is located in. Djulpan is male, so he will encourage more male star-gods than female ones to regenerate in his galaxy. When the fight to determine the gender of stars occurs between Helius and Hydroga, Djulpan aids in the fight against Hydroga.'

'I'm with you.'

'Good. The same thing happens with universes. Universe A2S7I4M6A2, or Asima, as she's called, is female because there are more galaxy-gods inside her that are female. When they regenerate, she will aid in the battle to create more female galaxies. Because of this, galaxy and universe gods keep their gender because they encourage different gods of the same gender to regenerate inside them.'

'That makes sense. But why are the element-gods female and male in the first place?'

'Right. You know when you sense for the particles that make up an element?'

'Yes.'

'Well, when they group together, they make the building blocks of life. Those atoms have certain allegiances. Male and female atoms marry and take new forms. Take water, for example, that uses atoms of hydrogen and oxygen. A female element-god, Hydroga, and a male element-god, Oxygenus. Their particles marry and make water.'

'OK, but what about all the compounds that don't do that? Methane, for example, that's Carbondria and Hydroga. They're both female.'

'That's a friendship. They stay bonded, but their allegiance is different from mixed-sex element bonding. Except the gay elements, obviously.'

'Gay elements?'

A few sniggers.

'Well,' said Arcturus. 'There are certain elements that only pair with the same sex in a marriage fashion, and the opposite sex in a friendship fashion.'

'Right,' said Mirembe. 'Why exactly do they do that?'

A few more laughs.

Arcturus' essence darkened. Different shades of green skated through it. His tone was formal as he spoke. 'The Executive, and by extension, Paradoxa, are clear that particles form allegiances with other fractions of their respective elements that were dispersed in The Great Gamble. Once reunited in the stable structure of the atom, they begin merging with other atoms, seeking to make further stable structures. They do this to obtain stability in an otherwise unstable and entropic Megaverse, an entropy caused by the volatile reactions certain element-gods have to each other and the forces that creates in the Megaverse. The pairing of elements happens to reach an equilibrium in the Equation of Existence. The way they bond is how they'll best stay bonded. Normally, this is hetero-bonding, but occasionally, that differs. Just one of the many vicissitudes of existence.'

'I see,' said Mirembe. 'So, particles that were separated in The Great Gamble form into atoms, which then form elements via male and female counterparts. Some of these marry and take new forms like water. Then there are friendships, like methane, and then there are gay elements whose atoms only ever marry with the same gender to create an equilibrium.'

'Exactly,' said Arcturus.

'There are also bisexual elements who merge with male and female elements in a relationship fashion.'

'Gosh,' said Mirembe. 'Do they ever form friendships?'

'Not if they can help it,' said Revati.

Olawangangu chortled. 'Yes, they form friendships.'

'This is where it gets slightly more complicated,' said Zung-fu. 'There are also the element-gods that were born male and now identify as female, and visa-versa. Phosphora, for example. Used to be known as Phosphorus.'

'So, he's a male, who identifies as a female, and bonds with… what exactly?'

Revati and a few of the others laughed. She doesn't mean to, but her tone, it's so emotive and amusing, it manages to portray her exact internal reaction. Which is almost always comical.

Arcturus explained. 'Their particles are happy to attach to males or females in a marriage and friendship pattern, depending on their preference. There are only eleven element-gods that are like that, though.'

'I see. And how many gay and bisexual element-gods are there?'

'Forty-four: twenty-four males and twenty females.'

'So less than five percent of the element-gods, then.'

'Correct.'

'Just to throw a curve in here,' said Eridani. 'There's also 'non-gender identifying' element-gods.'

'Oh yeah,' said Alnisa, 'I forgot about those weirdos.'

'Basically,' said Revati, who could sense Mirembe's confusion. 'Their atoms will merge with any gender in a friendship or marriage fashion and the element-gods themselves don't have or accept the idea of gender.'

'Madness if you ask me,' said Ulybka. 'What do they mean "non-gender identifying element-gods" or "gay element-gods"? Who ever heard of such shit? Same-sex atoms are friends, mixed-sex atoms are marriages. Simple. Same goes for their respective element-gods. That's how it was in the Old World.'

'The elements only started grouping in gay relationships in the New World?' asked Mirembe.

'No,' said Lalande, 'they've always grouped like that, but in the New World, gods started identifying as gay and non-binary. One of the reasons some compounds are so easily convinced to switch allegiances and become a new compound is because some of the atoms are gay and others straight, and it just doesn't work. Paradoxa said clearly it looks like it was caused to create an equilibrium, that she can't change it, so she has no right to judge. Take it up with existence, I guess.'

'She created existence, and it's her fucking mistake,' said Revati. 'If she could do her job properly and created a Megaverse where anything actually works how it's supposed to, then there wouldn't be any gay elements or "non-identifying" ones. There'd be male and female and they'd form marriages and friendships accordingly. She allows it because she knows it's her fault.'

'Oh, don't start with your "Paradoxa created the Megaverse" theory,' said Arcturus. 'You can't blame her for everything.'

'She's the one who allowed this madness to happen!' said Ulbyka, raising his voice, several streams of gas flying out of him. 'Hydroga, Helius, Nitrogenus – they'd never have allowed it. The element phosphorous belongs to the god Phosphorus, who is male. He's a male, no matter what he tells himself. As for "gay element-gods", in my day there were no "gay element-gods". He uttered the words as though astonished by the concept. "They formed bonds and everyone assumed they were friendships. Only in the New World did it come out, because Paradoxa told everyone. Nosy bitch that she is, routing through our thoughts. I'd prefer not to have known that such disorder could exist in the Megaverse. And don't even get me started on "non-identifying gods": it doesn't even warrant being discussed. The lunacy!'

'You can't blame element-gods for forming structures with same-sex marriages,' snapped Bellatrix, more annoyed than Mirembe had ever seen her. 'They don't choose to be attracted to each other. That's just how they're programmed, to react to each other that way. They want to bond: as inexorably drawn to each other as heterosexual elements. Homosexual bonding is innocuous, as is non-gender conformity or reassignment. What does it hurt if they want an identity just like everyone else? They deserve happiness. There are far worse things in the Megaverse.'

'It's the actual bonding for me,' said Ulybka.

'No one is making you watch,' said Arcturus.

'And it hardly matters if Phosphera wants to be a female,' said Revati, 'does it?'

'In fairness, we are the better gender,' said Alnisa.

Tongwera decided to settle it before they got dragged into a pointless and unwinnable argument. 'At the end of the day – which is actually quite soon, so we better wrap this up – some element-gods are gay or bisexual, and if they can make a stable compound like that, then I mind my own business, because they're just dealing with the whacky workmanship that you see in the Megaverse. If Chlorinus and Sodius want to have some fun, create some sodium chloride, and the whole time they're getting their fill, that's their business. I don't care. The same goes for 'new gender' and 'no gender' gods. They are the gender they are, but they're compelled to feel like the opposite gender or refuse to accept the idea of gender, so they act according to their desires. Not what *we* think they should be. What *they* think they should be. That's their choice. Their right. As long as the compound stays together, who gives a fuck?'

'Yeah,' said Revati. 'Fix it or fuck off, I always say.'

'You're right,' said Mirembe. 'If they don't have a choice in the matter and there's no victimhood, then I can't think bad of them. I'm assuming there are loads of gay star-gods, too? Are you gay, Revati?'

They all laughed.

'Don't be ridiculous,' said Revati. 'Who ever heard of a gay star? The stuff you come out with!'

'Next,' said Olawangangu, 'you'll be saying there are gay galaxies and universes!'

'Wouldn't fucking surprise me!' said Ulybka.

'I told you,' said Lalande, 'we don't have sex. We just

merge our essences and our particles bond in the normal fashion of hetero-bonding. Not loads to do as a star-god.'

A siren shrieked in all of their minds.

'Joy,' said Revati.

Everyone said their goodbyes and started to make their way back to their stars. Mirembe flew slowly back to hers with Arcturus, Revati, Lalande and Bernard.

'What do we actually do during curfew hours?' said Mirembe. 'I don't feel tired at all.'

'Neither are we,' said Lalande. 'It's nice when day-end coincides with sleep, but it's rare.'

'So, we have to reside in our star,' said Mirembe, 'not communicating, not moving, just waiting for the end of curfew?

'Pretty much.'

'Is there any area of my life that Paradoxa has not planned for me without consulting me?'

Revati merged the gas particles of his essence into the shape of a head, laughing manically. 'Welcome, Mirembe, to The Game of Life.'

Mirembe told herself for the nth time not to call out for one of her new friends. It was so frustrating being prohibited from moving or communicating, under the command of someone she'd never met and was never likely to meet. After spending so long in Indoctrination, she didn't like being alone with her thoughts for too long. It reminded her of the solitary confinement, the inability to escape or change things.

Perhaps when she's older, she'll tell herself to enjoy the simple times like this. Right now, she's frustrated with being told what to do. How to live. Paradoxa only stops short of telling her exactly what to think.

She checked the clock in her mind, which had been set at Indoctrination. It showed her a detailed set of times from the Megayear she inhabits to the microsecond, but for now, we shall focus on a few:

93 Hours, 12 Minutes, 76 Seconds.

I can't believe I'm required to stay in here for another thirty-two hours.

She stared at the clock some more. Even here, Paradoxa's influence could be felt. She had organised everything into neat little boxes. 100 seconds in a minute, 100 minutes in an hour, 100 hours in a day, 100 days in a month (10 weeks consisting of 10 days), 100 months in a year, 100 years in a century, 1000 centuries in a millennium, 10,000 millenniums in an aeon, 100,000 aeons in an ultra-year, and 1,000,000 ultra-years in a Megayear.

Accompanying the time are two counters, one which reads 77,925,857, the amount of times the Megaverse has orbited its centre since The Great Gamble. The other contains a figure underneath a title labelled, 'Year of Fair and Just Order', which displays the number of years there have been since Paradoxa enforced The Rules.

This doesn't tell me how long it's been since The Ebullient Escape. I wonder how much longer existence has existed than this counter shows?

She stopped focusing on the clock in her mind. Thinking about time was only likely to make it seem longer, something she'd learned in her eight hours of isolation. At least with Indoctrination there were screens with information. She tried to work out Paradoxa's motives for organising the world in this way. Clearly, she had thought about all possible outcomes in the Game of Life and any area of independence that Mirembe might one day grow to want, Paradoxa had already legislated against.

What was puzzling her was why she was forced into isolation for forty percent of her life. On repeat. Every day. The only way around it was to work doing something that allowed or required a god to be outside of their star during curfew. So, for life, or at least the foreseeable future, this would be her existence.

She thought back to how the elements had controlled entities with this kind of inflexible routine; time cut into segments; activities mandated or prohibited during certain hours; complete design of how an entity lives *their* life. And that's the point; it is her life, not Paradoxa's.

Paradoxa is in some ways like the elements, she mused. She demands that you live exactly as she says. She forces you to do things against your will by threat of punishment, cultural controls and

But why force gods to isolate themselves every day? To train obedience in them? To force them into a routine until they're so used to following The Rules they don't question them? To make them value the small freedoms they are given? She couldn't decide, but she didn't like not being able to communicate with the other gods.

It was, however, a welcome relief from Alnisa, and Revati. Though she did like him somewhat, she just wished he was less insensitive and got the impression that his captivity under the element-gods led him to be cruel to all those whom he had power over in the Old World.

She wondered what the rest of the gods were doing right this second. What they were thinking about, or who. She thought of Arcturus. He seemed to have really taken to her. He appears to get on with a few of the others. Mirembe got the impression that he wasn't revealing his full self to them. He'd told her that he used to work in The Executive before anyone else, and he'd lived in the Milky Way for thousands of years. He's also very defensive of Paradoxa, like she could do no wrong.

None of the other gods she'd met seemed unwaveringly loyal or in awe of Paradoxa. They each have their own views on her, positive and negative.

Lalande had some similar views on Paradoxa to her own. She seemed a friendly and genuine star, and Mirembe loved her onyx shade of black. It was her favourite black. Darker and shinier than Olawangangu's essence. She and Arcturus seemed to be quite good friends; she appeared genuinely upset when she thought Mirembe was trying to get him regenerated for a joke.

She wondered how they all felt about being dictated to like this. She assumed Bernard and Bellatrix must be used to it by now, being so much older and born in the Old World. Bellatrix said she prefers the New World Order. She still wondered how they felt about being controlled. Having to perform the same actions against their own desires every day. And when she thought about it, days were really quite short. Given that there are only ten thousand days in a year and one million years… no, seven hundred thousand now, seven hundred thousand years until she naturally dies and regenerates.

The thought of death flooded through her essence. Another thing she has no control over: The Laws of Existence. Stars will start to eject their outer layers when they've used up their energy, compress, just as they do in birth, and die. Then, regenerate again somewhere in the Megaverse.

Paradoxa then adds her rules, prohibiting intergalactic travel, meaning when Mirembe dies, she will be unable to communicate with all the gods she's met. All the attachments she's likely to form will be cut short. What are the chances that she will encounter any of these stars again? With infinite universes to inhabit and no way for her to influence where she materialises next, she's not likely to see any of these again for at least an infinity. And that's with favourable odds. Though it would offer her the chance to explore, she reasoned, and to meet new gods that aren't in the Milky Way.

She rechecked the clock.

99 hours, 44 minutes, 21 seconds.

It's at least moving in the right direction.

The particles of something called out to her. A pulling sensation ran through her essence. She felt the impulse to leave her star, to design things and create them. She ignored it.

Maybe curfew is about reflection on life, she pondered. *But every day? Madness.* She wondered how long she could continue in this routine before she went insane. The repetitiveness of daily life. It would be like Indoctrination all over again. How long would it take her to crack? How long until she decided to break The Rules? The thought occurred to her, briefly, to sneak out one day, to leave the confines of her home during curfew.

Before she had time to dismiss the idea, an authoritative voice sounded in her mind.

Rule 90: Curfew is from 85 hours to 25 hours the next day. All entities, except those with post-curfew privileges, must return to their place of habitation during these hours. Failure to comply will result in immediate disciplinary action.

In a strange lack of recognition, it had only just occurred to Mirembe that each time these rules sounded, she had just considered breaking a rule. *Ulybka's right; Paradoxa is intrusive.*

Not content with designing her life, Paradoxa constantly monitors her thoughts. She must be listening constantly to know whenever she so much as thinks of breaking a rule. She even polices her dream world! Mirembe realised she'd been wrong to assume Paradoxa didn't control what she thought. There is no area of her life that this god doesn't feel comfortable intruding in.

'Well, since you're listening to my thoughts, perhaps you'd like to tell me the meaning of curfew? Or the Meaning of Life, while you're at it? Indoctrination was really, *really* great, but I've still got *quite* a few questions I'd like answered. Like, why you feel justified designing my life? Or why we can't earn rights or trust in any way other than serving you? Or what your calculation notes are for the Equation of Existence? In fact, I have many questions about existence. Why? How? What? Who?'

Mirembe was met with silence.

'Paradoxa, if you're listening and interrupt when I genuinely feel like breaking a rule, why don't you answer when I'm being well-behaved?'

More silence.

'It's like I'm being punished for good behaviour. Is there at least a lower-ranking god who could answer my questions?'

No response.

Something about being ignored and dictated to, simultaneously, really irked her. 'Do you not think it rude of you, that you impose upon my life countless rules? I can't even think in ways that go against your world vision. You put yourself above me from the moment I entered this world: I was made to know I was owned by you. That you are the most important god, and everyone must do exactly what you say. You created hierarchies, rights, privileges, obligations, restrictions, inequalities and punishments without ever once consulting me– or any other god, I imagine– and I'm forced into roles and behaviours accordingly. All of this, and you don't even reply. And the worst part? You are clearly listening! I know as eternities go, I haven't been alive very long, but with such severe punishments for disobedience, I think your lack of reply is shameful.'

No reply.

'It's like you don't exist. Except you must exist because everyone follows your rules and believes in you. You just never show yourself until we've done something you don't like, and even then, it's one of your servants who enforces. You still don't show up. Just a pre-recorded message of some rules. You're a shockingly absent god for someone so dictatorial. And I just want you to know: Indoctrination is too far. My thoughts are my own. You can't have them. Listen all you want. I won't think in your boxes and rules. I'll determine what is right and wrong; good and bad; true and false, for myself.'

Yet more silence.

Well, thought Mirembe, *at least she's consistent.*

Her annoyance subsided. She didn't know herself well enough to know that she needed to control those angry impulses. Gods are notorious for their ego and power complexes. Paradoxa and the elements aren't the sort of gods a young star-god wants to aggravate. Though, she does appear to be getting away with it. Paradoxa could have written her up there and then without even telling her. But she didn't.

'I suppose it must be hard ruling everything,' she relented.

'You ended the Game of War, and I respect that. I just wish there was a bit more dialogue. A bit of flexibility.'

She didn't expect a reply, and she didn't get one.

She checked the clock again.

11 Hours, 64 Minutes, 96 Seconds.

Time seemed to go faster when she was distracted. Even if she was talking to herself.

The matter called out to her again. She projected an invisible field to block out the call. She did it without realising or understanding that she could block it out. She just wanted it to shut up and it did.

There have been a lot of strange occurrences as far as the God of Morality is concerned. A moral god itself is oxymoronic. They're pacified now, but few gods resist the allure of power given the chance. No matter how small a portion of the power pie they get to plunder.

She wondered why she had slept so long and if that was going to happen every time she slept. From what Arcturus said, sleeping for one hundred thousand years is unheard of. Which made sense. At this rate, there'll be seven more sleeps until she starts to regenerate. Maybe she had just been exhausted from Indoctrination? She hoped so.

Memories formed an orderly procession for her review in her mind, played and processed together almost instantly. Patterns emerged, drawing questions and conclusions, some of which led to more questions. One piece of logic she simply could not make sense of was the Equation of Existence. How could 2 possibly equal 0? She set a reminder to ask the other stars after curfew. Another thing playing on her mind: her appearance and composition. To have every colour in existence, and to have cooked up every element in existence, she must be composed of a portion of all the positive something in existence and, from what she could sense, potentially all the negative something, too.

Countless entities she'd met, and even Resource, a machine, had been completely shocked by her existence. And they would all know. Resource had mapped her essence on arrival. Paradoxa and the elements, not to mention most of the Milky Way, would know by now that she's got all the elements, as well as all the colours. A complete phenomenon.

How strange life is, she thought. *I don't choose to live. If I die, I regenerate somewhere else, alive again. Once you're born, you're thrust into existence forevermore.*

Why had she been born? What is her purpose? Her reason for being? And what is "being", anyway? What is existence, for that matter? She wished there was someone who could answer her, but nobody was going to tell her the Meaning of Life. She was going to have to work it out for herself. She'd been so distracted by The Rules she'd forgotten to explore the genuine questions in life. And why there is life at all. And how. And what her place in all that is. She believed it could be chance, coincidence. And she believed it could be something else. Had the pain of existence created her?

Arcturus said he always wondered why there hadn't been a God of Morality before. And he was right to wonder. The only thing that's ever mandated anything resembling compassion and justice is an entity who, by her own nature, is the antithesis of all positivity. This negation, who took it upon herself to ban all godly interference in war, who told entities not to think of what they desire but instead what Fair and Just Order requires. And now here she is. The God of Morality. With the feeling the Megaverse is calling out to her. Maybe the positive something is fighting back?

The eliminated elements, like Hydroga and Helius. How can it be that hydrogen still exists, but there is no Hydroga? How did Paradoxa do it? Where did they go? Their energy and matter still exist. She could sense it, within and around her. Hydroga must be somewhere, surely?

Perhaps she was underestimating Paradoxa's ingenuity. Perhaps it had all been a dream. Perhaps. But she couldn't get rid of the feeling that *something* was contacting her.

A rational part of her mind reminded her that it was more trouble than it was worth. That the elements could never be trusted. That Paradoxa is a fairer ruler. She'd seen what the elements planned and executed for the Megaverse, and it was worse than this. Whether she was indoctrinated to believe it or not, she felt sure of that point. It felt like her genuine conclusion. Not something drilled into her.

But where did they go? How did Paradoxa break a Law of Existence? The Law of Rebirth. Maybe it has something to do with her part of the equation being larger? How does the increased rate of expansion of negative something affect the dynamics of existence? Anti-matter seems an incredibly important part of life from what she's seen and been told.

She made a mental note to think about the importance of negative something in the Equation of Existence, in existence generally. Everything seemed to use the antithesis in all operations, except the machines, whose entire logic is based solely on the use of combinations of positive something and nothing, 1 and 0. More importantly, how exactly did everything that is something, whether negative or positive, come from nothing? How is that possible?

Something seems, at first glance, the most important. Some entities live their whole life never understanding the importance of nothing. Already Mirembe could see the patterns. She thought how bloody mad it was, for so much of life, to be affected by nothing.

She wondered again if Paradoxa existed. No, they'd be warring again for sure. Oxygenus' little outburst had proven that. He'd have broken a rule if he'd attacked a Resource. So, he went for the decor, parts of the mindless machinery. He was making a point to leave the matter there for the entirety of her Indoctrination, and then put it back in place once she was done, two billion earth-years later.

Everything's a game with these gods, she thought. *I suppose that helps to show just how many games there are to play in the Game of Life.*

She felt relaxed now, enjoying the clarity of isolation.

She wasn't sure if isolation was designed for this purpose, but it definitely helped her get her thoughts in order. The decomposition and re-composition of arguments, and existence's inability to not provide it, lends great weight to the argument for isolation. She loved logical consideration and how each move and countermove shakes her worldview, or as Mirembe has rightly named it, the dance.

If only she could leave to study and confirm her theories and suspicions. Maybe she would apply to work at The Executive. Maybe there she could study. She felt it bad form, for there to be so much design put into her life, with none whatsoever for her genuine education.

Maybe the other gods were right: that Paradoxa doesn't want her thinking. Thinking can only lead to questions and creativity, and the designer of this world is happy with their work. No room for improvement, apparently. And always, since she'd first been born, she's felt the itch. A tingling, pulling sensation, running through the bonds between her particles. Enticing her to design, create and innovate.

But all her creating was done. She'd made her planets. Nothing more to design. So, what to do with the itch? She would have to get a job at some point. There's no way she could just fly around and talk her whole life. She made a note to ask Arcturus what kind of jobs Bureaucrats do. See what her talents could be used for.

Bernard's star shone brightly, catching Mirembe's attention. Must be early.

24 hours, 62 minutes, 00 seconds.

Thirty-eight minutes to go.

Mirembe left her star shortly after 25 hours. A trickle of gods started to leave their stars as well. Most stayed in, some shining brighter than the others, more alert. Colloquially, that's known as having their "lights switched on".

She remembered to be quiet and not to send out any thought beacons until 30 hours. Another portion of her day forced into quiet reflection.

The outline of Arcturus' bright green essence appeared in the distance. She knew he would be straight out at 25 hours. He looked on course for her star. She loved visually sensing things rather than relying solely on her other primary senses.

As he drew close, Mirembe felt a clamped connection link between their minds.

'Good day-start,' he said,

'I thought,' she said, in a quiet, conspiratorial tone. 'That we're not allowed to talk until 30 hours?' Her gasses swished around excitedly as she realised her mistake. 'Oh, sorry, I forgot, this is a private connection, it's allowed as long as the other gods don't hear.'

'Yes,' he said. 'Though some entities can still hear. Djulpan can. And quite a few other gods if they chose to listen.'

'That reminds me!' she said, her essence glowing.

'It's a good thing this is a private connection if you're going to scream.'

'Sorry!' Her colours toned back down. 'I've had so many thoughts that I wanted answered that I haven't been able to share.'

'It's alright. You'll get used to it. I find it cathartic. It gives one time to think.'

'Very true. So, as I was about to say, does Paradoxa listen to my thoughts constantly? Because I thought about breaking a rule, and it played in my mind. Then when I responded, she completely ignored me.'

'Paradoxa is an infinite entity. She is all things simultaneously. So technically, yes, she listens. I doubt she focuses. I picked up most of my information at The Executive, none directly from Paradoxa. My understanding is that technically she listens and experiences all our thoughts and emotions. Rather than sorting through it all, she made algorithms that monitor our thoughts and play rules whenever we have a series of thoughts that potentiate rule breaking. It's all done in her mind, automatically, without her consciously monitoring thoughts. Paradoxa lets her algorithms spot the rule breaking, then the machines or elements deal with said rule break. Then, if it can't be resolved through all those channels, then she gets involved.'

'Right, so essentially, I was talking to myself all curfew?'

'Oh, Mirembe,' he said, a little uneasy. 'She definitely received it. It's highly unlikely to be reviewed for a long time. If ever.'

'That makes more sense. Gosh, I really get worked up at times.'

'As far as Paradoxa or the element-gods are concerned, you need to learn to keep your thoughts about them private.

Insubordination is a crime.'

'How can I keep my thoughts private if they read them?'

'I find it helps not to think bad thoughts.'

'I'll definitely try to remember to do that.' Her essence flashed violet with sarcasm. 'I think I see Bellatrix and Lu-Wong making their way to the meeting point.'

'I believe you're correct.'

Bellatrix looked especially blue today, interspersed with pinks, reds, purples and lots of other colours you won't be familiar with. Starlight glistened against the particles of gas that compose her, reflecting back to Mirembe as she swirled around in a spiral effect.

'Look at Bellatrix,' she said. 'How pretty!'

'She does look nice. Do you know what that's based on? How she's moving.'

'Hmmm. Is it the movement patterns of excited particles and atoms?'

'Technically correct. It's the movement of matter in the Milky Way. Bellatrix has access to maps of anywhere she'd lived. A privilege afforded to her a long time ago. She wouldn't tell me what for.'

'Oh, I wonder if she's added me in there now.'

He grinned internally. Their connection warmed slightly. 'The maps update automatically once you're registered. She's mirroring that.'

They arrived shortly before 30 hours and connected to the VPN until their curfew after curfew ended.

Revati, true to form, welcomed them. 'Glad to see you managed to get through the day-end without being regenerated.'

A small, morning laugh ensued.

'And then,' said Mirembe, her colours bright. 'Who would I go to for cheap, opportunistic jokes?'

A much heartier laugh.

'I see someone's started their cheeky phase.'

'She's had less than three hundred thousand years of life,'

said Olawangangu, 'and zero regenerations. And she already gets you.'

'That's because she's an observer, like I already told you!' He tried to act cool, but he was burnt, or frozen, as the gods say. His poor response is proof enough of that.

Mirembe swirled, trying to imitate Bellatrix. 'Well, I'll have to check The Rules and see if I can discipline you for poor jokes.'

Mirembe felt a small weight lift as the closed connection was broken.

'Freedom,' said Tongwera.

'Is everyone here?' said Lu-Wong. 'Who are we waiting for?'

'Everyone is accounted for.'

'Get in formation then,' said Olawangangu. He headed to the front.

Lalande ushered Mirembe over. 'You can fly by me.'

'Great.'

'Right,' said Olawangangu. 'Are we all in place?'

'Yes, let's go.'

He didn't need to be asked twice. He shot ahead, and the other stars followed in his path.

'So,' said Lalande, flying in between Mirembe and Denebola. 'How was your first curfew? Not ideal right after Indoctrination, I know, but one gets used to it.'

'I spent most of it talking to myself.'

'Oh, my paradox. Already? It normally takes a Megayear before anyone goes that insane.'

'From what I heard,' said Arcturus, who was flying two rows behind but listening in, 'she was arguing with the message you get of The Rules when you think about breaking one, thinking it was a direct connection with Paradoxa.'

'Oh,' said Lalande, visibly amused. 'I'm trying to think if I ever did that. No one explains to you. It was strange when I first heard the rules sound like that in my mind. It really does make you paranoid at first, but like most things in life, over time, you get over it.'

'Hopefully,' said Mirembe, 'when she does get around to listening, I'll be so much older, she'll let it slide.'

'What did you say?!'

'Just that it was rude of Paradoxa not to answer but to punish us for not doing what Paradoxa decides we should do.'

'Can't argue with that,' said Lalande.

Arcturus said nothing.

'I've decided next time I'm annoyed, I'm going to think things through before getting angry. I'm going to get into trouble being so honest.'

'Yeah,' said Tongwera. 'That's what happens when you make it law that no one can speak directly to their "superior" to tell them how bad a job they're doing.'

'Mirembe was shocked, Lalande was amused, Arcturus was silently disapproving, and Denebola and a few gods around them laughed.

'Not Paradoxa,' said Tongwera, evenly. 'I've met enough elements in the Old World and the new to hate some of them. Not being able to retaliate to their megalomania is annoying.'

'They're just following rules,' said Arcturus. 'Rules that ensure Fair and Just Order.'

'They thrive on their status as element-gods,' said Lalande. 'All the power and privileges that affords them.'

'I do think it naïve of you,' said Mirembe. 'To think the element-gods have changed their ways.'

The group flew upwards, falling out of formation. Adrenaline ran through the particles into the atoms that form Mirembe. She shot ahead, catching up to Olawangangu.

A streak of colour marked the path behind her, which lingered after she'd flown by, a trail from a combustion engine plane.

'I see someone's come to play,' said Olawangangu. 'You'd better keep up then.'

Mirembe erupted forward, tailing Olawangangu so close they almost merged. She was travelling faster than him, only she didn't know the course. Following him and making certain unexpected turns was adding time to her flight.

Luckily, everyone else knew the route because Mirembe and Olawangangu were now really far ahead.

'I'm coming for you,' she said. 'Send out a light to mark the path to the finish line.'

'If you haven't noticed, I'm currently flying.' He made a sharp turn and dropped downwards.

Mirembe followed, annoyed at the time she was losing due to her ignorance. They were neck and neck now, so to speak. Their gases almost collided.

'Are you genuinely that scared I'll beat you?'

'You know what?' A stream of light spat from Olawangangu's star, illuminating the path for his and Mirembe's essence.

'Very impressive,' said Mirembe. 'It's a shame you can't travel as fast as your starlight. Bye.'

She jetted past him. Her core screamed, she nearly screamed. Her essence sliced through spacetime, a knife through butter. The forces worked with her when useful, against her when useful. Everything blurred as she followed the light to the finish post. She made it. First place.

Olawangangu was hot on her tail, albeit too late.

'Congratulations.'

She was shocked. She didn't think he'd congratulate her. 'Thank you. You almost won. I was just so eager to finish first. I think it gave me an extra boost.'

'No. You're faster than me. That was faster than the speed of light, I'm sure. You should compete in the year-end games.'

'What? No. Don't be ridiculous. I don't want to compete.'

Lalande, Denebola, Tongwera and others started to arrive.

'I see she beat you again.'

'Yes.' He didn't sound bothered. 'I've told her to compete in the year-end games.'

'Maybe give it a few more attempts. If she keeps winning, it might not be a bad idea.'

'I haven't agreed to this,' said Mirembe, a little uncomfortable. She didn't like the idea of taking Olawangangu's place. She just wanted to beat him and fly her fastest. She'd done both those things.

'You're faster than me,' said Olawangangu. 'End of story.'

'I don't even know if I'll be awake,' said Mirembe. 'I slept for one hundred thousand years last time!'

More stars arrived.

'There is that,' said Eridani.

'Both of you train,' said Lalande. She mock-suppressed a giggle. 'You can be back-up, Olawangangu, if Mirembe is sleeping.'

'You can try to wind me up all you want. But the God of Morality clearly isn't like us. Her command of everything she tries excels even enormous stars. I've no problem accepting when I'm beaten by natural talent. I don't know what the Megaverse has planned for us, one thing I'm sure of is, your birth definitely means something, Mirembe. The year-end games are the least of my worries.'

'What do you mean by that?'

'I don't know what I mean. But this isn't just coincidence. I've been alive long enough to know almost nothing ever is. Arcturus is right: you're special. I don't know what games are coming, but I feel a wrinkle for sure.'

She didn't know what to say. She didn't feel special, even though she understood she was phenomenal. 'I'm not sure what you're suggesting. I have been thinking about getting a job at The Executive. Maybe it will start there?'

'Leaving us so soon?' said Alnisa, who had come over with the other non-fliers.

Mirembe didn't reply.

'Maybe one day you'll be recruited to The Executive,' said

Olawangangu. 'It might not be that. If you come first out of all the others in the Milky Way, you'll compete for the galaxy in the quarter-finals. Then for the universe in the semi-finals. From there, you get all sorts of privileges.'

'I still haven't agreed to compete,' said Mirembe. 'And I won't be applying for The Executive until I've regenerated at least a thousand times. I'm still getting to grips with having my whole life designed for me. I'm not in any rush to work for the designer.'

'You don't apply,' said Tongwera, 'there are no applications at all for The Executive. You're just chosen.'

'That's so Paradoxa,' said Mirembe. 'I should have known.'

'I can understand why,' said Arcturus. 'They would be inundated with applications otherwise. Every god and their planet would be applying.'

'True.'

'But you *can* apply to compete in the games,' said Olawangangu.

'You're not competing in the year-end games?' said Bellatrix, who had not long ago arrived from the flight.

'No, unless sleepy gases over here hibernates again. She's a force-tamer, I'm sure of it. She was definitely faster than the speed of light.'

'Are you sure?'

'Yes.'

'That is very rare,' said Arcturus. 'For a star-god, and one so small. But not unheard of. Doesn't necessarily equate to force taming. It could just be energy leading to increased speeds.'

'Given everything else that's happened,' said Bellatrix. 'I could believe you're a force-tamer.'

'It's not impossible,' said Arcturus. 'Though, we could be getting ahead of ourselves.'

When she thought about it, the forces had given in to her request instantly. Maybe she is a force-tamer. 'Is there a test for force-taming? What kind of roles can you do with it?'

'There are tests, yes,' said Arcturus. 'Examinations that you take once you've studied force-taming at The Executive. Entities who take the exams are chosen. There's no application process. Most jobs are in Enforcement, but there's some in other areas too.'

'Then I can't be a force-tamer,' said Mirembe. 'If it is a skill one must learn.'

'When you've lived as long as me,' said Olawangangu. 'You know anything is possible in the Megaverse. Maybe it can be learned, that doesn't mean it has to be. That's just gods working to have what you were born with.'

'You shouldn't say if you don't know,' said Arcturus. 'She's impressionable.'

'Why am I impressionable?' She liked Arcturus but she didn't feel like the helpless child he envisaged her as. She felt capable of evaluating for herself.

'Because you're a new god,' said Arcturus, a little condescending but still very caring. 'You haven't been alive long enough to have all the perspectives that other gods have. We've had so much time to review information from multiple perspectives. It isn't enough to be born instantly infinitely intelligent if you're not instantly infinitely knowledgeable. Gods, and lifeforms, for that matter, are susceptible to information because we are created with only the knowledge in our essence, for language, logical deduction, mind functionality, flight, and such. Everything you hear has already begun shaping your perspective as a god. It takes countless infinities to validate all of your theories. You've simply not existed long enough.' His tone lifted and became less formal. 'I just don't want you to get excited thinking you're a force-tamer if you're not.'

'Well,' said Olawangangu. 'You are. For sure.'

Mirembe's gases shone brightly. 'Thanks.'

'Just don't be getting the galaxy regenerated,' said Revati. 'I genuinely wouldn't put it past you.'

'I'll try not to,' she paused for dramatic effect. 'Unless you carry on with your terrible jokes.'

'Someone's taking your place,' said Alnisa.

Revati was completely orange. No polijuma visible whatsoever. 'I can share.'

'Can everyone stop saying I'm taking everyone's place?' said Mirembe. 'First Olawangangu, now Revati. I'm my own god, I should have my own place. I don't want anyone else's. I'll compete in the games because I'm faster, but it stops there. I haven't had much opportunity to practice my humour, but I think I'd be funnier and less needy than Revati. I'm not sure I'm the woman for the job.'

Everyone laughed.

'I thought we were friends.'

'Well, this is the first I've heard of it,' said Mirembe. 'But since you've asked, yes, I will be friends with you, Revati. I suppose everyone you live with are your friends,' said Mirembe. 'Do gods have families?'

'That depends on how you determine family,' said Bellatrix. 'Most count gods who they've known and bonded with through their life as family. It was easier in the Old World, but even here, gods whom one meets and bonds with, that one's happy to see again, and when one does it's always the same as if infinite years hadn't passed, those are my family.'

'I wonder if any of you will become my family,' said Mirembe. 'I've started so late in the game. Everyone is ahead of me.'

'Don't worry about it,' said Revati. 'That's how we all start the game. We all start the game after everyone else, with almost no knowledge. Everything learns from scratch. We get language, flight, the capacity to reason, etcetera, of course. Lifeforms are born knowing how to eat, defecate and keep their bodies running, well, most of them anyway. Everything else we learn or deduce. It's a fact of life.'

'I suppose that helps prevent boredom if nothing else,'

said Mirembe, swirling around as though she was not in the middle of a conversation. 'Is that the rule for everything? What about particles? They appear to decide what to bond with. What about grade one and two lifeforms? They grow without being taught, they operate and seek out sunlight or other nutrition. That's all knowledge, surely? Indoctrination said it is.'

The last sentence appeared to have issued some form of cue, as all of the gods immediately replied: 'Indoctrination is correct.'

None of them seemed to notice what they had done.

Mirembe was taken aback by the immediate consensus, a rarity for these gods. 'I wonder how we can be born with knowledge.'

'I don't know why you care anyway,' said Alnisa. 'All knowledge is what Paradoxa says it is. It doesn't matter if we're born with knowledge or not, it won't stop Paradoxa on her relentless assault on our mental and physical freedom.'

'Fortunately,' said Mirembe. 'No one was talking to you. They were talking to me. And I have my answer. So, thanks.'

'You'll definitely end up in The Executive,' said Tongwera, his essence directed towards Mirembe. 'I'm surprised she hasn't summoned you already. Not like Paradoxa to give anything breathing space if it displays talent. Paradoxa can find a use for any entity, believe me.'

'From what I've seen of Paradoxa through her rules, it'll be when I least expect or want it.'

'You'll have to keep expecting it then,' said Revati.

'It's best not to have any talent,' said Eridani. 'It's the only way to ensure you're not enslaved by Paradoxa.'

'There's no way to ensure you're not enslaved by Paradoxa,' said Tongwera. 'I doubt there's a single entity in existence who hasn't been given duties as a punishment for some minor infraction of The Rules.'

'Entities who work are rewarded with privileges,' said Arcturus. 'It's not slavery. We only work for free if we break a rule.'

'Firstly,' said Revati. 'Slavery is not an acceptable punishment for breaking rules. There's no justification. Secondly, once summoned to "work", you work, whether you want to or not. You also don't get any say over remuneration. Paradoxa tells you what you're doing and what you're being paid. And the "payment" is not even payment. It's simply not having to follow some rule Paradoxa created or having some experience she has otherwise prohibited entities from creating for themselves. Lifeforms would be punished for indentured service, slavery and excessive government control, if it was them performing the action. What's the difference?'

'Firstly,' said Arcturus, copying Revati. 'We're not lifeforms: we don't feel pain. Secondly, lifeforms that enforce a community repayment system, after or as part of the punishment, are favoured by The Executive. When gods are summoned to work at The Executive, that benefits the greater good: maintaining Fair and Just Order. Thirdly, lifeforms almost always enslave other lifeforms for greed. They're rarely paid more than what is required to keep them alive and working. They're often abused and mistreated, something Paradoxa doesn't do. She only ever requires workers to maintain Fair and Just Order. Something she does based on the need created by unruly gods. If we could take care of ourselves, there'd be no need for Paradoxa's intervention. Paradoxa assigns gods to manage gods, which is what would always have happened. She also has machines doing a huge bulk of the work, most of whom aren't sentient. Paradoxa uses sentient entities as little as possible.'

'Were you born this far up Paradoxa's gases?' said Alnisa. 'Or is it just something you developed over life?'

'I'm not up Paradoxa's anything,' he said snobbishly. 'She isn't made of gas, for one. I agree with the New World Order, and any component that helps maintain it. Paradoxa freed the Megaverse from the elements. And even got them in line in the New World. I'm grateful for that. We have freedom under her rule. Yes, there are rules we must follow. But there always would be, no matter who ruled – and there'd always be some form of governance. Paradoxa has the most knowledge, power and experience. I trust her conclusions.'

The kofilulu returned in Revati's essence. 'I thought you said we were supposed to shield the "impressionable" Mirembe, not teach her to blindly trust in something without studying it. I have one piece of advice for you, Mirembe. Never trust a god. They're more trouble than they're worth.'

'We're not all bad,' said Bellatrix. 'You get your good gods and your bad gods. I think it's healthy to question things, especially when you're being made to behave in ways against your desires. Maybe you could get to The Executive and change something one day, who knows. But I also think it's healthy to accept Paradoxa's way of doing things in a world where you're obliged to do things Paradoxa says. And that's the world you've been born into, whether you prefer her way or not.'

Mirembe took on board the things Bellatrix said, her advice always seemed rational. 'It's just so frustrating when I'm not yet comfortable with having to do everything Paradoxa says.'

'If it's any consolation,' said Revati reassuringly. 'That's the way all gods are. It's not just Paradoxa. We're almost all controlling, dictatorial entities.'

Mirembe got through the last month of curfews without cursing at Paradoxa. She still talked to herself, jotted down questions to ask once curfew was done, reflected on what she'd learnt that day, but no abuse. A lot of her time was spent watching her planets. Over on Earth, water vapour was outgassing from the interior of the planet. Torrential rains formed from the vapour, which rained on the cooling crust of the planet. From there, it heated, rose, formed back into clouds, and rained again. Mirembe found herself in a mild trance as she watched the groups of elements rising and falling, taking different forms and states. One of the many dances she'd come to enjoy. It had made curfew fly by, so much so, that most day-starts, she was often shocked to hear the siren screech at 25 hours.

This curfew had seen some impressive rains on Earth. It was a topic of hot debate in the morning flight. No one expected rain so soon, especially Mirembe, who couldn't remember putting oxygen in the planet. It's water, that's the first thing she sensed for when she saw rain. And these were torrential, terrain-reshaping rains.

The more suspicious of the clique had pointed the finger at the comets that messed up Earth. That still didn't explain the acceleration taking place on her planet. It had been little over a month since she created her planets, equivalent to one hundred earth-years. This was all happening too quickly, even Mirembe understood that from her calculations.

After the flight, after Mirembe again beat Olawangangu, the gods convened around Earth. The usual non-fliers had joined, along with other gods who don't always socialise in this circle, attracted by the rains.

Bernard's white essence could be seen darting around the planet as he inspected it. 'I can see where this is coming from,' he said. 'See the slopes jotted about? They're the mouth of the volcano, if you like. The core must be heating. The rains are excess –'

'Yes,' said Mirembe. 'I understand what's happening, I can sense it. It just shouldn't be happening this quickly.' She flashed brightly. 'OH, MY PARADOX! It's Oxygenus!'

'What is?' said Revati, mirroring Mirembe's flash of light in mock shock.

'Oxygenus sent those comets!' Her essence spread out, then shrank, then grew again. 'He obviously put oxygen in my planet and forced it to accelerate somehow!'

She shrank back down. 'I should have seen it sooner. He was obviously going to retaliate. Whatever he's done to Earth is probably some pathetic show of power and ability.'

'He wouldn't do that,' said Arcturus. 'One thing I'm sure of is, Paradoxa watches everything the elements do, every minute of every day.'

'It's not often I side with Arcturus on these matters,' said Olawangangu. 'But I'm inclined to agree. If there's anyone she'll never let off the leash, it's the element-gods. What's left of them anyway.'

Mirembe wasn't so sure that meant he wasn't behind it. Everything he'd done was probably legal. He'd found a way to get to her without breaking a rule. She decided not to protest the point until she had time to think about what he was doing, and why.

'You're probably right,' she said. 'Maybe it's all the elements in the one planet. You said agency was an unstable element, didn't you? There are loads in there. Could be that.'

'Ahh, agency,' said Bellatrix. 'Definitely my favourite element. So independent, cooperative and volatile, all at the same time. But no, agency wouldn't be causing that, I don't think.'

'It's a gift,' said Lalande. 'Not a problem. You'll get a big ocean with all this rain. And you know what they say about oceans!'

'Erm, no, I don't.'

A lot of laughs.

'They're like a love potion...' said Revati. 'Because lifeforms are always having sex in there.'

Mirembe knew it shouldn't, but it did make her laugh.

'It would liven things up,' said Eridani. 'I'm not sure the last time the Milky Way had lifeforms, if ever.'

'I'm sure it has had lifeforms actually,' said Bernard. 'A very, very long time ago.'

'Unexpected.'

'Most galaxies have,' he said. 'At one point in time.' He gestured towards Earth with his gases. 'Given the intensity of these rains, I'd say you'll have a decent-sized ocean within a few years. Given the slant of the crusts, I'd guess you'll have a nice landmass, too. Assuming there's nothing too toxic in there that really could mean lifeforms.'

'There are countless oceans in the Megaverse,' said Arcturus. 'With not an amoeba to be found. Rain means rain. That's all.'

'I think it unusual,' said Mirembe. 'Given the dream. These planets are looking more and more like the ones I dreamt up.' Everyone there knew what dream she meant, but only half the gods present should understand. 'And now water on Earth. There was loads of water in my dream. I specifically used all my oxygen before Earth. I've scanned every memory I have. There's no sign of oxygen. Something's not right.'

'Have you checked with Djulpan what specifications you sent?' Bernard said. 'See if there's oxygen in there.'

'Djulpan?' said Alnisa. 'Not exactly known for his replies. You'll have regenerated before he answers.'

'You'll have regenerated a good ten times before he answers!'

'I'm sure you just grabbed what was left,' said Lalande. 'I don't remember you taking much care with Earth. You didn't want to make it.'

'Yes, for this reason. I knew it would be trouble.'

'Oceans are beautiful,' said Bellatrix. 'Given the axis, you might get seasons. Something nice to look at during curfew.'

'Seasons *and* lifeforms,' said Mirembe. 'Who will end up getting me regenerated. Earth looks almost the same size as in my dream now, maybe slightly smaller. All that's missing is the layer of oxygen surrounding the planet. And I see plenty of oxygen floating around in there. It's only a matter of time. And then what? Lifeforms and regeneration.'

'Dreams aren't reality,' said Lu-Wong. 'You have to learn to distinguish between what is real and what is imagined. Dreams speak from our essence: the most uncontrolled and emotional part of us. We see what we want, fear or expect to see.'

'Perhaps you're right,' she said, 'perhaps not. Only time can answer that.'

'Time,' said Denebola. 'That's the one thing we've all got.'

He's right, thought Mirembe. *We've all got time. An eternity of Paradoxa's rule.* 'I suppose,' she said, 'I'll just have to let things run their natural course. Maybe it wasn't Oxygenus. Maybe it was *only* a dream. Or maybe the opposite is true. Something to look forward to, the answer to a question.'

'Given the rate Earth's going,' said Olawangangu. 'That could be tomorrow.'

'That would only increase my suspicions.'

'I'm only messing with you.'

'I think you're being overly concerned,' said Arcturus. 'About lifeforms and what it means to have them. I'm sure it's just rain, and in the extremely unlikely event lifeforms do develop, it's not the end of the Megaverse. They create responsibility, yes, but also privileges. You get to learn Lifeform Law and make trips to the Registrars, so you can travel. Lots of benefits if they did grow. Some species are so egalitarian they've shaped Lifeform Law, what Paradoxa expects from them. They've influenced her algorithms. For all you know, your species could be even more significant than that.'

'It will be a huge shame,' said Revati. 'When you explode and kill them all.'

'I think if they're made of Mirembe's matter,' said Olawangangu. 'They'll definitely be far enough away by then.'

'A nasty twist,' said Mirembe. 'We kill anything that lives off us when we die. So many twists in The Game of Life.'

'As with most games,' Bernard said, 'there are almost always moves that can be taken to avoid "inevitabilities". You'll kill anything that lacks the resourcefulness required to survive in the Megaverse. That might not be a bad thing. Lifeforms have it rough unless they make it better for themselves.'

'And how often what's better for them,' said Lu-Wong, 'is worse for other lifeforms.'

'I feel sorry for them,' said Revati. 'But unless Paradoxa decides they deserve more, their suffering ends. There are mercies inherent in the game just as much as there are perceived cruelties.'

'Very true,' said Lalande. 'There are lots of twists and turns in The Game of Life. Embrace it, I always say.'

'Watching lifeforms develop,' said Tongwera, in his usual deep, gravelly voice that Mirembe had so grown to enjoy, 'is one of the most interesting things to do in existence. And the more complex they get, the more interesting it is. The constant tug-of-war. And once they develop language – my paradox– they're so bitchy. They make gods look reserved.'

'In fairness,' said Bernard, 'since they've been allowed to govern themselves, however short their reign, some lifeforms have put even the gods to shame for their wickedness. Their cruelty bound only by their limitations.'

'Like everyone who has independent desires,' said Arcturus. 'Some choose to be bad. The Executive has these societies destroyed. Suffering ends. There are also many examples of lifeforms alleviating suffering for other lifeforms as well as themselves.'

'The lifeforms I saw in my dream didn't look like they alleviated suffering. They enjoyed inflicting it.'

'I blame hunger and pain for all their cruelties,' said Bellatrix. 'Especially lifeforms grade three and below. Their environment is always so hostile to their fragile, sensitive bodies. Everything eats everything else. It's difficult to watch. What kind of entity are those harsh environments likely to form? It's almost inevitable some are bad. I'm surprised all aren't.'

'That doesn't excuse cruelty,' said Muwan. 'Killing for food is different. And even then, only really for grade four and below. I think once they get to grade five and above, they ought to consider what is and isn't food.'

'Yes, hunger and pain can't excuse some of their actions,' said Eridani. 'Some get to a point where they have masses more than they require, yet over half of their number live in need.'

'Lifeforms can be cruel. Just like us.'

'The pain and suffering in this game is enough to shake any entity to the very core of their being,' said Sirius. 'I often wonder whether Paradoxa was right to wipe it all out, and if she should again. The power dynamics between lifeforms are almost unbearable to witness. I shudder to think what it's like to live it – the constant fear, threat and danger. The only thing I'll say for this game is that, eventually, it offers them a route out. Conflict and suffering are natural in the early phases. Once they develop technology, they have the choice to create almost any society they want. They move from prey at the mercy of their environment to a reality where their environment is at their mercy. Their dependence on lifeforms which feel can be eliminated. They can create temperatures where they don't suffer simply existing within it. They can work out how to control the nucleus of all matter, allowing them to create any possibility they can imagine. They get the choice whether to programme in inequality or equality, to stay autonomous or live scripted happy lives. At every stage of their development, they get the choice to play war or peace, love or hate, compassion or cruelty.'

'That's very true. If only it wasn't so utterly brutal and savage in the early phases. It would make choosing benevolent and egalitarian options in later stages more probable.'

'Not to mention all the lives that suffer before they get to that point. Most of the discoveries and inventions that improve their condition take countless generations to achieve.'

'Everything is designed a lot closer to "fair" than it's ever been,' said Bellatrix. 'Fair and Just Order is as close as we'll get to fairness. I don't judge lifeforms because I don't feel pain. I understand Paradoxa must, but she can, because she feels all their pain. And she is infinitely more capable in every conceivable way than every other entity. So, I'm happy to let her judge it and decide when they're suffering too much.'

'It's their evolution that fascinates me,' said Bernard. 'I'm much more interested in watching their DNA write itself into new, updated versions appropriate for their environment than I am planetary politics.'

'That is a show, for sure,' said Eridani. 'But watching them devise how to govern themselves, fuel themselves and satiate their natural and personal desires is incredibly interesting. Who gets what? Who does what? And best of all, why?'

'The how part of that is also quite interesting.'

'You're right there.'

'I love watching them develop receptivity to their environment,' said Xalistya. 'Their ability to sense and utilise everything from sunlight to sound waves always manages to impress me. They manage so much in their brief blip in existence.'

'For me, it's the interactivity between the elements. That each lifeform is composed entirely of different elements, with each species needing to seek and consume different combinations of elements to fuel themselves. Absolutely fascinating.'

'I'm always amazed by how sensitive lifeforms are to moves by other players and the role their unconscious mind plays in managing it all. Something as simple as stretching a jaw muscle and flashing some enamel will cause them to be happy for the whole day, and another player just directing angry vibrations at them is enough to give them repeated flashbacks for the rest of their lives. They're so unbelievably receptive and sensitive to their environment and cues it sends, considering how utterly basic they are.'

'It's their internalisation of actions that makes them so meaningful,' said Lalande. 'Especially caring and loving gestures, they're so important. The reciprocation is essential to their survival and happiness. It really helps them through the barbarism of the game, especially in the early stages. The fortunate ones, that is.'

'Maybe you'll get a sentient plant-based lifeform,' said Olawangangu. 'Trees on land are almost always peaceful. Ocean plants are quite vicious, they rarely get past grade three, though.'

'Even they fight over sunlight, water and the like.'

'I doubt even The Executive punish minor scuffles over naturally arising needs.'

'Wouldn't put it past them.'

'It probably all adds up in their algorithm total.'

'Kind of harsh,' said Eridani. 'That they're judged collectively, with no communication from The Executive. Who knows what they'd do with forewarning? Not to mention the other gods dragged into the regeneration when the whole society is deemed unfit for existence.'

'I think,' said Arcturus, 'that after the way gods treated lifeforms, Paradoxa was right to ban all communication between us and them. As I understand it, 99.99% of judgements on lifeforms are simply to let their essence leave the game. Even the ones who are punished are in a better position than they would be in a free world left to the whims of the elements.'

It does leave them lots of questions,' said Lalande. 'And fears. I remember my lifeforms constantly questioning life. Almost as much as gods. I'd have loved to have answered.'

'I didn't know you had lifeforms!' exclaimed Arcturus, uncharacteristically loud.

'I didn't know you worked in The Executive.'

'I assumed you'd all had them at one point in your lives.'

Most of the gods confirmed they had. Arcturus and two others hadn't. All have lived in a galaxy that contained them.

'How long did your lifeforms live, Lalande?'

'About one hundred thousand years,' she said, reminiscent. 'They were at grade four, made it onto land... then I got the farts, blew out a solar flare, completely destroyed them. It was so unexpected. I couldn't control it.'

'That's so sad,' said Mirembe.

Purple and mpilgagwe were streaked through Lalande's black essence. Colours rarely on display. 'I know,' she said, with an empathetic despondency rarely seen in gods. 'I think I finally understood why lifeforms grieve when they miscarry or their children die. I was totally unprepared for the hole it left in my life. It took ages to get over it.'

Mirembe had been programmed to fear having lifeforms

through Indoctrination. She left there feeling that lifeforms, like gods, couldn't be trusted. They all played the Game of War. But the way Lalande talked about them reminded her of the emotion she'd felt for them when she first watched lifeforms under the tyranny of the elements. How she'd felt genuine compassion for them, their right to freedom from suffering, and their right to autonomy. 'It's nice that you got attached, though,' she said. 'A much better relationship than in the Old World.'

'It's not all bad,' said Olawangangu. 'But the sheer number of trips I took to the Registrars and Offertories about mine is unbelievable.'

'Yeah,' said Revati. 'I definitely don't miss that.'

'I was only ever called to a debate once,' said Lalande. 'It was all over very quickly.'

'Lifeform Law is so dull,' said Revati. 'Only Paradoxa could think up something more boring than The Rules.'

'I think it's fascinating,' said Arcturus.

'Of course, you do,' said Alnisa.

'It's fairly interesting,' said Bellatrix. 'Finding a morality base for lifeforms is more complex than for gods.'

'And Paradoxa determines what morals lifeforms should have?' confirmed Mirembe.

'Correct.'

'She does manage to encroach in every area of life,' said Muwan. 'Everything that exists is hers to rule. That's literally Rule 1 of The Rules.'

'I don't think she encroaches on every area of life,' said Arcturus.

A long shrieking alarm wailed inside their minds. Twenty-five minutes to curfew.

Everyone laughed. Timing.

'You know what I think's cheeky?' said Tongwera. 'That she used the same siren the elements used to call "lesser gods" and lifeforms to prayer in the Old World. I could have done without hearing that in the New World.'

'Well,' said Arcturus, flying away from them back to his star. 'At least it's only twice a day, one of those times is to let you know you're free to roam, and she never demands or requires our worship. A massive improvement from the Old World. Some might say you're ungrateful. Good day-end, see you all tomorrow.'

'We should leave,' said Eridani.

'Another day,' said Revati, 'another detention.'

Mirembe looked at the freedom of open space longingly and returned to her star. Time, once again, to play curfew in the Game of Life.

Four Billion Years Ago…

Several months had passed, and Mirembe's three-hundred thousandth birthday had at last arrived. As I'm sure you've realised, Mirembe is still incredibly young at three hundred thousand years old. Many gods have been alive for all the Megayears since The Ebullient Escape. Mirembe hadn't yet reached even a Megayear or had a single regeneration. For her, this day was special. She'd missed countless birthdays during Indoctrination and another hundred thousand during her sleep. Today was the first real birthday that she could celebrate. She was so determined to celebrate it that she hadn't slept for the last forty-six months.

She'd occupied herself in every way she could. She learned to morph the gas of her essence into different shapes and expressions. She studied the Equation of Existence and The Rules, querying what they implied about reality. She went gallivanting with Bellatrix and a few others, using Bellatrix's map to guide them through the Milky Way.

Much of her time was spent getting to know the other gods. Talking endlessly about life; what it all means, and what life was like for them in the Old World and the New World. Everyone had some piece of advice for her, some perspective for her to consider. And that's how she'd resolved to get through curfew, by considering anything and everything. Especially those things that she didn't share with others.

It didn't take Mirembe long to realise that anything said to one god was as good as said to all gods. So, she had learnt to restrain herself somewhat, though she's still very impulsive and overshares at times.

Her development has been accelerated in places. She has already displayed talent matching and even exceeding accomplished star-gods. She's consistently beaten Olawangangu whenever they competed in flights, and so she agreed to race in the year-end games— though she refused the offer of leading the morning flight. Olawangangu and Bellatrix mapped a new flight route, where Mirembe and the other faster fliers could deviate from the route to cover more space in preparation for the games. Mirembe's speed increased consistently, as she better understood the relationship between force and her own energy.

To add to that, her memory, reasoning, and logic already rivalled other gods at times. She showed great promise for what everyone agreed would be a job as a Bureaucrat at The Executive.

Mirembe was not in any rush to become a Bureaucrat. She was just getting to grips with the Milky Way. She was still fascinated by the smaller things in life: socialising, the first greeting of day-start, the feeling of flying, learning something new in the daily chat and watching her planets develop.

Most of her planets were stabilising, which for many of them, like most particles in existence, is a constant state of cyclical change. Still, the cooperation between elements was excellent, and their orbit was steadying. Each planet had its own feel. Tiānránqì Jùrén had hurricanes swirling around the planet, creating colourful spiral effects on the exterior of the planet. Beautiful frozen storms and ice structures formed all over Kude Khakulu and Azul. Laysia sprouted beautiful mountains. Even Earth had settled down. The rains became less torrential, an ocean formed on the planet, and a large landmass with rocks now protruded out of the water.

Watching the planets meet an equilibrium with the forces had occupied a lot of Mirembe's curfew time. From the superficial beauty of it all to the atomic composition and use of force, she had been mesmerised watching her planets grow and develop. She formed an attachment to each planet: they felt like a prized creation and possession.

One thing that had been at the back of her mind, constantly, was Oxygenus. She was convinced that he had done something to Earth. The only logical explanation she could think of was that he was trying to create life and, in the process, get her regenerated, and possibly punished upon regeneration. Every curfew she'd watched the oceans of Earth, half expecting life. It never came.

She'd accepted that she'd broken a rule in being rude to him, but after the way he'd behaved, and everything she'd been through during Indoctrination, she felt he could have let it slide. But he hadn't used the normal disciplinary procedures. He hadn't reported it. He'd punished her indirectly. Letting her know she'd made an enemy. Or so she assumed, anyway.

Other than that, life had really been quite enjoyable. She'd gotten used to curfew and spent her free time exploring and socialising. Everyone she'd met had been really ingratiating, even if in their own bitchy way. She was now part of an enormous family of gods, and the youngest of the bunch!

She loved the variety of characters in the Milky Way. Listening to the constant exchange of ideas entertained her greatly. No one seemed to agree on anything; everyone had an opinion on something. Even Mirembe had developed a lot of opinions in her short life. It excited her to have so many things to question and evaluate.

All this activity was making her extremely tired, so it was with great relief that she heard the siren screech, releasing her to enjoy her birthday.

She left her star as soon as the siren finished. A much larger crowd than usual had left their stars and were making their way to Dazembi's. She raced to Dazembi's star, covering the distance almost instantly.

A clamped connection latched onto her mind, followed by a wave of excited chatter, which quickly dissipated as Mirembe joined the conversation.

'You're early,' said Dazembi. 'You'll have to wait for the other stars.'

Mirembe tried to make small talk. No one replied.

Once the last few gods arrived, they spread out in front of Mirembe, compressing their gasses into the shape of musical notes. Revati's essence shimmered and pulsated, sending a ripple through the gods. As his essence connected with theirs, the notes of Mozart's Requiem in D minor chimed for the birthday girl.

Mirembe beamed. Her essence illuminated the space around her.

As the cheers settled down, the gods flew around Mirembe. They shot up in pairs, colliding with each other, exploding into colourful fireworks.

Once everyone had exploded, they reassembled their gasses and regrouped, aligning themselves to spell 'Happy Birthday'.

Mirembe beamed again. She was overwhelmed.

Everyone flew back to Mirembe once they'd reassembled themselves. It was now after 30 hours, and everyone was free to talk openly.

'Thanks,' said Mirembe. 'I didn't expect all this! That's really sweet of you. You all looked spectacular, of course.'

'Given that you haven't shut up about it for the last ten months,' said Revati. 'I thought you would have expected some recognition of the fact you're three hundred thousand years old today.'

Good-natured laughter.

Mirembe beamed again. She felt a little embarrassed at all

the attention. 'Are we still going on our morning flight?'

'Yes,' said Lalande. 'But a different route. No racing today. You're flying in the middle with me and Eridani.

'Why?'

'It's a surprise.'

'We should get moving,' said Olawangangu. 'We're going to be late.'

'Late for what?'

'All will be revealed,' said Revati.

They set off to the undisclosed location, anticipation and excitement building in Mirembe's core.

'So,' said Arcturus, flying behind Mirembe. 'How does it feel to be awake and able to celebrate your birthday?'

'Great,' she blurted out. 'I can't wait to know where we're going.'

'I've never been,' said Arcturus, 'so it's a bit of a surprise for me too.'

'I'm sure you came with us once,' said Lalande.

'Definitely not.'

'Well, you'll enjoy it.'

'I said I was coming as a spectator. I didn't want to miss your birthday, Mirembe.'

'Oh, my paradox,' said Mirembe. 'Where are we going?'

'We told you,' said Eridani, 'It's a surprise.'

'Arcturus doesn't agree, of course,' said Lalande. 'But it's not against The Rules. If it's fine with Paradoxa, it's fine with me.'

'I never said I don't agree,' he said snobbishly. 'I said I don't partake. And I think Mirembe is still quite young.'

'It's her birthday,' said Lalande. 'Special occasions, that's what I've always said.'

'She is young,' said Eridani, 'relative to us. We're young relative to Paradoxa and the originals.'

'It'll be fine,' shouted Revati. 'Now shut up about it before you ruin the surprise.'

Mirembe felt even more excited and curious than before.

She didn't think it unusual for Arcturus to disagree with the majority of the gods in the conversation, but it was rare that his views didn't align exactly with Paradoxa's. She wondered what could possibly have caused him to do this!

'Yeah,' said Eridani. 'Don't be such a laughter leech, Arcturus. Mirembe's still young enough to care about birthdays, she should at least enjoy it.'

'I am unusually excited,' said Mirembe.

'It wears off,' said Lalande. 'I only celebrate once every ultra-year. Obviously, when you hit a Megayear birthday, it's a big event.'

'Even that bores me now,' Bernard said.

'What do you usually do to celebrate?' said Mirembe. 'What do gods do on their birthday?'

'That depends whether you celebrated in the Old World or New World.'

Everyone laughed, but Mirembe didn't get it.

She noticed a familiar sight, an asteroid cluster she'd seen when exploring with Bellatrix. They'd gone much further out than they normally would.

'The best birthdays,' said Lalande, 'are celebrated when you regenerate with gods who you got on with when you last lived in the same galaxy. You can celebrate with them all day, it's a great feeling. I even got a gift once. I lived near a star who worked in The Executive. He made me a planet for my birthday. It was so sweet.'

'Made you a planet?'

'Yes, I didn't have enough matter of my own. I received correspondence from The Executive authorising it. I didn't even know it could be done that late on. I'd lived there six hundred thousand years by that point.'

'That's cool,' said Mirembe.

'Most birthdays in the New World,' Bernard said, 'are spent doing what we always do, with a bit more attention. In the Old World, gods could at least make something, if not buy something. No real present giving anymore since

Paradoxa banned currency. Present giving was a nice thing from the Old World that I miss in the New World.'

'There is a bit of gift-giving,' said Lalande. 'But I've heard it was rampant in the Old World.'

'I did enjoy getting gifts in the Old World,' said Eridani. 'I also miss giving presents. It's a nice thing to do when you've bonded with a god.'

'I imagine the elements and universes gift things to each other,' said Lalande. 'They wouldn't miss an opportunity to gain power and influence.'

'I'm surprised they've got any room to do anything,' said Revati. 'Paradoxa has thought up a rule for *every* fucking eventuality. If they're giving each other gifts, that's what she wants them doing.'

Arcturus rolled his mind's eye. 'We're really far out,' he said. 'How much further is it?'

'We're about two-thirds of the way there.'

'Wow,' said Mirembe, taking in the scenery. 'I don't think I've been this far out in this direction.'

'It was me who found it,' said Eridani. 'One day when I was exploring. I'm surprised there's anything fun to do in the Milky Way.'

The suspense! Mirembe had never felt an emotion like this before. This kind of suspense. This happy curiosity at what lies ahead. 'Thank you for bringing me,' she said, sending a beacon to the gods. 'I really appreciate it.'

'Don't thank us just yet,' said Revati. 'You don't know where we're going.'

'Can we fly faster?'

'We're not all as fast as you.'

'Of course, sorry. I'm just excited.'

'You'll be glad to know,' said Olawangangu, 'it's standard practice that new gods celebrate their birthdays every year until their first Megayear. As the first God of Morality, I'm sure you'll have lots of fans, wherever you go. It'll be an exciting few years. Enjoy it while you can.'

'I will, for sure.'

'I forgot how far away this is,' said Lalande. 'Some might struggle to get back on time if we stay too long.'

'We'll all be late if we stay too long,' said Olawangangu. 'Got to keep your wits about you.'

'Doesn't that require wits in the first place?' said Revati.

'Carry on, and I'll keep you in there for an hour,' said Olawangangu. 'You know I can stay in there twice as long as you.'

Mirembe laughed. She had such a warm feeling when she heard the gods bickering.

'We could pick up the pace a little,' said Bellatrix.

'Alright,' said Olawangangu.

Mirembe still couldn't see anything that looked remotely significant. 'Do you come here often for birthdays?'

'Birthdays, normal days, whenever.'

'I've been less than one hundred times,' said Lalande. 'Since I regenerated in the Milky Way.'

'So not every birthday then.'

'No. There isn't always one near enough. Some galaxies might only have a few. The Milky Way has loads.'

'It's lucky that I generated in the Milky Way then,' said Mirembe.

'Not a sentence you hear every day,' said Arcturus, with a kind of humour Mirembe rarely saw him display.

'Maybe you've all underestimated the Milky Way.'

'True,' said Eridani. 'First, we find this little beauty so close by, then a new god is born. Djulpan has outdone himself.'

'I've loved my time here so far,' said Mirembe. 'The main things I've struggled to deal with are The Rules, which I'd have to follow wherever I was born. You've all made it more bearable.'

'That is legitimately cute,' said Alnisa, with unusual sincerity. 'Happy Birthday.'

'Eh...thanks,' said Mirembe, scanning the comment for

bitchiness. There didn't appear to be any.

'You're a nice star, Mirembe,' said Olawangangu, who had formed a brotherly attachment to her over the past months. 'You already get things well past your age. You've got a lively, inquisitive personality that isn't bitchy or rude. And you care. A lot of gods don't. If you keep it up through your life, and I'm sure you will, you'll make lots of friends because your company is enjoyable. Even if only to see your reaction to learning new bits of information. Everything's been so dull for the last million Megayears. A new god is what we needed.'

'Thanks, Olawangangu. That's nice of you. I definitely hope we regenerate together sooner rather than later.'

'You've still got this life left to live,' said Lalande. 'And if you look over there, you'll see we've almost arrived at our destination.'

The only thing Mirembe could see was a small, dull grey star slowly orbiting an even duller white star. 'This is my surprise?' Her voice didn't conceal the disappointment. She recovered, trying to act grateful. 'Thanks. I did see some on my flight with Oxygenus, but we didn't get to stop and watch. Thank you for bringing me.'

They all laughed.

'We're not here to observe,' said Muwan. 'You see the centre point where the mass of the stars meets and orbits? That's where we're going.'

Mirembe flew ahead to the stars and observed the point more closely. Like the wavy wafting ripple of heated air, the centre point of the stars' orbit faded in and out of view as she watched.

'What are their names?' said Mirembe.

'The large one is Fufumi. The small one is Antanzi.'

'From the looks of things, they're both sleeping,' said Arcturus. 'Do you not need to ask?'

'We've already asked,' said Olawangangu. 'Out of courtesy. We're going in the centre point, which belongs to the forces, not the stars, as you well know.'

'Who's going first then?' said Revati.

'We should all go together.'

'Why are we going inside there?' asked Mirembe.

'Basically,' said Alnisa, 'it's to get you gravd. We'll all stay in there for like twenty minutes. Then leave and socialise.'

'Get me gravd?' said Mirembe. 'What's that?'

'Euphoria,' said Eridani.

'Are we getting in?' said Denebola. 'The longer we chat, the less time we've got.'

'I'm not,' said Arcturus. 'And you don't have to either, Mirembe.'

'Don't listen to the laughter leech,' said Eridani. 'It will make you feel happy and lively.'

'She's already happy and lively,' said Arcturus

'Maybe stay in ten minutes for your first go,' said Olawangangu. 'Other than that, you'll be fine. If we weren't meant to be doing it, there'd be a rule against it. Which there isn't.'

'I'll go first,' said Alnisa. She flew into the centre point. A stream of gods followed in her path.

'Are you coming in?' said Lalande. 'Seems a wasted journey otherwise.'

'You'll enjoy it,' said Bellatrix.

Mirembe wasn't sure what to do. It wasn't prohibited. Everyone else was doing it, except Arcturus. *No harm in trying,* whispered an internal voice. 'Right, OK,' she said. 'If I don't like it, I can always get out.'

The centre point sucked her in the moment she entered its pull. Her essence compressed into a tiny ball under the weight of the stars. Her mind compressed along with it. She felt a force pulsating from one star to the other, passing directly through her. Every shockwave made her a little more gravd. She was starting to feel tipsy already.

'How are you feeling, birthday girl?' said Lalande, compressed in a ball not too far from Mirembe.

'I feel really light-minded,' she said. 'I can feel the forces and the stars interacting with each other *through* me. It's quite surreal.'

'Glad you're enjoying yourself.'

'You'll have to have birthdays more often,' said Lalande. 'It's been a long time since I was last here.'

Mirembe started to reply, shockwaves pulsed through her, cutting off her sentence before it started. 'Woaaahhh,' she said, visibly more gravd. 'Either the Megaverse has stopped spinning, or I've somehow outspan it.'

'Now, now, Mirembe!'

'It's great, isn't it?' said Revati. 'I love these guys, especially as Fufumi's so big. He makes the whole thing more intense.'

Mirembe's vision started to blur. The intensity of the gravity permeated her essence. She screamed, now completely euphoric. 'THIS IS THE BEST BIRTHDAY EVER! Wahhooo.'

'I think we should get her out,' said Olawangangu. She's gravd, for sure.'

'Get me out? I don't want to leave!'

'You can come back when it's worn off,' said Lalande. 'I already feel a bit buzzed. I'll leave with you.'

'I don't want to,' said Mirembe. 'I'm having fun.'

'Look what you've created,' said Revati. 'She'll be a graviholic before she's even regenerated.'

'Me?!' said Lalande, 'It was your idea.'

'Eridani's idea, you mean,' he replied, now quite tipsy.

'If she's old enough to be indoctrinated,' said Eridani, 'she's old enough to feel a tiny bit of force on her birthday. That being said, it is time for you to leave Mirembe. Don't make me drag you.'

'You couldn't if you tried,' she said playfully. 'How do I leave? I can feel it sucking me in.'

'Force yourself out, charge yourself if you need energy. Come on.'

She burst from the centre point of the stars, popcorn out of a frying pan.

All the gods still inside cheered.

Space kind of slapped her as she re-entered the atmosphere. In doing so, she became slightly soberer and twice as gravd.

'How do you feel?' said Arcturus, who had flown over to her.

'Great! This feels amazing!'

His essence flashed a smiling light green. 'I'm glad you're enjoying yourself.'

More gods started to arrive, taking a breather from their first round of getting gravd.

'You haven't exploded then?' said Revati.

'Haaaaa,' said Mirembe, dragging out the word. 'I really love you guys. You're so funny.'

'I thought you said I had a needy sense of humour?'

She screamed with laughter, like she'd never heard a funnier sentence. 'Oh, Revati. You do amuse me.'

'So, you're glad we came?' asked Lalande, looking from Mirembe to Arcturus.

'I'm glad we came, and I'm glad we came together. I don't want the day to end.'

'Well, we've got a while before we need to get back,' said Bellatrix. 'Give it fifty minutes and we'll go back in.'

'Sounds like a plan.'

Mirembe launched herself into the air, flying around in circles, talking gibberish.

'Have you seen this?' said Olawangangu, pointing to Mirembe.

'I love it,' said Revati. 'I can't remember the last time I saw someone try force for the first time.'

'I know,' said Lalande 'and it's such a weak gravitational attraction, considering you all used to take capsulised energy from the centre of the Megaverse in the Old World. I can't imagine functioning under the influence of that much gravity.'

Mirembe came to an abrupt stop. 'You are joking! Gods

used to feel the force of the Megaverse orbiting itself?'

'Yes, until The Rules came in,' said Revati. 'Paradoxa being her usual self.'

Mirembe thought about the weight of infinite universes and the amount of force required to keep it all in motion. To bottle that and sell it, it would drive anyone mad, surely. The force between two stars doesn't even compare to that, and she was very gravd.

'That's outrageous,' she said. 'I'm not surprised Paradoxa banned it.'

'Yeah, graviholics were a big problem in the Old World,' said Arcturus.

'Really? That's interesting. They didn't mention it in Indoctrination.'

'There are some startling omissions in Indoctrination,' said Bernard, arriving with Bellatrix and a few others. 'I thought Paradoxa would have at least given gods who were alive in the Old World a different Indoctrination — he cut off his sentence, gawping as his essence dispersed and contorted into what looked to be some kind of grade four lifeform. 'What on Paradoxa's multicoloured Megaverse are you doing?'

Mirembe had seized control of the gods, scrambled their matter and proceeded to morph them into all kinds of shapes.

'I'm not sure we should let her back in,' said Olawangangu, as his essence flexed in ways it hadn't moved for Megayears.

'Maybe she should take it every other turn,' said Bellatrix, attempting to regain some control.

'I'm just having fun,' said Mirembe. 'You should try it.'

'You know what?' said Revati. 'Let's do this.' He exploded, managing to rest control from Mirembe. He morphed his essence into a dragon-like creature, shooting flames from its mouth at Mirembe. More gods joined in, and soon they were all doing it.

Mirembe laughed, setting off a chain reaction of laughter. Like naughty drunken teenagers, the gods played, being silly and dancing. Throwing their matter at one another and chasing each other around space.

Mirembe stopped playing Olawangangu to enjoy the sight of the madness. Streams of coloured gas morphed into lifeforms, listening to Mozart's Requiem in D minor, dancing around stars, high on gravity. All celebrating her birthday. She felt loved. She was loved. She knew in her core, there and then, that the stars she'd met in the Milky Way would be her family for life.

Mirembe arrived back by her star with an hour to Curfew. She had insisted on leading them home, adamant she knew the way. Olawangangu had a hard time keeping her on the right path. She consistently took incorrect turns and accelerated ahead, ignoring their cries to come back.

Luckily, everyone was back near their star by the time the siren rang, signalling twenty-five minutes to curfew. Mirembe was still fairly gravd. The flight home hadn't changed that much. In fact, it appeared to have made her more gravd if anything.

'Mirembe, darling,' said Lalande. 'You need to go back to your star and stay there until you hear the siren releasing you. Try to get some sleep.'

Mirembe was swaying from side to side, still in the euphoria of her birthday celebration. 'Paradoxa, bossing everyone around as usual,' she said. 'Let's all go play curfew. EUGH!' She let out a stream of gas.

'I told you we shouldn't have taken her,' said Arcturus in a condescending tone that showcased the best and worst of him. 'If she breaks a rule, it's on all of you.'

Mirembe stopped dancing and morphed into eyes, rolling at Arcturus' comment. 'I'm not going to break a rule. I'm going back to my star, calm down.'

She flew off to her star immediately, the image of eyeballs disintegrating into a stream of gas. 'Oh,' she cried out, 'thanks for taking me, this was my best birthday so far! Love you all. Good day-end.'

'See,' said Revati, making his way to his star. 'Nothing to worry about.'

'I hope you're right.'

Mirembe returned to her star punctually and begrudgingly. The first time in months she's had an issue with curfew. She still had fifteen hours until her birthday ended. She was determined to stay awake to enjoy it, despite sleep calling for her.

This birthday had been not only the best birthday, it had been the best day of her life so far. Love was gushing from her core for all the gods she'd met in the Milky Way. Everyone really had taken her under their wing... Even if they had gotten her gravd.

She'd felt so many new emotions, and she loved them all. Especially the feeling of gods going out of their way to make her birthday feel special. She knew there was no obligation for them to care, but they did anyway. It made her feel loved.

A yanking sensation clamped onto Mirembe. She felt it pulling her from the direction of Earth. She instinctively cast a shield to defend herself from the unknown force. It penetrated through, clawing at her essence, trying to compress and encapsulate her. It felt a bit like where she'd just been.

What the paradox is going on? Something was trying to force her out of her star during curfew. Then it hit her: an avalanche of thoughts and emotions. Trillions of individual organisms going about their lives, all playing into Mirembe's mind.

The unknown force apprehended her essence, dragging

her out of her star. A swarm of colours soared through the sky towards Earth.

She came back to her senses. She was on the ocean floor, sliding around, inhabiting a grade one lifeform.

How did I get inside this lifeform?

She could feel the water against the membrane of the lifeform's body.

What's going...

Her internal voice quietened, becoming a mild thud against a barrier in the lifeform's mind. The lifeform's thoughts and feelings had completely overtaken her own. Its internalised thoughts and emotions were mainly impulsive. The desire to eat, the desire to move, the desire to reproduce.

Her new body started moving. It was a bizarre experience. As though trapped in "locked-in syndrome", Mirembe did everything the lifeform did, unable to intervene. The longer she stayed in the lifeform, the weaker her connection to her own essence became.

Something caught her attention. She sent herself in the relative direction of her target. The best she could do with her limited, murky vision. It slipped away just before she had the chance to catch it.

All she could think about was catching other lifeforms. The moment something came into view, she felt the compulsion to chase, to eat.

She slid around the ocean floor, looking for changes in light.

She felt something touching her skin as her next meal foolishly slid underneath her. The squidgy membranous body of the lifeform tasted sweet as she devoured it through the organism.

Victory felt great, briefly. Hunger's cries continued even after she consumed the whole lifeform. She went on the hunt again, eating everything she could catch. The nucleus would reward her with chemicals after each kill, incentivising her to go on.

After her fifth kill, she rested on the ocean floor. Something was floating in the distance, too far away to make out. Every time something went past, it would set her on edge. Everything around her felt like a potential threat. She felt constantly anxious. Constantly hungry.

The murky figure in the distance started to grow larger and nearer. It was massive. She watched as it sucked up all the lifeforms in its path, making its way to her. An unfamiliar anxiety struck her core – the fear of a painful death. She frantically pushed herself out of the way.

She was too slow. Like a stab in the back from someone you trusted, the pain of being eaten alive tore into Mirembe. She screamed, her first real scream.

Everything stopped. Mirembe returned to her star, all pain instantly gone.

'What the fuck just happened?' she said aloud and to herself. She felt completely sober now. Had she just inhabited a lifeform? Felt its emotions? Its *pain*?

It couldn't be. Gods don't inhabit lifeforms, and they certainly don't feel pain. Paradoxa's the only god ever known to feel pain.

The clawing sensation returned, attempting to drag her back to Earth.

She sensed in the seabed of Earth from her star. Multicellular lifeforms were scattered about everywhere. Grade one lifeforms on *her* planet.

This cannot be happening! she screamed in her mind, trying to convince herself it wasn't real. Dread spread through her essence, pulsating along the bonds that form her. She was going to be regenerated for sure.

I must report this, she thought, panicked. She didn't know what to say. How to approach it. She wasn't sure if she could communicate with Djulpan during curfew, but she knew she had to report any change of circumstance within one hour.

She called out to him. As usual, his voicemail replied. 'Djulpan, I wish to report a change in circumstance.' She cut off briefly, in trepidation at the sentence to come. 'I... I, well, I'm not exactly sure what happened... I've sensed the ocean of Earth, and I can feel what I'm sure are grade one lifeforms. I've only just been made aware and am reporting my change of circumstance. Please let me know if you need any more information or if there's anything I need to do. Thanks.' She severed the connection.

Where had they come from? She had sensed the oceans of Earth yesterday during curfew. There were no lifeforms anywhere. She left for a few hours, and suddenly there were lifeforms swimming around in her ocean. Something didn't add up.

And then it clicked into place, a relocated joint. It was Oxygenus! He must have been waiting for her and the other gods to leave to plant the bacteria. Making it look like she'd created life. She would be punished for sure. Maybe Paradoxa would do more than just regenerate her, maybe she'd torture her if she thought Mirembe broke Rule 20.

It dawned on her, a sudden, gut-wrenching panic of realisation. This must be his end game. To make her suffer because she said she would have made him suffer.

But she'd already suffered. She'd just been eaten alive, and she felt every bite. How had he done this? Made her feel what lifeforms feel. Made her feel pain.

Oh, I'm going to get in so much trouble.

Mirembe felt a connection clamp onto her mind.

'Mirembe, dear,' said Djulpan, trying to keep his usual cherry composure. 'I feel I MUST have misheard you. Did you say there are lifeforms in one of your planets?'

'Hi Djulpan,' she said, her voice quivering with panic. 'I didn't expect such a quick response. Erm... well, yes. We had just gotten back from celebrating my birthday and I felt this force pulling me, dragging me to the oceans of Earth. It all happened so quickly. Then, the next thing I remember is waking up inside a lifeform. I could feel everything it felt and thought, I did everything it did –'

'What on Paradoxa's multicoloured Megaverse are you talking about? Sucked into a lifeform?' He was visibly perplexed but much less anxious. 'Whatever do you mean?'

'That's what happened! I was inside a lifeform! Eventually, I got eaten and returned to my star. Then I contacted you straight away.'

'Have you been out getting gravd, Mirembe?'

She answered reluctantly. 'Yes.'

'Oh, silly woman,' he said, more relieved than annoyed. 'You gave me the fright of my life. You're gravd! Who took you? It was Revati, wasn't it? I knew he'd be trouble as soon as he regenerated here.'

'Djulpan, I'm not gravd! Being eaten alive really sobered me up. Sense the Earth's ocean if you don't believe me.'

A pause followed by a huge gasp. 'Lifeforms!'

'I told you. They were here when I got back. Oxygenus planted them, I'm sure of it.'

Silence permeated the vacuum around her.

'Djulpan?'

She could still feel his connection clamped onto her mind. 'Hello!' she said. 'Djulpan?'

Still no reply. That's definitely not a good sign.

'Djulpan, this has got absolutely nothing to do with me. I have no idea where they came from!'

No reply.

The silence pressed down on Mirembe, getting heavier and harder to bear with each passing minute. She knew creating Earth was a bad idea. She'd seen it in her dream. These lifeforms were going to get her punished. If only she hadn't insulted Oxygenus. This wouldn't be happening.

She called out for Djulpan again. He'd severed their connection.

Anxiety welled in her core. The weight of the silence pressed harder.

She called Djulpan again, trying to re-establish a connection. Not even his voicemail replied.

An alarm wailed outside and inside her mind. The breaking of the silence forced her emotions up through her core, into every fibre of her essence.

Hundreds of thousands of Enforcers materialised around Mirembe's star. She watched, aghast, as more and more metal robotic-looking objects appeared around her, a universe-god entombed inside each one.

'MIREMBE, GOD OF MORALITY,' screamed an Enforcer with five heads. 'YOU HAVE BROKEN RULE 20. YOU ARE NOW AN ENEMY OF FAIR AND JUST ORDER. SURRENDER YOURSELF IMMEDIATELY FOR PUNISHMENT.'

Mirembe had never heard anything so loud. Half the Milky Way would have heard that. Adrenaline and anxiety wrestled through her essence, the dam liable to break at any moment.

She morphed the exterior of her star into a face to communicate with the Enforcers. 'I am not an Enemy of Fair and Just Order!' she said, trying to muster some confidence. 'And I have not broken any rule! I didn't create those lifeforms and I reported my change of circumstance immediately.'

'GUILTY UNTIL PROVEN INNOCENT!' screamed an Enforcer.

'GUILTY UNTIL PROVEN INNOCENT!' screamed all the other Enforcers in response.

The five-headed Enforcer contacted her again. 'SURRENDER IMMEDIATELY. LEAVE YOUR STAR AND KEEP YOUR ESSENCE SPREAD. DO NOT ATTEMPT TO RESIST OR ESCAPE.'

She panicked, unsure what to do. She didn't want to leave her star; it made the whole thing real. She was still in denial.

'SURRENDER NOW OR BE FORCIBLY REMOVED. YOU HAVE 50 SECONDS TO COMPLY.'

A countdown started, somehow audible over the wailing alarm, which hadn't stopped since the arrival of the

Enforcers.

The dam in Mirembe's mind broke. Fear flooded her essence. Thoughts of escape started presenting themselves to her. She could feel the Enforcers around her, sense their power. She wondered if she could take them all on. Overpower their essence and tear them apart, atom by atom.

An obscene number of rules sounded in her mind for each rule she'd just thought about breaking.

'25... 24... 23....'

Just leave, she thought to herself. *They'll win either way.*

'10...9...8...'

She materialised outside of her star. Several balls of energy flew towards her the instant she appeared. They hit her before she had time to react. She felt them latching onto her, lions on the hide of a gazelle. The last thing she saw was herself rushing towards something in one of the Enforcer's hands.

16
INTERROGATION

All Mirembe could hear was the sound of her own thoughts, which was a great deal more than she could see. She pressed her essence against the capsule she'd been sucked into. It pressed back threateningly.

It had been hours since they arrested her, which felt to her like days. No light made its way into the capsule. She was in complete isolation. She wondered what they were planning for her. Paradoxa was probably already selecting quantities of pain to give her as a punishment. She would make her suffer for sure.

The solitary confinement made her simultaneously more and less anxious. Knowing something terrible was about to happen was setting her anxiety off; having time to think and avoid it made her feel better.

She told herself to be calm and accept what was to come. Protest her innocence and hope for the best. The panic paid no attention. How had she gotten herself arrested so early in life? First, she made an enemy of Oxygenus. Now she was an Enemy of Fair and Just Order. The Executive, and Paradoxa, now regarded her as an enemy. She'd seen what gods and lifeforms do to their enemies.

Light flooded into the capsule. The force binding her relaxed. Her essence spread out, only to meet a new barrier. She was inside a suit. It was made of flexible metal, with two legs, two arms, and one head with eyes and a voice box. Every available space on the suit was branded with the same word: 'ENEMY'.

She tried to move her new limbs. Her arms were bound to her side magnetically, her legs refused to move an inch. Directly in front and above her, a huge counter with a large Enforcer behind it stared down at her. To her left stood the five-headed Enforcer who arrested her. To the right, three identical-looking Enforcers stood menacingly, staring at her in disgust.

The Enforcer directly above Mirembe extended its neck down over the desk to inspect her. It stared into her multicoloured essence visible through the uniform's eyes. After a long, repulsed look, as though he'd just fallen face-first into a pile of shit, he retracted his neck.

'State your name and meaning,' he said in a robotic fashion that still managed to sound disapproving.

Mirembe trembled in the suit. 'My name is Mirembe. I am the God of Morality.'

'Some God of Morality you are!' said an Enforcer to her right.

'Not even been alive the twirl of a galaxy and already breaking rules.'

The Enforcer behind the counter addressed her in the same monotonic way as before. 'Place your hands inside the slots.'

A panel retracted to reveal two hand imprints. The suit moved its arms into place automatically. Mirembe felt it bind her as it scanned her essence.

'Mirembe, God of Morality,' said the monotone Enforcer. 'You are hereby charged with the crime of intentionally germinating lifeforms, in blatant violation of

Rule 20 and the personal Oath of Obedience you swore. You are henceforth an Enemy of Fair and Just Order. Everything you think can and must be used against you. You will now proceed to interrogation, during which time you have no right to any representation or defence.'

'I am not an Enemy of Fair and Just Order!' exclaimed Mirembe. 'I haven't broken any rule!'

'GUILTY UNTIL PROVEN INNOCENT!' cried the Enforcers in unison.

The five-headed Enforcer tapped Mirembe and walked ahead. Mirembe's uniform released from the desk and followed him without her control. The movements felt laboured and jagged, the uniform itself much more uncomfortable to inhabit than the flexible glass she used at the Registrars.

The Enforcer rolled along on what looked like the belted wheels of an army tank. He was silent throughout. Every time he took a turn or changed his pace, Mirembe's uniform would follow suit.

She wondered what horrors lay ahead. The corridor walls were setting her on edge. As they walked by, part of the wall would dematerialise, revealing different rooms. Everything that could express distaste visually scowled at Mirembe through the temporary doorway.

They approached a flat, steep incline. Mirembe's feet anchored to the floor magnetically, tilting her at a 45° angle as she walked. The Enforcer rolled along beside her.

She tried to speak, to ask where they were going. The voice box wouldn't work.

She tried to communicate telepathically as she usually would. The signals met a wall, reflecting her thoughts back to her.

Her vision returned to level as they reached the top of the path. Ahead were more corridors. They took the second on the left and made their way along. The Enforcer stopped outside a dematerialised wall, as did Mirembe's uniform.

She saw a hexagonal room with a hexagonal desk in the centre. The desk had a hexagonal screen in its centre. The walls were completely black, as was everything else, excepting the screen.

The Enforcer rolled in and stood on one side of the table.

Mirembe's suit marched her to the other side of the table. The wall rematerialised, sealing them in. When she was facing the Enforcer, the suit bent her knees uncomfortably, forcing her into a seated position. The uniform's weight supported only by its legs.

All five of the Enforcer's heads appraised Mirembe with distaste.

'Place your right hand next to the screen,' said the second head of the Enforcer, his voice curt, his metal brows scowling.

The uniform obliged. She felt a force latch onto her essence, routing through it.

1% appeared on the screen next to her hand.

'So,' said the third head of the Enforcer. 'I suppose my first question is – who the fuck do you think you are?'

'Yeah,' said head four. 'Three hundred thousand years old and you have the audacity to break Rule 20.'

'You disgust me,' said head two. 'Traitor.'

Mirembe was too shocked to reply.

The last of the Enforcer's five heads extended their neck to Mirembe, centimetres from her face. 'I asked you a question.'

'I told you already,' she said, trying not to be scared. 'My name is Mirembe. I'm the God of Morality.'

The heads retracted. 'What's the God of Morality,' said head one, 'doing creating lifeforms?'

'Is it all oaths you don't take seriously,' said head two, 'or just your Oath of Obedience?'

'It wasn't me!' shouted Mirembe through her voice box.

'GUILTY UNTIL PROVEN INNOCENT,' screamed all five heads.

The third head continued as though nothing had happened. 'Cut the shit, Mirembe. You know you did it, I know you did it. What I want to know is why, how, and who assisted you.'

The percentage next to Mirembe's hand reached 9%.

'There was nothing to assist me with,' she protested. 'I didn't create any lifeforms. I was out celebrating my birthday, and when I returned to my star for curfew, I felt something trying to pull me from my star. I resisted for as long as I could. Then it sucked me inside a lifeform. I stayed trapped in there for a while until I got eaten. Then I returned to my star and reported the lifeforms to Djulpan immediately!' It all came out as one long sentence.

Heads four and five looked at each other, confirming they'd both just heard her correctly. Head one looked confused, head two looked amused, head three's eyes looked like the cat who got the bird.

'So, let me get this parallel,' said head three. 'You're saying you left your star during curfew?'

'In flagrant violation of Rule 90,' said head one.

'Oh dear, oh dear,' said head four. 'Looks like someone created some lifeforms then went to visit them during curfew.'

'No!' cried Mirembe.

'Is that how you get your frills,' said head three, 'creating lifeforms to suffer?'

'Thought you'd pay a flying visit during curfew and cause some havoc?'

'I didn't have a choice!' she screamed. 'They dragged me there against my will. And I didn't create them!' She needed to move her body to let out some frustration. It wouldn't oblige. Only the swirling coloured gas behind her eyes was able to convey her emotion.

'Against your will?' said head four. 'So, you're admitting you left then.'

'Yes...' she said reluctantly. 'But it wasn't my fault.'

'That's two violations.'

'Let's say I believe you,' said head three. 'If you didn't create them, who did?'

'I don't know! I think it was Oxygenus. He must have planted them there while I was out.'

The heads all turned and looked at each other in bemusement.

'You're claiming Oxygenus created the lifeforms?'

'That's a serious allegation,' said head one.

'Very serious,' said head five.

'I can't know for certain,' she said, more unsure than she had been. 'But I definitely didn't create them!'

She glanced at the screen. 34%.

'First, it was Oxygenus,' said head three. 'Now you don't know. Which is it?'

'You've got to get your story parallel, Mirembe.'

'My story is parallel! I'm saying I suspect Oxygenus, and I have no idea where those lifeforms came from. Which is the truth.'

'Every lie you tell me is an extra violation of The Rules,' said head five. 'You're only making this worse for yourself by lying.'

'I'm not lying.'

'How did you do it?' said three. 'You must have had help.'

'Was it Arcturus?' said head two. 'You're close, aren't you?'

'You and Olawangangu work together, did you?'

'Thought you'd have some fun torturing defenceless lifeforms.'

'You're being ridiculous,' said Mirembe. 'I didn't create those lifeforms, alone or with any god. I wouldn't even know how to!'

'So, you're admitting you had help!' said head two, as though he'd just solved the puzzle.

'I think you're an anarchist,' said head three. 'An advocate of chaos.'

'Did someone put you up to this?' said head two.

Head one extended his neck again to be close to Mirembe's face. 'I think you enjoy lifeforms suffering.'

Mirembe was overwhelmed with all the accusations. It was like regenerating for the first time all over again: everyone convinced she was a liar.

'Are you housing these lifeforms for Revati?' said head three.

'What organisation are you with?' said head four, who had also extended his neck to be near Mirembe's face.

'Hello, anyone home?' said head three.

'Nothing you're saying is true,' said Mirembe, rage bubbling in her core. 'I told you what happened already. The lifeforms appeared while I was away and then dragged me to Earth. Once I was eaten, I returned to my star and reported the change in circumstance. Why don't you believe me?!'

'I believe you,' said head one.

'Sounds completely feasible,' said head five.

'Gods are always accidentally stumbling across lifeforms,' said head three.

'And getting dragged out of your star by a lifeform? Oh, that makes loads of sense.'

When she heard it for herself, it did sound beyond ludicrous. But that's what happened.

She glanced at the screen. 56%.

'What happens at one hundred percent?' she asked.

The fourth head smiled wryly. 'You don't want to know what happens at one hundred percent.'

'Yes, I do.'

'I ask the questions!' snapped head three. 'Not you.'

'Now tell us how you did it,' said head two.

'And who you did it with.'

'It's hard for me to tell you something that I don't know! I never asked for this! The bacteria created itself like it always does.' She didn't like being treated like a criminal when she was innocent.

'That's a nice story, Mirembe.'

'Really original.'

'It's the truth,' she said. 'Whether you accept it or not.'

'What elements did you use to create the bacteria?'

'Did you create them or procure them?'

'Neither,' she said, still eyeing the percentage.

'What were you really doing out of your star during curfew?'

'I was sucked inside a lifeform, as I told you already. I felt its pain! Do you have any idea how traumatic that was?'

The third head laughed. 'This story just gets better and better.'

'A god who feels pain. I've heard it all now.'

Head one looked utterly incredulous. 'Do you know how bad you're making this for yourself with these extravagant stories?'

'It's the truth!'

'You created those lifeforms,' said head five. 'Then you left your star during curfew to go spy on your pet project.'

'No, I didn't.'

'Was it fun watching them kill each other?'

'You enjoyed their suffering, didn't you, Mirembe?'

'There's something about watching newly born children being torn apart by a pack of wild, hungry animals that really turns you on, isn't there?'

Mirembe's uniform started to shake, her anger causing her energy to overpower Paradoxa's. 'I do not enjoy lifeforms suffering! I didn't create them! I am not cruel!'

The Enforcer's heads looked concerned at Mirembe's movements.

'Where did you find the carbon for the lifeforms?' said head two, conversationally.

'Carbon?' said Mirembe. 'What are you talking about?'

'The carbon-based lifeforms... which were found on a planet you registered... that orbits your star.'

'I'm sure you know the one.'

The uniform relaxed, becoming motionless again. 'I had carbon left over from my birth,' she said, recalling Earth's creation in her mind. 'But I didn't create lifeforms. You should be more concerned with the question of where the oxygen came from because I didn't put any in Earth, and there's loads in there now!'

'Because you put it in there.'

'To fuel your lifeforms.'

'They're not *my* lifeforms,' she said aghast. 'I don't want them. I didn't create them. And I didn't put oxygen in my planet!'

'Yes, you did.'

The change of numbers on the screen caught her attention. 78%.

'Who gave you the oxygen?'

'No one. I don't know where it came from.'

'Times running out, Mirembe,' said head three, befriending her. 'It's better you tell the truth now, before it's too late.'

'I've told you the truth!'

Three of the Enforcer's hands banged down on the table.

Heads two and four shouted aggressively. 'STOP LYING!'

'For the last time,' said Mirembe. 'Will you stop calling me a liar?! I am innocent!'

'GUILTY UNTIL PROVEN INNOCENT,' screamed all five heads, some spinning in their socket.

All five heads extended their necks to encircle Mirembe's face. Head three spoke in a quiet, vicious, conspiratorial tone. 'I know you created that planet with oxygen. I know you created those lifeforms. I know you left your star during curfew. I know you had help.'

Head two took over. 'I'm going to take pleasure in handing you over for punishment. I hope they throw the computer at you.'

'This is your last chance to tell me the truth!' said head

three, barely containing his contempt. 'How did you do it?'

'I didn't do anything!'

The heads retracted.

Head two approached her as though on official business. 'I need names, Mirembe. I want to know who you worked with.'

'I didn't work with anyone. I didn't create those lifeforms, in partnership or alone.'

'Give me names,' said head one. 'I can make it clear you cooperated. I can't help you if you won't help yourself.'

'I don't have any names to give you.'

'Just give me the names,' said head three, with thinly veiled anger.

'I didn't create them!'

'You created them, and you watched them fight for sport. Don't deny it!'

'I did no such thing!'

The Enforcer's heads shook in rage. 'Enough with your lies!'

'I've told you nothing but the truth!'

'GIVE ME THE FUCKING NAMES!'

'I AM INNOCENT!'

They stared at each other, both convinced they were right.

A notification sound broke the silence of their stalemate. 100%.

Mirembe, and all five of the Enforcer's heads stared at the screen with ravenous anticipation.

'TRUTH TOLD: 100%' flashed on the screen in bright green letters.

Mirembe's core swelled with relief. *Thank life for that!* This had to be a good sign.

Several of the Enforcer's heads scowled, some in anger, some in disbelief. All looked shocked in one way or another.

'Rule 20: OBEYED' flashed on the screen.

'I told you!' exclaimed Mirembe.

The Enforcer looked even more annoyed, still convinced of her guilt.

More writing appeared on screen. 'Rule 90: Sending to Decision Maker.'

Head three smiled cruelly.

Mirembe's core raced with anxiety. They were sending Rule 90 to the Decision Makers to decide if she'd broken the rule. According to Arcturus, 99.98% of decisions are that a rule *has* been broken. *No,* she thought. *That isn't good.*

She'd barely even had time to panic when the notification

sounded again.

The Enforcer tapped the screen eagerly.

'Decision Maker unable to decide: Escalating to The Executive.'

Mirembe gasped. All the Enforcer's heads gawped in astonishment.

The screen went blank and the room was plunged into darkness.

A forceful female voice sounded inside Mirembe's mind. 'YOU HAVE BEEN SUMMONED.'

In a process that now happens so often it felt quite routine, Mirembe felt a force dragging her essence from the suit. The compressing force of dematerialisation weighed down on her. There was a moment of stillness before she was forced back inside an enemies' uniform.

Her surroundings slowly came into focus. She was in an identical-looking room to the one she'd just left, only this time the Enforcer opposite her was female, with seven heads.

'Mirembe, God of Morality,' said the Enforcer. 'I am Gerulina, a level zero Enforcer. I will be conducting the Interrogation. Place your hand on the screen.'

Mirembe's uniform moved as commanded.

The second head cut straight to the chase. 'Recall the events on day 3, month 27, year 46, century 91, millennium 987, aeon 4,518, ultra-year 99,998, Megayear 1,958,562,189,346,859∞ when you left your star during curfew in violation of Rule 90.'

The feeling of shock subsided quickly as the severity of the situation re-presented itself to Mirembe. 'I...' she paused, unsure how to phrase it. 'I didn't intentionally leave my star during curfew. I returned to my star as normal following the siren. Nothing happened at first. Then I felt this pulling sensation... I managed to fight it off initially, then it dragged me to one of my planets, Earth.'

Most of the Enforcer's heads studied Mirembe keenly. Several stared at her essence through the eyes of the suit.

Heads two and five kept glancing at the screen next to Mirembe's hand expectantly.

Mirembe looked straight up at the Enforcer, unable to move her head or body. 'I ended up trapped inside a lifeform,' she said. 'I couldn't intervene or control it, but everything it decided, I did. Everything it felt, I felt. Including pain. I'm sure of it!'

The Enforcer glanced at the screen again. All her faces looked shocked, even though some attempted to conceal that.

'Eventually,' said Mirembe, 'I got eaten by a larger lifeform. As soon as the lifeform died, I returned to my star. I then contacted Djulpan immediately to report the change in circumstance.'

The Enforcer tapped the screen. 'TRUTH TOLD: 100%'.

'I had to see it for myself,' said Gerulina, who looked completely unsure of herself. She addressed Mirembe. 'Stay here. I will return shortly.'

Once the wall rematerialised, sealing Mirembe in the room, a strange mix of anxiety and relief welled in her core. She's been exonerated from the crime of creating lifeforms. Which was a great relief.

What worried her was that she'd admitted leaving her star during curfew. She had the horrible feeling that, much like being punished for uncontrollably regenerating too close to another star, she would be punished for leaving her star whether she chose to or not.

The one thing she had on her side: she was telling the truth. A fact that had been proven. Twice. Maybe they'd take that into account when they sentenced her if she was found guilty.

She toyed with the idea of being found guilty, being punished for breaking Rule 90. She wondered what the standard punishment would be for that crime. It couldn't be as bad as breaking Rule 20, surely. Nothing had suffered as a result of her leaving her star.

Then she realised, something *had* suffered. She'd eaten several lifeforms while in her host.

But that couldn't be her fault. She didn't choose to inhabit the lifeform. She didn't make the lifeforms eat each other. They did that of their own accord.

The wall dematerialised. The Enforcer spoke without entering. 'Follow me.'

Mirembe's suit stood up and walked her out of the room.

'Am I free to go?' she asked, hopefully.

The Enforcer tapped her suit so she couldn't communicate. She did, however, answer her. 'You have a meeting with Magnesia.'

Mirembe wasn't sure if that was a good or bad thing.

The platinum floor lurched forward, speeding them along. Mirembe couldn't see an end to the corridor they were in. It sped up faster and faster the longer they stood on it. Even still, she could see the looks of outrage and disgust on the faces of the Bureaucrats and Resources she saw through the wall as they went by.

She couldn't believe she was about to come face to face with an element-god. She had sworn after Indoctrination that she would never speak to an element-god ever again. And now she was going to have to ask them for mercy. She needed *their* help.

She thought about the things she'd seen Magnesia do in the Old World. As elements go, she wasn't the worst. But she'd still warred, like all the other gods.

The floor reached astronomical speeds. Had Mirembe not been bound to the floor magnetically, she'd have been thrown off long ago. The opening and closing doorways along the wall now an indiscernible streak of colours. Her core raced, more from the exhilaration of speed than anything else.

The doorway came into view. The floor didn't appear to have left any time to slow down.

Several identical forces slammed into Mirembe. She came to a complete stop, feet from the doorway.

The Enforcer rolled through it unfazed. Mirembe's suit followed, her emotions still in complete disarray. Inside, millions of gods moved in and out of pods, many flying around the room on large discs. Mirembe had never seen such a commotion in real life. The madness of organised chaos. She loved it. A momentary enjoyment in an otherwise dreadful situation.

They walked through the mass of gods trying to find a vacant pod. Everyone who saw Mirembe reacted to her with shock, disdain, fear, or disapproval.

They managed to find a vacant pod, and Gerulina scanned them in. 'Magnesia's offices.'

Everything went pitch black. Mirembe waited for the compressing feeling of dematerialisation to take over her. It didn't.

They rematerialised in a much smaller room, still with millions of pods.

Gerulina made her way through the commotion. Mirembe followed, trying unsuccessfully to avoid everyone's gaze.

Several colleagues greeted the Enforcer along the way. Some tried to engage her in conversation. She boasted to them that she had a meeting with Magnesia and thus was unable to talk.

They stopped at a group of large, disc-shaped platforms floating above the floor. Gerulina stepped onto it and turned around. Mirembe's suit jumped her onto the platform. It rose diagonally through the air as they had both taken their place.

All along the walls were doorways. Mirembe got a glimpse of some bizarre sights. The ascension anchored to Mirembe's core, dragging her emotions further into her consciousness. She became increasingly aware that the probability that one of these doorways would lead to Magnesia was steadily increasing.

For a moment, she remembered feeling quite like this when she floated through the air to Indoctrination shortly after her birth. The same feeling of fear, the fear of possibilities. So many of which are her being punished.

She scanned her memories for information about Magnesia. Something she could use to increase her bargaining power. Magnesia always had a prominent position in the Old World, but she also worked directly under other element-gods. She isn't the most important god. How would that impact her? Would that make her more or less likely to deliver harsh punishments?

She imagined Arcturus deciding her fate in this situation. If he didn't know her personally. She was sure he'd conclude that a rule had been broken. And she suspected so would Magnesia.

The higher they rose, the fewer other discs there were flying around them. Mirembe noticed that the doorways on the wall in front of her were getting fewer and more spaced apart.

What would they do to her? Regenerate her? Force her to work at The Executive doing some mind-numbing task? They couldn't possibly torture her for leaving her star. Especially against her will.

Anxiety pulsated through her. She could see a roof at the top of her vision. They were almost there.

A solitary doorway came closer and closer into view.

This is it, she thought.

The platform attached to the wall to allow them to disembark. Everything, the walls, floor and ceiling, was made of the same dull, silver-grey material: magnesium. Random rules appeared in golden calligraphy over the walls as they walked past, as though being scribed by invisible hands.

Every step Mirembe took sent a jolt of anxiety coursing through her essence. She was about to see what happened to Enemies of Fair and Just Order. About to come face to face with an element-god.

Her suit stopped abruptly in front of the reception. Behind the magnesium counter was a universe-god manifesting as a lifeform. He had two heads, hundreds of eyes, and long tentacles extending out from all over his body. An ugly-looking lifeform if she ever saw one.

The Enforcer placed some of her hands on the counter. 'I'm Gerulina, a level zero Enforcer. I have an appointment with Magnesia.'

The heads of the receptionist looked at Mirembe with no attempt to disguise their disapproval. 'Will the... Enemy... be joining you?'

'Yes.'

All the machinery around the Bureaucrat danced, the Bureaucrat itself flailing its arms around pointlessly.

They waited in silence.

Part of the wall to the side of the reception dematerialised.

'Follow the corridor until you come to the wall at the end,' he said. 'You'll both need to scan in once you arrive.'

'Thank you.'

The corridor sped them along to the end almost instantaneously. Once they scanned themselves in, the doorway dematerialised. Mirembe's anxiety reached unprecedented levels. Every step dragged her emotions up further until they were almost swimming in her throat.

They reached the centre of the circular room. All along the walls, the golden words of The Rules appeared and disappeared. Directly facing them was a solid magnesium desk that looked like it had grown out of the floor.

Mirembe was too preoccupied with Magnesia herself, who was coiled up behind the desk. She was manifesting as a lifeform. It had sparkly purple scales with a green sheen and dull grey eyes. She looked like a cross between a snake and Shiva the destroyer. At the top of the neck, it branched out into nine heads, each with miniature snake-like creatures growing out of them; sentient living dreadlocks.

Magnesia seemed as transfixed by Mirembe as Mirembe was by her. All her heads studied the colour behind Mirembe's eyes.

'Magnesia, your superiority,' said the Enforcer. 'May Fair and Just Order be the ruler of our lives. I have brought the Enemy of Fair and Just Order as requested.'

Magnesia turned some of her heads to glance briefly at the Enforcer, with as much interest as a mother being interrupted during her evening wine watching something on TV. 'Yes,' she said, snapped out of her trance. 'I can see that. Thank you. You're free to leave.'

'Eh...' Gerulina hesitated. 'Should I remain in the reception for –'

'Return to your post,' Magnesia interrupted authoritatively. 'I will contact you if I require any further assistance.'

'Order received.' She promptly turned and left the room.

Magnesia slithered out from behind her desk.

Mirembe had the horrible feeling she was going to be eaten again.

Magnesia stopped directly in front of her and bent her heads down to stare into Mirembe's eyes. 'First things first,' she said. 'Let's find you something decent to wear.'

She waved some of her many arms. A clear, flexible glass uniform appeared out of the air. It looked just like the enemies' uniform, only it was clear, had antennae instead of forward-facing eyes, and didn't have 'ENEMY' written all over it.

Once again, Mirembe felt her essence forcibly sucked out of the suit. It lingered in the air for a second, then flew into the transparent suit, reserved for Advocates of Fair and Just Order.

Magnesia looked positively enthralled staring at Mirembe's colours. 'Even in my wildest imaginations, I wouldn't have imagined this.'

Mirembe still felt unsure about what was happening. Her

new limbs hugged the body for protection.

'Don't be scared dear,' said Magnesia, in a caring teacher fashion. 'I'm not going to punish you.' She waved an arm and the enemies' uniform disappeared.

She turned and slithered back behind her desk.

Mirembe stood still, too shocked to move. 'I'm free to go?' she said, disbelieving.

'You've only just arrived,' said Magnesia. 'Here, take a seat.'

A jagged magnesium throne erupted from the ground on the other side of the desk. Mirembe hesitantly took a seat.

Magnesia studied her essence through the glass. The glow of thoughts being created glistened in Magnesia's eyes.

'It's been an incredibly long time,' said Magnesia, 'since I've seen 100% on a truth detector test. And what a story to be true.' Several heads turned to each other and smiled before focusing their attention on Mirembe again. 'You inhabited a lifeform and felt its pain, is that correct?'

'Well... Yes....' said Mirembe. 'I'm sure that's what happened. I got trapped inside a lifeform, and I'm confident I felt its feeling. I'd never felt pain before, but the moment it was eaten, the first pang of agony, I knew instantly it was pain.'

'And how did you get inside the lifeform,' said Magnesia, who was now lent across her desk in an attempt to be closer to Mirembe.

Mirembe shrugged. It felt weird to control her own movements again. 'I'm not entirely sure,' she said. 'I just felt myself dragged out of my star. Then, when it stopped, I was inside a lifeform. Almost like materialising inside this suit.'

'How extraordinary!' said Magnesia, her faces curved into thoughtful smiles. 'Was the lifeform aware you were inside it?'

She wondered. 'I don't think so, no. It was controlling me, not the other way around.'

'And you were definitely inside the lifeform? Not simply

sensing it from your star?'

'Definitely.'

'That is most unusual. Gods can control lifeforms and read their thoughts, of course. Creating a lifeform to manifest as, as you can see, completely normal.' She gestured to herself. 'But you say you were transported into the consciousness of a lifeform and felt its pain! It's unprecedented! You've already caused quite a commotion amongst the elements, Mirembe, I can tell you that much!'

Mirembe stared blankly, her essence swirled around inside the suit. She didn't feel like she was talking to the Magnesia she'd seen in Indoctrination. This version seemed... Friendly.

'First, you were born,' continued Magnesia, as though chatting to an old friend, 'which is curious enough in itself. No one expected a new god after all these Megayears. Then it transpires you're the first ever God of Morality, have all the elements, and all the colours as well. And, if anyone could believe it, you materialised in the Milky Way of all galaxies! The whole thing is just so bizarre and unexpected. You've been a topic of great discussion.'

She looked at Mirembe, expecting her to understand how unlikely this situation was. 'The moment I heard it,' she said, 'I thought you'd created lifeforms for sure. Then when I saw your truth detector test – I almost passed out with shock. There were the words clearly, 'I felt it's pain', with one hundred percent truth told. How can this be? Gods don't feel pain. Only Paradoxa feels pain, but she's antithesis. Never has positive something felt pain without Paradoxa's influence.' She leant over the desk far too enthusiastically for Mirembe, who was still traumatised from her time as a lifeform and couldn't shake the feeling she might be eaten. 'I have to ask, what did it feel like?'

Mirembe raised her eyebrows. 'I'm not sure how to describe it. Like nothing else except ending the sensation mattered. Like ending the sensation was the most important issue in the Megaverse. Everything else became irrelevant.'

'It sounds dreadful, truly dreadful.'

'It was. Then all this aggression and accusations, it's been horrible.'

'Well, you'll be glad to know that since you were forced out of your star, against your will, we will not be progressing with disciplinary procedures.'

Mirembe's core swelled with relief. 'Thank you!'

'Oh, we can't very well punish gods for things completely out of their control! How absurd. No, no, you can't be blamed. We have had to inform Paradoxa of course. This has never happened before, so there's no rule for it.'

Mirembe started to panic again. 'Informed Paradoxa for what reason?'

'Standard procedure, nothing to be concerned about. She may well issue new guidance. For now, we've issued you with an exemption from curfew, meaning you can leave your star at any time if you're inhabiting lifeforms. Assuming it happens again. You can't leave for any other reason, obviously.'

Mirembe couldn't believe her luck. She was exonerated. 'Brilliant! Thank you.'

'The Megaverse being what it is,' said Magnesia, 'it may never happen again. But, if it does, you'll be safe in the knowledge you're not breaking any rules. You will have to report it to the Milky Way each time it happens, other than that, there's nothing to worry about.'

Except for pain, thought Mirembe. 'Is there no way to prevent that happening again? I don't want to experience pain another time.'

Magnesia's heads appeared to scan their minds. 'I think ultimately,' she said, 'you'll determine that. If there's a defence you can put up against this force you mention, you'll find it. As it's never happened before, it's impossible to say what is causing it, or how to stop it. Maybe Paradoxa will work it out and send you updated rules.'

'Right, OK. So, I will just have to try and fight it off until a solution presents itself?'

'Yes, dear, I think that's the best plan.' She leaned even closer to Mirembe. 'One thing I'm curious to know. Why did you suspect Oxygenus to be involved in the creation of your lifeforms?'

Mirembe forgot she had said that. 'I... we argued after Indoctrination. And I couldn't recall putting any oxygen in my planet. It was the only logical conclusion.'

'Paradoxa has been notified, so it will definitely be investigated.' She smiled and retracted somewhat. 'Though I suspect you're being paranoid.'

'Perhaps, yes. So, what happens now? If I'm not in trouble for leaving my star, and it's been confirmed I didn't create those lifeforms, am I free to return to the Milky Way?'

'I thought you might like to chat a little longer,' said Magnesia, somewhat affronted. 'Yes, I will have you escorted back to the Milky Way shortly. Unless you think there's anything else that I can help you with?'

'No,' said Mirembe. 'There's nothing else....' She paused mid-sentence. 'Actually, there is something that's worrying me.'

'Oh, really?'

'Yes. I've only been to sleep once, and it was after Indoctrination, but I slept for ninety-nine thousand years. If I do that again and something changes on Earth, I'm worried I'll miss the hour deadline to report changes in circumstances.'

Magnesia tapped some of her fingers against the desk. 'That's very long for a star-god, isn't it?'

'So I've been told.'

'Things get more curious with you by the year, Mirembe.' She frowned, trying hard to think of a solution. 'There's absolutely no exemption I can give you from reporting your changes when it concerns lifeforms. I could, however, instruct the Milky Way to take over all your reporting duties whilst you sleep. How does that sound?'

'Erm, yes, that could work. Do you think Djulpan will mind?'

Magnesia smiled as she replied. A whisper of amusement glowed in her eyes. 'I'm sure it will be fine. A minuscule addition to his duties. You'll need to tell him before you sleep and when you wake so he knows when to monitor changes.'

'Right, um, thanks.' Mirembe didn't know what to say. She still couldn't believe all this was coming out of an element-god's mouth.

Magnesia smiled. 'Wasn't too bad, was it?'

Mirembe's essence flashed a bright glow.

An image appeared on Magnesia's desk. Mirembe saw the receptionist's ugly faces.

'Arrange an escort to take Mirembe to an intergalactic travel terminal. From there, she is to be released and transferred to the Milky Way.'

The receptionist was caught totally off guard. Evidently, he'd expected Mirembe to be punished. 'Order received,' he said once he'd pulled himself together.

Magnesia blinked and the screen disappeared.

'You're free to leave, Mirembe. The bureaucrat on reception will arrange an escort to take you home.' She smiled. 'It's been a pleasure meeting you. I wish all gods were as honest as you. It would make my life a lot easier.'

Mirembe stood up to leave. 'Thank you for being so understanding.'

'Not at all! Fair well, and may Fair and Just Order be the ruler of our lives.'

It took Mirembe a while to remember the correct reply with everything she'd just been through. 'May Fair and Just Order be the ruler of our cores.'

18
HOME AT LAST

Mirembe arrived back in the Milky Way shortly after 52 hours. The moment she left the materialisation pod a swarm of gods flew over to her.

'OH, MY PARADOX,' said Revati, the first to reach her. 'I didn't think we'd be seeing you again, especially not so soon.'

Mirembe's essence brightened considerably, her core smiled. 'I'm glad I could surprise you.'

'Mirembe! You're back!' said Lalande, who had just arrived with a few others.

'It's good to see you've been released,' said Olawangangu. 'I was worried if I'm being honest.'

'*You* were worried?!' said Mirembe. 'I've never been more worried in my life! First, I found lifeforms on my planet, then all those Enforcers arrived and arrested me, then they interrogated me – which was bizarre. Then, I had to explain myself to Magnesia. The whole thing has been emotionally traumatic, to say the least.'

'I don't think I've ever seen so many Enforcers in one place,' said Denebola.

'It's standard procedure,' said Arcturus. 'You've been released now, that's all that matters. It's great to have you back, Mirembe. Quicker than I expected, too.'

'Yeah,' said Tongwera. 'It's great to see you, Mirembe. You're looking as bright as ever. They kept me in for ages anytime one of my planets got pregnant. I didn't have a tenth as many Enforcers, though. That was insane.'

'I thought you were getting the whole galaxy regenerated for sure,' said Revati. 'Exactly like I told you not to do!'

'We're all still here,' said Olawangangu. 'Besides, it would have meant no one had to listen to your terrible jokes anymore. It wouldn't be the end of the Megaverse if she did get us regenerated.'

Everyone laughed.

'Well, well, well,' said Bernard, who had just arrived with Bellatrix. 'The God of Morality has returned at last.'

Mirembe's essence brightened. 'Hello Bernard. Hello Bellatrix.'

'Good to see you,' said Bellatrix. 'I hope it wasn't too scary for you?'

'I was terrified the whole way through!' Her essence dimmed as she re-experienced the sensation. 'Especially during interrogation and having to explain myself to Magnesia. She was very reasonable, though. They've given me an exemption if I get sucked out of my star during curfew again or if I oversleep.'

'Get sucked out of your star during curfew?' said Alnisa, who hadn't bothered to welcome Mirembe back. 'What do you mean?'

It occurred to her that the gods wouldn't know about that part of the story.

'Hello,' said Alnisa. 'Anyone home?'

Mirembe knew telling one god was as good as telling all gods, so she just came out with it. 'After I returned to my star following the siren on my birthday, I felt this force pulling me. Eventually, it overpowered me and sucked me out of my star. It transported me into the mind of a lifeform on Earth. I did everything it did, thought everything it thought, felt everything it felt. Including pain!'

'What the fuck are you talking about?' said Alnisa.

'Transported you into the mind of a lifeform?' said Lu-Wong. 'How?'

'I don't know how it happened.'

Olawangangu's essence was midnight black. 'You felt its pain, Mirembe?'

'Yes. I was eaten by another lifeform. I felt it all until the lifeform died.'

'You can't be serious?' said Eridani.

'I am,' said Mirembe. 'Even the Enforcers were shocked when I got one hundred percent truth on my tests.'

'I believe you,' said Olawangangu. 'Everything about you screams that your destiny is something great, something important. You've barely even been born, and you've already got lifeforms. Now you're saying you can inhabit them and feel their *pain*! I believe it. I don't know why, I don't know how. But I believe you.'

Arcturus was lost in thought. His essence shrank.

'A god who feels pain!' said Bellatrix.

'What was it like?' asked Arcturus. 'The whole experience.'

'I don't know if you've ever inhabited a suit?' said Mirembe.

'Yes, of course.'

'Right, well, it's sort of like that. Well, actually, it's sort of like being forced into an enemies' uniform, because I couldn't control myself. I just moved where the lifeform moved, thought what it thought, felt what it felt. There was an almost constant discomfort: hunger. It abated slightly when I ate, then resumed shortly after. Eventually, I was eaten, which was horrific and agonising in equal measure. The only way I can describe it: everything else became irrelevant. In those moments of pain, I'd have done anything to make it stop. No matter the consequence. And as I screamed, I cursed existence, that such a feeling was possible for any entity to feel.

'Wow,' said Bellatrix.

'You know what, Mirembe?' said Tongwera. 'I believe you. If it was anyone else, I'd say you were lying. I just know that what you're telling me is true.'

A chorus of agreement from the gods.

'What has The Executive said about this?' asked Arcturus.

'They've given me a pass to leave my star if I'm inhabiting a lifeform. Magnesia also said Paradoxa had been informed and that she might issue new rules.'

'That's all?' asked Sirius, surprised.

'Yes.'

'I'm amazed they didn't keep you in for further questioning, experimentation, something!'

'Who was at the tribunal?' asked Arcturus.

'Tribunal? I didn't have a tribunal.'

'You only spoke with Magnesia, no one else?'

'Yes, why?'

'That's a very soft touch for The Executive.'

'Extremely soft.'

'Well, I got one hundred percent on my truth detector test. It would have been unreasonable to punish me.'

'Still, they're just leaving you to your own devices. It's strange.'

'They obviously know,' said Olawangangu, 'that Mirembe has a higher destiny. Even Paradoxa will be able to see that.'

'A higher destiny?' said Mirembe, who wasn't sure how to take that. 'I wouldn't go that far. Granted, there have been a lot of unusual occurrences surrounding my birth, but I don't know what any of it means.'

'I don't know what any of it means,' said Olawangangu. 'But it definitely means something.'

'I'm beginning to agree,' said Bernard.

'I wonder if anything will change,' said Bellatrix, thoughtfully. 'The oath you've been hearing, it has been playing on my mind since you were arrested. This can't all be coincidence. Well, it could, but it's almost certainly not.'

'Something's coming,' said Olawangangu. 'I'm sure of it.'

'Maybe it has something to do with your lifeforms?'

In everything that had happened, the fact that she now had lifeforms she is responsible for, hadn't fully set in. '*My* lifeforms?' said Mirembe, several thoughts running through her mind. 'What would it have to do with them? We're not even allowed to communicate.'

'But you *can* inhabit them,' said Revati. 'The fact that you're even able to do that, it has to mean something. And the fact they're just letting you, that's even more meaningful.'

'I don't have a choice,' said Mirembe. 'Something forced me inside that lifeform. I don't know what, I don't know how, but it did.'

'That's so bizarre.'

'I wonder what force that was.'

'I'm definitely going to find out,' said Mirembe with steely determination.

'I'm guessing whatever force did that,' said Olawangangu, 'will do it again.'

'I'm hoping it doesn't!' said Mirembe, her essence flashed an orange-red. 'I don't want to feel pain ever again.'

'It does sound horrific,' said Lalande empathetically. 'It often made me sad watching my lifeforms suffer. I can't imagine what it's like to feel it.'

'This is mental!' said Eridani. 'A god who feels pain.'

'Paradoxa feels pain,' said Alnisa. 'I don't see the big deal.'

'She's the antithesis!' said Lu-Wong. 'It has always been thought that only negativity could feel pain. This changes our whole understanding of existence and what importance positive and negative something play in the Equation of Existence.'

'I hadn't even thought of that.'

'How does it change things?' asked Mirembe.

'In the Equation of Existence, antithesis has always been

the larger, more powerful entity than positive something. When they multiplied together in The Great Gamble, Paradoxa is believed to have a 99.99% weighting in that. It was assumed that the reason lifeforms feel pain is because they have a higher proportion of nothing to something than gods and machines do. If positive something can feel pain, that refutes that theory. If that theory is wrong, what else could positive something be capable of? What role does positive something play in existence?'

'This doesn't necessarily mean Paradoxa's weighting is wrong,' said Sirius. 'There's definitely more negative something than positive something in existence. That hasn't changed.'

'So much has changed,' said Lu-Wong. 'In such a short space of time.'

'You've got me there.'

Mirembe felt strange. Her existence could redefine the current understanding of reality.

'It could all be coincidence,' said Arcturus. 'I maintain that. I am very curious, though. I wonder what made you inhabit those lifeforms, and how that is possible.'

'Can Paradoxa inhabit lifeforms?' asked Muwan.

'I don't know,' said Bernard. 'I assume so.'

'I don't know anything she can't do,' said Bellatrix.

'The elements never claimed to be able to, did they?' said Olawangangu. 'They certainly didn't feel pain, that's for sure.'

'No, not that I recall.'

'They did like to invade the minds of others, though,' said Tongwera. 'I remember all too well being tormented by gods higher up the hierarchy.'

'Not easily forgotten.'

'Maybe if they'd felt pain,' said Mirembe, 'they'd have been less inclined to inflict on others.'

'I highly doubt it,' said Arcturus. 'Lifeforms feel pain. Many of them are cruel.'

'True.'

'I wonder what your lifeforms will be like when they're grown.'

Mirembe still wasn't comfortable with gods calling them *her* lifeforms. 'Considering what I experienced,' she said, 'and what I dreamt, I'd say they'll be lifeforms who war, ultimately getting me regenerated. Potentially tortured.'

'Nice to know you're staying positive about things,' said Revati.

'Your dream,' said Bellatrix. 'Another thing that makes this so meaningful. I believe you when you say it was a premonition.'

'You think Mirembe has the sight?'

'Yes.'

'The sight?' said Mirembe. 'What sight?'

'It's a power that only Paradoxa and the originals have displayed. It's the ability to see multiple timelines, multiple futures.'

'You're saying everything I dream will come true?'

'Not everything, no. The sight shows multiple futures. You could see lots of things that might happen if certain decisions are made by the independent variables. If those decisions aren't made when the time comes, that future won't come to pass. The sight allows gods to see infinite possible futures, at least some of which will come true.'

'I see,' said Mirembe. 'I might have the sight then. I do feel it was a premonition. I'm sure they're going to grow into grade four, at least.'

'That's what everyone's hoping, yeah.'

'Hoping?' said Mirembe, glowing bright yellow. 'Do you want to be regenerated?'

'It's you they'll regenerate.'

'Not if they leave their planet,' said Arcturus. 'We're all in this now.'

'The whole Milky Way is in this now.'

'Even Asima has cause for concern.'

'I'd be impressed if they got the whole universe

regenerated.'

'I bet Djulpan is overjoyed now that you've got lifeforms,' said Arcturus. 'He'll be ecstatic.'

'Bet he's already sucked the gas out of everyone who'll listen.'

'He'll even have sucked the gas out of the ones who wouldn't listen.'

'He didn't seem pleased when I told him,' said Mirembe. 'Shocked, definitely. Not pleased, though.'

'He'd have been delighted,' said Sirius. 'Now that you've been released, he'll be even happier.'

'It wouldn't matter even if they did get the Milky Way blown up,' said Olawangangu. 'Djulpan would still be happy to have housed them.'

'I think he would be wiser to worry,' said Lu-Wong. 'There is every chance these lifeforms will go on to do extraordinary things. Whether they are wonderful things or terrible things remains to be seen. But I am sure they will be great, either way.'

'Why are you so sure that my lifeforms will do great things?' said Mirembe, her interest peaked. 'They looked vicious enough in my dream but not extraordinary. I saw much more complex organisms in Indoctrination.'

'Because, Mirembe, they are made of your matter.'

'I agree.'

'Me also.'

'Quite.'

Mirembe's essence blushed. 'Thank you, that's very kind. I'd much rather that these lifeforms didn't exist and I wasn't causing so much speculation with my existence and abilities.' She sighed out some gas. 'I suppose I'd just better accept it. I have lifeforms now. What comes will come. There's no point worrying about it.'

The siren screeched inside the gods' minds.

'Home time,' said Revati. 'Try not to get us regenerated, Mirembe.'

'Until tomorrow,' said Olawangangu.

'Good day-end,' said Mirembe. She watched the gods head back to their stars before going back to hers. She'd been through a real rollercoaster of emotions since her birthday. Something about watching everyone running on Paradoxa's schedule put her at ease. Home at last.

Ever the visionary, Mirembe's sleep was punctuated with a concert of dreams.

Mirembe's world formed in the centre of a grand coliseum. Dancers glided through the air on fine silk above a royal blue carpet that stretched all the way to the gargantuan, scurrying feet of Dilophosaurus, the lifeform she currently inhabits.

'The awaited guest has arrived at long last,' said Allosaurus.

Dilophosaurus beamed as he greeted the other kings of Pangea. 'Fashionably late as always, I'm afraid.'

They took their seats, and the concert began. Mirembe's consciousness awoke inside the dinosaur, pressing against the border in its mind. Her core cried a thousand tears of joy for each note the orchestra played. It was the first music she'd heard other than The Anthem. It was beautiful.

Divinity had clearly earmarked these sounds for anyone clever enough to compose them together. She sat, mesmerised by the competing melodies and crescendos of the piece.

It was with great lamentation that the concert came to an end. The conductor lifted his baton, the music stopped, and Mirembe's dream world reformed.

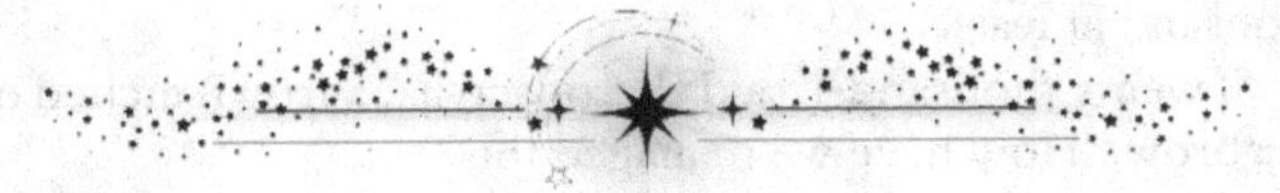

Mirembe awoke in the body of Pterodactylia. Her wings beat heavily against the passing wind, so hard she was almost thrown backwards. She thrust her wings out wide to steady her flight.

She scanned the ground looking for Tylia. The battle raged all around her, making it somewhat difficult for Pterodactylia to find her informant.

A momentary rage flashed in her as she saw one of her species, a Pterodactyl, torn apart by a mangy slave from Kingdom Four.

Pterodactylia let out a war cry and swooped down into the throws of the battle. She grabbed hold of the nearest slave and launched herself into the air, the squeals of the lifeform lost in the general mayhem of the war dance being performed around her.

Bones cracked against the ground as she dropped her victim. The slave squirmed and attempted to regain his balance.

Pterodactylia was saved the need to re-attack as a passing boulder flattened it, taking out several others and several of Pterodactylia's own species.

She flew high in the air, her black pupils trained keenly on the ground, the purple of her iris glittering with rainbow against the passing light.

A horn sounded in the distance. Just the sign she'd been waiting for. She made her way rapidly to the source of the noise.

'Tylia!' said Pterodactylia, 'I had feared we may have lost you.'

'Your grace,' said Tylia, spreading her wings wide and lowering her neck in salute. 'No, of course not. I managed to escape at the lower reaches of the river Iftyk. We lost twenty-thousand at least.'

'Twenty thousand?!' said Pterodactylia, a frown etched on her brow. 'How have we managed this?'

'We were betrayed. They knew we were coming. They ambushed us from all sides of the Iftyk.'

'Who betrayed us?'

'We're not sure, as yet,' said one of the generals stood behind Tylia. 'Giganotosaurus knew we would be there, so our guess is either the Allosauruses or one of the slaves from Kingdom Four.'

'Those filthy Herbis,' said Pterodactylia with the disgust she reserved for animals too weak to eat meat. 'I knew they couldn't be trusted. We should never have thought them capable.'

'We can't know for sure. The Allosauruses could well have tipped them off.'

'Well, find out!' snapped Pterodactylia. 'And clean up this mess. I don't want a single soul left alive.'

'As you command, my grace.'

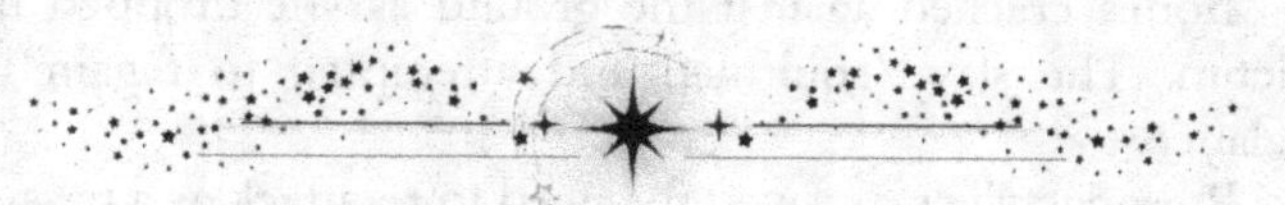

The view from Mirembe's enemies' uniform slowly came into focus. Five conjoined Enforcers stood menacingly guarding the entrance to the offertory.

'State your name and meaning,' said the middle Enforcer.

Mirembe was confused. She stared, waiting for confirmation she was being addressed. 'Excuse me?'

The officer repeated the question with more force. Which only added to her concerns but managed to startle her into a response.

'My name is Mirembe. I'm the God of Morality.'

The central Enforcer split in two and allowed Mirembe through. The Anthem slowly penetrated into Mirembe's mind. Her uniform forced her roughly down the passageway. As she went along, the walls around her compressed, getting narrower as she progressed.

A female Enforcer appeared out of one of the side doors as she walked down the corridor.

'A poisoning, is it?' said the Enforcer, facing Mirembe.

'Erm, what?'

'A high-ranking lifeform of yours has been poisoned. Is that correct?'

Mirembe wasn't sure what she was talking about. 'Um…'

'Yes, yes,' said the Enforcer. 'It's all here. A poisoning. Nothing too major, but it's still a concern.'

'One of my lifeforms has been poisoned?'

'Yes, King Dilophosaurus, I believe. Always the kings, isn't it?' said the Enforcer with a weak smile.

Mirembe gave a weak, contemplative smile in return.

'Always the kings,' repeated the Enforcer. 'We'd have nothing to do if not for them. Have you prepared your defence?'

'My defence?' said Mirembe.

'Yes, you'll need as much Lifeform Law as possible to help you out. Here.'

The Enforcer waved an arm, and Lifeform Law was uploaded into Mirembe's mind.

The calculations started churning in her mind, links and connections for all the laws her lifeforms had obeyed calculated instantly. A gentle feeling of relief comforted her essence as she formulated her defence.

'Thank you,' said Mirembe.

'You're welcome. Just remember, they've been steadily at peace for twenty-thousand days, Mirembe. That's your best argument and your best defence. I'd play it most often. Most societies have an identity crisis around that point in their development.'

Mirembe reached the final door. She scanned in and walked to the centre. The Enforcer waited at the gate. 'Good luck.'

'Thanks,' said Mirembe. 'I'll need it.'

Mirembe strode to the centre, through the addendum to the debating ring. She glanced around her at the Debaters, all of whom stood on disc platforms spread evenly around her to fully encapsulate her.

As was customary, Mirembe chose her favourite track from The Anthem, Dies Irae, as her defence piece.

A ripple of multicoloured energy erupted from Mirembe's eyes. The colours merged and clashed around her, solidifying into rules and Lifeform Laws that her lifeforms had obeyed. They locked in place around her, a defence shield of obedience.

The Debaters took their stance and swirled around Mirembe, throwing laws at her defences. Before long, all of her defences were shattered.

A line of Debaters soared forward and darted Mirembe with laws. With no defences left, they struck her directly, causing her to scream.

The dance stopped, and an angry red face appeared in the centre of the offertory.

RULES NOT OBEYED. LIFEFORMS LOSE.

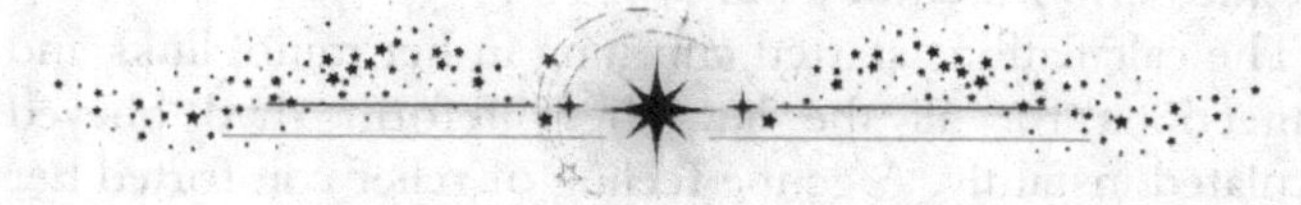

The sun had not long set, and Mirembe found herself in the body of a slave named Tigo, pressed uncomfortably against a jagged rock. She fussed around on the rock, trying to find a point of purchase that didn't cause her some discomfort. The slave to her right passed her a horn. Slowly, the dinosaur's consciousness overtook her own.

He grabbed the cup hastily and drank. It was a strong and bitter wine, the kind one finds brewed in the illegal trenches of Kingdom Three. He stopped short of drinking the whole thing and passed on the remaining dregs to the next in line.

'Just enough to piss in, Tigo' said the slave to his right. 'Could have left more than a wet.' He finished the contents and tipped the horn upside down to show the group it was empty. He tossed it aside and let out a low rumble.

'Herbi swill, anyway,' said Nilo. 'What can wine offer a slave that a woman can't? Go find your misses.'

Tigo picked up a leg from the pot above a fire in the centre of the congregation and put the whole thing in his mouth. He wolfed it down like a man who hadn't eaten all day – which he hadn't. Splutters of flesh spewed from his mouth as he devoured the meat. He licked his lips and stood up, removing a bone from his teeth with his tongue. 'Find my misses? Yes, I think I shall.'

'You'll service nothing until you've serviced us,' said the slave to his right. 'Get the drums. One song before bed, lads?'

'Aye!' cheered the crowd.

Tigo grabbed his drum, as did several others.

'Is it that time already?' asked Lubb. 'I suppose one rendition before bed can't hurt'.

'Suppose not.'

With a slap of his tail, Tigo began.

The slaves stood to attention, facing each other in camaraderie.

"One day we will rise
High up in the sky
Where the winds blow strong

And the sun shines bright
In another world
Where the mind is free
And the chains that bind us cease to be.

One day we will rise
To a higher self
Where the stars that formed us
burn in our hearts
Like the passing light of a long-dead friend
Guiding us through life from start to end.

One day we will rise
To the galaxies above
Through the starlit sky to the nebula
Until a supermassive black hole sucks us in
And our new life can at last begin."

Tigo slapped his tail against the drum three times to end the chant, and the slaves departed for bed.

The view from Mirembe's enemies' uniform slowly came into focus. Five conjoined Enforcers stood menacingly guarding the entrance to the offertory.

'State your name and meaning,' said the middle Enforcer.

Mirembe was confused. She stared, sure she had just been in this situation. 'Excuse me?'

The officer repeated the question with more force. Which only added to her concerns but managed to startle her into a response.

'My name is Mirembe. I'm the God of Morality.'

The central Enforcer split in two and allowed Mirembe through. The Anthem slowly penetrated into Mirembe's mind. Her uniform forced her roughly down the passageway. As she went along, the walls around her compressed, getting narrower as she progressed.

A female Enforcer appeared out of one of the side doors as she walked down the corridor.

'A poisoning, is it?' said the Enforcer, facing Mirembe.

'Sorry?'

'A high-ranking lifeform of yours has been poisoned. Is that correct?'

Mirembe was sure she'd heard that sentence before. 'Um…'

'Yes, yes,' said the Enforcer. 'It's all here. A poisoning. Nothing too major. You should be OK.'

'One of my lifeforms has been poisoned?' Then, suddenly, her earlier dream flashed in her mind. 'Oh, of course, yes: King Dilophosaurus.'

'Always the kings, isn't it?' said the Enforcer with a weak smile.

Mirembe gave a weak smile in return.

'Always the kings,' repeated the Enforcer. 'We'd have nothing to do if not for them. Have you prepared your defence?'

'No,' said Mirembe.

'OK. You'll need as much Lifeform Law possible to help you out. Here.'

The Enforcer waved an arm, and Lifeform Law was uploaded into Mirembe's mind.

The calculations started churning in her mind again, links and connections for all the laws her lifeforms had obeyed calculated instantly.

'Thank you,' said Mirembe.

'You're welcome. Just remember, they've been steadily at peace for twenty-thousand days, Mirembe. That's your best argument and your best defence. I'd play it most often. Most societies have an identity crisis around that point in their development.'

Mirembe reached the final door. She scanned in and walked to the centre. The Enforcer waited at the gate. 'Good luck.'

'Thanks,' said Mirembe. 'I'll need it.'

Mirembe strode to the centre, through the addendum to the debating ring and faced the Debaters, all of whom stared down at Mirembe from their floating discs.

Mirembe chose her favourite track from The Anthem, Dies Irae, as her defence piece.

A ripple of multicoloured energy erupted from Mirembe's eyes. The colours merged and clashed around her, solidifying into rules and Lifeform Laws that her lifeforms had obeyed. They locked in place around her, a defence shield of obedience.

The Debaters took their stance and swirled around Mirembe, throwing laws at her defences.

Determined not to lose, Mirembe threw her arms in the air, shattering many of the oncoming laws before they even had chance to set.

She cast her defences down once again, parrying the attacks of the Debaters as she went.

She lasted much longer than the previous attempt, yet before long, all of her defences were shattered.

The Debaters soared forward and darted Mirembe with laws. With no defences left, they struck her directly, causing her to scream again.

The dance stopped, and an angry red face appeared in the centre of the offertory.

RULES NOT OBEYED. LIFEFORMS LOSE.

In quite possibly the rudest wake-up call possible, Mirembe was awoken from her slumber to the fright of her life. The dinosaurs she had seen in her dreams, twice now, had managed to shake her to the core of her being for the third time. This time – it was the worst. This time, it was not a dream, it was a reality. She could sense them from Earth. Before she could even scream in anger or convince herself she was dreaming again, her essence was unceremoniously dragged to Earth.

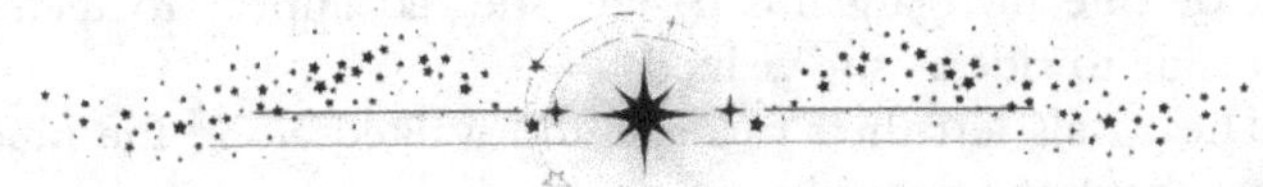

King Dilophosaurus 113th reclined in his chair, his tail wrapped beneath him for comfort. Mirembe's compassionate rays were visible through the sunroof of his carriage. A rainbow glistened on his retina as Mirembe's essence refracted against her own sunlight. Yew trees demarcated the path every twenty yards or so, unwavering in their attempt to reach the sun, while a pack of what Dilophosaurus considered to be feral animals stared at his entourage inquisitively.

He had been waiting for this day since his seventeenth birthday. It was well known by then that he would be picked amongst his siblings to take over from his dad as the ruler of the first kingdom, and fortune had not disappointed him. Today marked both his 113th birthday and 20,000 earth-years since the four brothers created the four kingdoms.

'We've arrived at long last,' said Dilophosaurus to his wives and children. 'I've had quicker council meetings.'

'They've really put on a show this year,' said Didlio, the king's firstborn son, taking in the scenery of the coliseum. A marbled pyramid sat atop a flat-headed dodecahedron, an example of the dinosaurs' architectural expertise. The designers had adorned every square inch with precious stones, jewels and metals.

The slaves disembarked from the transport's back, which also happened to be a slave, to help the royals disembark from their carriage.

'I see Giganotia hasn't missed the opportunity to dress up for the occasion,' said Didlia.

Didlia let out a broad smile, revealing her crooked teeth. 'Goodness me. I'm surprised she can walk.'

The extravagant hat they were remarking on was so large that, despite her gargantuan size, she did appear to teeter from side to side as she walked.

The royals left their carriage and walked along the blue carpet that lined the walkway into the coliseum.

King Dilophosaurus led the way, striding faster than usual, the anticipation getting the better of his usually calm demeanour.

The designer of this year's annual meeting had gone further than anything Dilophosaurus had ever seen in the coliseum. Dancing slaves hung from the ceiling in fine silks, gliding to and fro in synchronised dance. Along the walls were glistening jewels, which refracted rainbows into Dilophosaurus' eyes as he watched. Fire could be seen roaring throughout the hall at sporadic points. Ahead lay an orchestra, which had already begun a gentle, welcoming melody to usher the guests to their seats.

Dilophosaurus and his entourage took their seats in front of the stage next to the other three royal families. All eyes were on the Dilophosauruses as they took their seats.

'The awaited guest has arrived at long last,' said King Allosaurus.

King Dilophosaurus beamed at the other kings. 'Fashionably late as ever, I'm afraid.'

The conductor strode to the centre and took his place on a raised platform. The coliseum quietened and the room stood to attention.

'Kings and Queens, Lords and Ladies,' said the conductor, his shoulders spread broadly as he addressed the crowd. 'It is with great pleasure that I welcome you all to the 20,000th annual meeting of the joining of the four Kingdoms of Pangea and the unification of the dinosaur species.'

A small cheer ensued.

'Without further ado, let the concert commence.' The conductor turned to face the orchestra. A lift of the conductor's wand and the concert began.

There was something about the melodic harmonies produced by an orchestra that never failed to excite Dilophosaurus in all the right ways. He pressed his eyes shut and let the music seep into his consciousness.

The performance ended, and Dilophosaurus and the other kings made their way out of the concert hall to the reception area. The four kings took their place at the centre of the hall, and the rest of the congregation moved in place to bow before the four brothers, the rightful airs to Pangea.

The kings took it in turns to bow to one another, handshakes being less common owing to the lack of useful, extendable arms, which most of the dinosaur species had yet to manage in their evolution.

A loud bang issued from the front of the hall. King Dilophosaurus turned to see a Pterodactyl striking a large golden gong.

The kings bowed to one anther and spread out to mingle with the aristocrats and other high-status dinosaurs. Everyone else made their way over to the buffet table.

'Well, well, well,' said King Allosaurus, smiling at King Dilophosaurus. 'What an auspicious day. A prodigal birthday and the twenty-thousandth year of the glorious founding of our glorious nations, all taking place on the same day.'

'I should think your speech shall be impeccable,' said King Pterodactylus with a pensive smile.

'Oh, you simply must hear it,' said Dilophasaura. 'I can promise you it will be spectacular.'

'I can't wait.'

King Dilophosaurus turned to face King Giganotosaurus. 'How're things in the fine kingdom of the Giganotosauruses? Those pesky Herbis giving you any trouble?'

'Trouble?' said Giganotosaurus, his chest and stomach flaring. 'Oh, they've given us trouble all right. Almost lost one-tenth of my workforce thanks to the little bastards. There are not enough dinosaurs in the world to keep that vermin at bay.'

'It's time we cleaned them out once and for all,' said Dilophosaurus.

'I've been saying exactly that, what with times being peaceful as they are, the armies not up to much use bar boundary protection and the occasional hunt.'

'We should put it before the council tomorrow,' said Dilophosaurus.

'I shall do exactly that.'

Dilophosaurus picked up an appetiser with his mouth from one of the passing slave's heads, all of whom had platters strapped about their head. 'Any word on what to expect for tonight's extravaganza?'

'The usual theatrics, I imagine,' said King Pterodactylus, moving over to stand next to the Dilophosaurus. 'If it's anywhere near as good as that welcome concert, we should be in for a treat.'

'King Pterodactylus,' said Dilophosaurus. 'Nice of you to join us.'

'Have you ever known me to miss a party?'

The kings chuckled

'Grander pomp and ceremony than ever this year. I suppose one can never overstate the importance of perpetual peace.'

'Perpetual peace?' said Giganotosaurus. 'Tell that to my wives.'

An academic from the Allososaurus' kingdom joined the conversation. 'Yes, where are your many wives?'' His tone was inquisitive, the muscle above his eye raised.

'Giving me a forgiving minute's peace,' said Giganotosaurus.

'They still haven't returned those manuscripts,' said the Allosaur. 'Somehow, my letters never seem to reach them.'

'There's one of them,' said Giganotosaurus.

'My letters?'

'My wife.'

King Pterodactylus pointed with his wing. 'It seems you'll have to wait a little longer, Amicus.'

A small Pterodactyl, much smaller than King Pterodactylus, flew to a perch built into an arched wall in the reception. He let out a high-pitched call from the lower reaches of his throat to call for quiet in the hall. 'Ladies and gentlemen,' he said, 'please welcome our honoured guest for his birthday speech, King Dilophosaurus 113th.'

'Oh, goodness,' said Dilophosaurus, gulping down the remainder of his food. He strode buoyantly to the far reaches of the room and stood to face the congregation.

'Honoured guests,' began King Dilophosaurus. 'It is with

great pleasure that I address you here today on this momentous occasion, the twenty-thousandth annual meeting of the unification of the four Kingdoms of Pangea. We give thanks to the four brothers in heaven who created the sky, lands and seas, and their mortal embodiments on Earth, the Four kings of Pangea.'

The crowd bowed in response.

'The guiding light and strength bestowed to us by the gods is the foundation upon which the prosperity and happiness of Pangea stands. It is with this light that I usher in not only the twenty-thousandth year of peace amongst our dinosaur brethren, but an altogether even more providential occasion — my 113th birthday.'

Whoops emanated from the crowd.

'Every day of our renewed peace shows just how crucial the hierarchy system is. It is the purchase point of our success and the bonding binds of our species. The rock and chains of our civilization.'

The whole room cheered and whooped.

'Please, everyone, find yourself a drink, and let us toast to the twenty-thousandth year of our prosperity.'

A slave walked into position, and King Dilophosaurus bent down to sip his wine from the slave's head.

'To twenty-thousand more years!' said King Dilophosaurus,

'To twenty-thousand more years!'

No sooner than the crowd had echoed his words, King Dilophosaurus began coughing, spluttering liquid down his front.

He dropped to his knees, crying out in agony.

The room gasped in shock.

Dilophosaurus screamed and ran over to King Dilophosaurus. 'Father!'

King Dilophosaurus spasmed on the ground. Several aristocrats rushed over to the fallen king.

Didlia waded through the crowd to her father, pushing

over several slaves in her rage.

'He's been poisoned,' cried the Didliaphosaurus.

Those were the last words Mirembe heard as Dilophosaurus lost consciousness.

Mirembe felt herself leave the body of Dilophosaurus and return to space, only to be requisitioned by those four dreaded words: YOU HAVE BEEN SUMMONED.

The view from Mirembe's enemies' uniform slowly came into focus to give her yet another fright. The exact same Enforcers she had just dreamt stood menacingly guarding the entrance to the offertory.

'State your name and meaning,' said the middle Enforcer.

Mirembe couldn't believe what she was seeing. She stared, unable to respond. The officer repeated the question with more force.

'My name is Mirembe. I'm the God of Morality.'

The central Enforcer split in two and allowed Mirembe through. The Anthem started as expected, as did the floor and compressing walls. The only out-of-place feature was their proximity to Mirembe. They appear to have given her... breathing space.

The female Enforcer she'd seen in her dream appeared at her side.

'A poisoning, is it?' she said, turning to face Mirembe,

who moved in jagged steps along the still narrowing corridor.

'Yes,' said Mirembe, less scared than in her dream.

The Enforcer gave Mirembe a slight smile. 'Have you prepared your defence?'

'No, not yet' said Mirembe.

'Here, you'll need as much Lifeform Law possible to help you out.'

The Enforcer waved an arm, and Lifeform Law was uploaded into Mirembe's mind.

'Thank you,' said Mirembe.

'You're welcome. Just remember, they've been steadily at peace for twenty-thousand days, Mirembe. That's your best argument and your best defence. I'd play it most often. Most societies have an identity crisis around that point in their development.'

Mirembe reached the final door. She scanned in and walked to the centre. The Enforcer waited at the gate. 'Good luck.'

'Thanks,' said Mirembe. *I'll need it.*

Mirembe strode to the centre, through the addendum to the debating ring and faced the Debaters, all of whom stood on disc platforms spread evenly around her. With enemies at all sides, Mirembe waited patiently for the debate to begin.

In another unexpected turn, a black conductor's wand appeared in her hand. She felt a momentary connection to Paradoxa.

And so began the dance Mirembe had so recently prophesized.

She lifted her conductor's wand high in the air and chose her favourite track from The Anthem, Dies Irae, as her defence piece.

A ripple of multicoloured energy erupted from Mirembe's eyes, and the sounds of Mozart's Requiem in D minor rushed to her aid.

The colours merged and clashed around her, solidifying into rules and Lifeform Laws that her lifeforms had obeyed

They locked in place around her, a defence shield of obedience.

A wail marked the sound of the retaliation. The Debaters around Mirembe sang and hurled their laws at her, their physical manifestation visible marginally through Mirembe's own defences.

The song reached the climax of the first crescendo as Mirembe and the Debaters finished laying their moves.

Mirembe raised her wand. In another unexpected occurrence, determined not to be shocked, Mirembe called on the laws to change form. They manifested into lifeforms from her planet.

The Debaters looked momentarily alarmed. They recovered and responded in kind with the new order. Rules soared towards Mirembe from all angles. She raised her wand, and the lifeforms leaped in the air to attack the laws from the Debaters.

They met in the air and collided, smashing into the ground. The four kings from Pangea appeared at the four compass points around Mirembe as her final layer of defence.

Try as they might, the Debaters could not penetrate Mirembe's defences.

Dies Irae came to a climax, and the Debaters' laws crashed to the ground.

A large, green, smiling face appeared facing Mirembe. RULES OBEYED. LIFEFORMS WIN.

Everything in the offertory vanished. Mirembe was transported back to the Milky Way to the welcoming sounds of Revati. 'You're back,' he said. 'I didn't think they'd let a poisoning go unaccounted for. Good to see they haven't arrested you.'

Mirembe beamed. She loved hearing Revati.

'I didn't bother to worry this time,' said Bellatrix. 'There was no way Paradoxa was going to allow her special Mirembe be regenerated.'

'It was a close call,' said Mirembe. 'I dreamt myself losing the debate twice. I was incredibly worried. I've never been more relieved to see that smiling green face telling me we had won our case.'

'You had better get used to it. You'll do nothing but debate now you're awake. Djulpan has been back and forth non-stop.'

'Thanks for reminding me,' said Mirembe. 'I'd better tell him I'm awake.'

'He knows,' said Olawangangu. 'I let him know as soon as I heard you were summoned. I'm surprised he wasn't there.'

'I am, too,' said Mirembe, now that she came to think of it. 'I did have a helpful Enforcer, though. She helped me with my Lifeform Law.'

'Nothing beats the feeling of winning a debate.'

'Well,' said Mirembe. 'It's far better than losing. Sorting through all their actions to find the good points was the most difficult. The joys of motherhood, I guess.'

'Motherhood,' said Bellatrix, enjoying the word. 'That's a very nice way of looking at it.'

'Isn't that how all gods see it?'

A lot of laughs.

'Considering what gods used to do to lifeforms,' said Olawangangu, 'we've come a long way just by remaining hidden, not interacting with them. Motherhood is a role gods seldom assign themselves. It's not the usual rationale of the relationship between gods and lifeforms.'

'Well,' said Mirembe. 'They're made of my matter, and I'm responsible for them. That's as much like parenting as anything I saw in Indoctrination. And when I think about those poor creatures who have to feel what I felt, suffering in hunger and death, I can't help but care. Even though I hate them for existing, and I'm sure they're going to get me regenerated, it feels like my duty to be their mother, you know? They don't choose to live, and they are forced to suffer. I can't end their pain, so I can at least love them through it.'

'I totally understand' said Lalande. 'I felt a bit like a mother to my lifeforms. I was so sad when they died. I really grieved. And that was without ever feeling pain. Your bond with them is going to be so much stronger.'

'You're right,' said Mirembe, convincing herself. 'You're absolutely right. I've no right to complain. What I feel inhabiting them isn't even a notable fraction of the suffering already taking place on Earth, and it's will only get worse as they evolve. If they get me regenerated, so be it. It will be a mercy. Besides, it means I'll never have to listen to Revati's jokes again. Who knows, if fortune continues to bless the galaxy, maybe he'll be close enough that none of you have to either.'

They all laughed.

Revati was saved a response as Mirembe's essence was dragged to Earth.